Look for these titles by *Ursula Bauer*

Now Available:

The Eternity Covenant Series

Immortal Protector (Book 1)

Immortal Illusions (Book 2)

To Heidi-
I am waiting
to buy that Blaze!
Thanks for being such
great lunch company.
Enjoy Ursula
Bauer.

Praise for Ursula Bauer's *Immortal Protector*

RT Rating: 4 Stars "A fascinating look at the gods and their modern-day involvement in the affairs of Earth. ... an adventurous story full of romance, horror and mythology...a great job of creating an alternate Earth."

~ *Susan Mobley, Romantic Times Magazine May 2008*

Rated: 91- A KEEPER! "...a crazy whacked-out rollercoaster ride of non-stop fun....a near-perfect pace... kick-ass action romance... enjoyable from start to finish!"

~ *Mrs. Giggles, mrsgiggles.com*

Rated: 5 Kisses, Recommended Read! "Immortal Protector is a thrill a minute adventure story... Bravo to Ursula Bauer..."

~ *Barb, A Twolips Reviews*

Rated: 4 Angels "...a most delicious beginning to a new series...an intriguing world...and I look forward to more in this marvelous series."

~ *Trang, Fallen Angel Reviews*

"You just don't find too many original stories to rave about anymore."

~ *Avid Book Reader Reviews*

Rated: 5 HEARTS "...an exceptional tale of ancient Gods, Immortals, demons and zombies...a spicy suspenseful story of twists and turns that will keep readers on their toes to the very end."

~ *Sandra, The Romance Studio*

Immortal Protector

Ursula Bauer

A Samhain Publishing, Ltd. publication.

Samhain Publishing, Ltd.
577 Mulberry Street, Suite 1520
Macon, GA 31201
www.samhainpublishing.com

Immortal Protector

Print ISBN: 978-1-59998-756-9
Digital ISBN: 1-59998-501-2

Editing by Angela James
Cover by Anne Cain

First Samhain Publishing, Ltd. electronic publication: June 2007
First Samhain Publishing, Ltd. print publication: May 2009

Dedication

To the Bear, the Crit Group, and Boba Fett. You all know why.

Chapter One

The games of the Gods are played upon the chessboard of the mortal world, and the heavens hang in the balance. ~Book of Wardens

Venice, Italy

"Campbell located a deviation point for the timeline convergence." Salazar, the elder Warden, tapped the screen of his hand-held computer with a thin stylus. A grainy publicity photo of a woman's face appeared above on the video display at the far end of the polished chrome and glass conference table. "A mortal."

Gideon Sinclair considered the woman's oval face. It was plain, except for a pair of almond-shaped, silvery-green eyes. They were a soft contrast to the startling fire-red hair that wound in coils like angry snakes around her head. The hint of memory rose from the grave and he ruthlessly pushed it back amongst his dead. "Your message said the stakes are high."

"One doesn't call on a champion lightly. Particularly not a champion of the Tribunal."

"She's not one of us. She's not a player." Gideon looked back at the woman's picture. The more he studied her, the less plain she seemed. "The Tribunal handles our own kind."

"Campbell and several other mystics explored all available threads for this convergence. She's the only deviation point available. Should the convergence progress uninterrupted, the war between Seth and Horus will begin anew."

"The war never ended."

"The war is cold, as are most conflicts between rival Gods. Such are the rules we all now play by."

Rules? That was rich. Gideon wanted to laugh, but was suddenly tired of it all: the hidden agendas, the multiple convergences, the treachery, the endless game. The eternal stalemate.

"Okay, I'll bite. What have you and your cabal foreseen today, Salazar?"

"Archeologists, Gideon, they're the bane of us all. Some artifacts were meant to stay buried, but they can't seem to let the past rest." Salazar slid a thin flash drive across the smooth glass table. "Five items sacred to Egyptian Gods were recently unearthed from a new dig at the Valley of the Tombs of the Kings. Each item is concealed in a canopic jar that hides their true power. We dispatched a retrieval team, but the artifacts vanished from the site before we could secure them. Campbell saw her coming into contact with the one blessed by Isis. It all unravels from there."

Gideon considered Salazar's words, but he couldn't help stealing another glance at the mortal. "How exactly does this transpire?"

"We're not sure of all the details. A disruption at a deviation point will prevent catastrophe. You know how these things work."

"I do." Gideon shut his eyes for a moment, trying to banish the image of the woman and escape the strange thoughts coming to mind. He must still be fried from his last job. His body ached and his wounds were fresh. It stood to reason his brain suffered as well. He opened his eyes again and the harsh glare of the Venice sun blazing in through the arched windows of the sterile conference room threw everything into a stark, inescapable clarity. "You called me because you want her taken out of play."

The Spaniard smoothed out imaginary wrinkles on the jacket of his custom-tailored, midnight-blue silk suit. "You know the protocol for this scenario."

"I know the protocol." He couldn't face the picture again. Instead, he grabbed the flash drive from the tabletop and slipped it into the deep pocket of his biker jacket.

"We don't have a choice. The mortal must die. When convergences like this arise..."

"Save the sermon." Gideon stood and turned his back to Salazar and the picture of the mortal with the misty fey eyes. "I'll get the job done."

Patient expired at 0615...

"You can't save them all."

Meg Carter stopped typing, looked up at her boss over the screen of her laptop, and rubbed her tired eyes. "I know, Bill, but I can try." It was the same old argument they'd always had, except it surfaced more frequently as of late. "Someone has to fight the good fight."

Bill smiled, making his boyish features crease in a way that showed a more mature, handsome version and hinted at his true age. He stepped into her office and shook his head. "Doesn't the drug research we do here count as the good fight?"

"I have three patients left on my service." The glare from the single desk lamp and back-lit computer screen was nearly unbearable. The killer headaches she'd been having were growing worse. She really needed to see someone. None of her interventions were working, meaning the pain was symptomatic of more than a simple migraine. "I'm giving the clinic my full attention. These kids need me. I can't transfer them to another doctor."

Bill leaned his leanly muscled body against the corner of her desk and frowned. "You're working too hard. When was the last time you took a real break from the war? Had a vacation that wasn't tied to some conference on cancer or treatments or medicine? Come to think of it, when was the last time you had a weekend to yourself?"

Meg shrugged. Truth be told, she had no idea. "A few months ago?"

"Doctors love to lie to themselves." Bill pushed his glasses up on his forehead and turned the full power of his baby blues on her. "Dr. Carter, as your boss, I'm ordering you to take a break. Get out of here, and take a few days for yourself. Call in sick. Anything. Just recharge those batteries. I can't do this job without you, Meg. You're the lynch pin of the team. The next phase of the Melaniprin study's about to start. I need you on your game."

The hope of the new chemotherapeutic made her smile. "Our last results were pretty promising."

"They were outrageous." A strange look came over him. "Thirteen years ago this kind of drug was still experimental. If Angel could have lived just a little longer, she might have benefited from one of the early trials."

The wound of his daughter's death was still fresh to him. Had Angel taken that drug in the earliest experimental phases, she would have been as likely to die from its dangerous, then unknown, side effects as she would the inoperable tumor in her brain. "You did the best you could, Bill."

"Right. I know. I should listen to my own words." He stood abruptly, his skin suddenly flush. "I envy you, Meg. You have the strength to handle private practice. I can only deal in the miracle business these days. Delivering the news, watching them die, after Angel..." His words trailed off.

"Maybe you're the one who needs a break?"

"I wouldn't know what to do with myself. You, on the other hand, are burning out. Pack it in, Doc, and hit the road."

She glanced back at the computer. She had two more discharge summaries waiting completion. "I have to tie up some loose ends."

"You've been here every night until midnight for the last few weeks. Promise you'll tie up those loose ends and be out of here by nine?"

That gave her an hour. She winced as pain stabbed through her skull. Bill was right. If she wanted to lead the charge, be there for the clinic and kids, she needed to be there for herself first. She was no good to anyone in her present condition. That also meant scheduling a trip to her doctor to figure out the underlying cause of the last three weeks of hell knocking around in her skull. "Fine. Your clinic. Your rules."

"Don't make me call security and have you bounced."

"On my honor, I'll ease up on the stick tonight."

Bill seemed satisfied. "Fair enough. We can talk tomorrow about a vacation."

After he left, Meg grabbed her glasses again and gave a shot at finishing the discharge summaries. Her vision rapidly blurred, so she removed the glasses and set them aside. Giving herself a momentary break, she stood and opened the door to the small office terrace and paused for a moment, letting the hot night air roll over her in soft waves. She closed her eyes, and let sensation steal her away. Normally the hot June weather was hell on her asthma, but this year she seemed to have little trouble at all. Only the headaches plagued her.

A gentle breeze shifted around her, carrying with it a subtle, unusual scent reminiscent of sandalwood with an earthy, alluring note she couldn't quite place. How strange to smell something so exotic and otherworldly in upstate New York. It made her curious and tantalized her in a strange and exciting way. For a moment she wondered what it would be like to step away from the clinic, the work, her world, and try on something new. The moment passed, and she opened her eyes back to reality. The pain had receded sufficiently and she returned to the tasks at hand.

At precisely nine the phone rang. The extension was the main security post. Meg laughed lightly, then shut down her computer for the night. Good thing she'd wrapped things up. Bill was nowhere near as laid back as he appeared. He just might make good on the threat to have her tossed out of the building. She let the phone ring as she grabbed her bag and closed down the office for the night.

In the elevator she wondered if she should consider a more aggressive approach to her problem. Skip seeing the general practitioner, move straight to a neurologist. Perhaps John Mitchell. They'd gone to Albany Medical College together. John was top shelf and blunt. If there was something terrible lurking in her body, he would play her straight and find the most aggressive ways to treat the problem. Her vision blurred briefly as the elevator came to a stop and she had a moment of passing vertigo. When the doors opened she was fine again, but the vertigo hit her several more times as she walked through the building.

She decided rather than wait any longer, she'd call John discreetly at home tonight and make an appointment. The escalation of symptoms scared her. She didn't want her situation getting out into the community and she didn't want to waste any more time. If she was lucky, he'd slip her into his schedule within the next few days.

Meg ventured down a dimly lit corridor that bypassed some of the smaller labs and used the side exit to avoid running into any of the security guards. They tended to be chatty and she wasn't in the mood for company. Outside, the muggy air pressed in around her like the walls of a prison. She rummaged through her backpack for her phone as she crossed the first lot, then paused on the island separating it from the rear lot. The cell was in the far corner of the bag, hidden beneath two prescription pads and a tube of lip gloss. The lip gloss made her smile. It was a gift from Sherry Roth, the little girl she'd discharged this afternoon, and it smelled like cherry bubblegum.

She pushed the pads aside and was about to grab the phone when the sound of heavy footsteps caught her attention. Reflexively, she glanced behind her. In the dense mist was the unmistakable shape of a very tall, very large man crossing the lot and coming her way. She wasn't one hundred percent sure, but she thought he had a ski mask on. The hair on the back of her neck stood on end and her mouth went dry. She forgot the phone, grabbed her keys and started off again for her car at a run.

The man caught up with her before she'd gone halfway across the rear lot. He grabbed her bag and jerked her backward. She fell down and immediately started screaming and kicking. God help her, she was getting mugged.

Meg fought like a tiger, adrenaline dumping like rocket fuel into her blood. The guy couldn't get a hold of her. He wore a ski mask, and black clothes. She continued to scream, but it sounded dull to her ears, as if the thick fog was swallowing her cries. No one came to her aid. No one heard her cries. Where the hell was security?

Unwilling to be a victim, Meg aimed a vicious kick at his groin and brought him down. She struggled to her knees, got to her feet and started to run, but the man was up in an instant and grabbed her again. She screamed for help as he spun her around, and she clawed at his face. He was forced to hold her at arm's length while she struggled.

Instead of speaking, her attacker howled at her, and a puff of acrid black smoke rushed from his mouth. The world spun around her and for a moment she thought she might pass out. Sheer grit and fear kept her conscious. She held her breath and renewed her fight. The man reared back, opened his mouth again, sucked in an audible breath and let loose another one of the smoky gusts.

She went woozy for real this time, but just when she thought she'd pass out, a black blur leapt between them and knocked the man to the ground. The man dragged Meg along, but she was able to wrench free and fell to her knees. It defied logic and reason but somehow, a sleek panther, straight from the wilds of the jungle, had appeared. It wrestled with the man, slashing at him with blinding, powerful blows.

She crawled backward but was unable to tear her eyes away from the insane battle of mugger and cat. Sense set in and she reached again for her cell, but as her hands closed around it, the cat slapped at the man's head and the ski mask ripped free. The face beneath was not human. It was dark yellow, mottled with red blotches, and twisted with thick ropes of keloid scars. There were only holes where a nose should be in a strangely shaped bald skull. It had black lips and pointed scarlet ears. Some kind of Halloween costume, she reasoned. Except it wasn't Halloween.

The panther reared up once it had the advantage over the mugger, hissed, and then a thick mist enveloped it and swallowed it whole. The next moment, a man appeared where the panther had stood. Taller than her attacker, he wore a black leather biker jacket and held a wicked looking silver sword that gleamed with an unholy light. She couldn't see his face from her vantage point, but his buzz cut hair was black as sin, and so was his intent.

Sanity slipped into her madness. "No, wait, let me call the police."

Her attacker got slowly to his knees. He bled profusely from his wounds, but his blood was pus green and not red. He showed no signs of backing down and made an attempt to rise.

The swordsman moved his blade with an inhuman speed and severed the head of her attacker from the body. Putrefied green gore spewed out and then the body, head, and bodily fluids evaporated in a billowing cloud of ash.

Meg wanted to scream but she couldn't find her voice, like she was in one of those bad dreams where you ran and ran, but couldn't call for help and couldn't outdistance the monsters. But she wasn't dreaming. She was wide awake.

She sat down hard on the blacktop and stared, her numb brain trying to process what just took place. She was dimly aware of the sound of more people coming. And when she looked up, two with heavily scarred faces, and a third with that grotesque yellow mask rushed towards her. The fog thickened in their wake, closing out the real world, locking them all in a macabre grey prison.

A shadow fell across her. Before her stood the swordsman,

his blade angled down, his harsh, craggy face cast in a mix of darkness and light. His stark black eyes were as vast as the night sky and as cold as arctic ice. The instinct for self-preservation kicked in and she started to inch backward. The creatures were closing in. The man took a step forward and held out his hand. She caught the scent again, the same mysterious, exotic one that had drifted into her office earlier on a gentle summer breeze.

"I'm Gideon Sinclair, Dr. Carter. The police can't help you now." His rough voice rumbled through the night like thunder in a storm. "Come with me if you want to live."

Chapter Two

Meg froze. Fear gripped her, squeezing her heart until she felt it would burst. She wanted to believe tall, dark and dangerous. For one maddening, mindless second, she wanted to reach for him, have him take her away from this nightmare. It was insanity, of course. The sword wielding lunatic was even more threatening than the attackers converging on them. There was a coldness in his eyes, steel in his pose, an aura of strength and lethal intent that could not be ignored.

Think, Meg, think. You've got to get free. She stuck her hand in her bag and dropped the cell phone. Her fingers grazed her albuterol rescue inhaler and an idea struck.

"My leg," she said, her voice shaking with very real fear. "I don't think I can stand." She slung the backpack, palmed the inhaler in her other hand, and let him pull her to her feet. Her knees wobbled and he slipped his arm around her waist, holding her up and, more important, giving her a chance to get close.

"Stay behind me, and you'll be safe." His deep voice was hypnotic. This close his scent was a drug, swamping her senses. His face appeared carved from the most unyielding stone, in a harsh yet arresting manner. His rock hard, muscular body was pressed against her own, leaving very little to the imagination. Under any other circumstance she'd think she'd died and gone to heaven. This kind of man existed only in the hottest of midnight fantasies. But this was no fantasy, it was a nightmare, and she had to escape.

His dark eyes focused on hers, pinning her and burning through all her defenses. She almost lost her nerve, but the arrival of the rest of the thugs helped her find the courage. She brought up the inhaler and blasted him in the eyes with the aerosolized medicine. Albuterol wasn't as caustic as mace or pepper spray, but it did the trick.

He jerked back and released her, cursing in some foreign language and rubbing at his eyes with one hand. He never released the sword however, and moved that into a defensive position as he struggled to see.

Meg broke and ran. One of her sandals fell off but she didn't stop. The mist was now so thick she could barely see. She slowed her steps and focused on the ground, trying to follow the lines of the parking lot as a makeshift map to reach safety. She'd not gone too far when she ran into another body of solid muscle. A stench like a rotting corpse filled her nostrils and drew forth an involuntary gag. She looked up this time not at the swordsman, but at another creature like the one he'd killed.

It grinned down at her with razor sharp teeth, its black lips twisted into a sinister smile. This thing was real and not a man in a Halloween mask, a realization so frightening it chilled her very soul. The creature breathed down on her, smothering her in a black, noxious cloud. Her system went into overload. She lost control of her limbs and dropped to the ground. Agonizing pain rolled through her body. Her vision clouded as her mind began to shut down.

The creature, so far from human her brain could no longer deny what her eyes saw, bent over her as she groaned. It scraped a claw along her arm and puffed more smoke over her. Then it scooped her up off the ground and began to walk into the mist. She should have stayed with the swordsman, she thought, as her consciousness sank back in fear and pain and the world went dark.

Gideon's eyes burned like twin fires. The doctor was free and off running into the mystical fog conjured by one of the attackers. Three more jumped him and took him to the ground hard. Gideon kicked out at one, and sent it flying backward. His vision cleared in time to miss a death strike of another as it swung a Kriss dagger down at him. The blade glowed dull red and dripped with a viscous, black, magical poison, and was wielded by a zombified corpse. Gideon was immortal, but the right strike from the right weapon could slow him down, send him back to his Gods, or, take him out permanently.

Gideon rolled to one side, elbowed another zombie, and fought up to his feet. The first creature he'd killed was an Ash demon foot soldier. The one he'd kicked was the same make and it was getting to its feet as Gideon gained his own footing. Not wasting time, he brought up his blade and decapitated the demon. The head dropped to the ground, then it and the body disintegrated in a plume of fetid smoke. He hoped it was dead. Some demons you had to kill more than once, particularly depending on who was running the magical lead strings.

His sword heated in his hand, itching for the corrupt blood of the perverse creatures. That meant one more demon was still out there, if not more. Normally, he'd have sensed their kind, smelled them in his panther form as well as his human form. Tonight magic had covered the attack. Not the dime store kind, but big magic. The kind that did not come cheap, or easy, and always promised trouble. He had to find the doctor. There was no doubt in his mind they were after her because of her role in the convergence, and there was no doubt now that more was at work than the mystics had foreseen.

One of the zombies lunged and Gideon sidestepped the attack. As he dodged, he reached behind his shoulder, unsheathed the sawed-off shotgun, cut a quick arc and fired the first barrel at the thing. It blew a clean hole through the creature and sent a blue cleansing glow throughout, setting the imprisoned soul-energy free. The other backed off, but Gideon fired off the second shot before it could get out of range.

He holstered the gun and stared into the thick, impenetrable fog. He had to find Dr. Carter. He didn't have a second to lose. He focused and switched back to panther form. The were-magic given to him by Bast was based on the real creatures that traveled between the two worlds of human and animal. Their domain was the mists and as such, as panther, he could more easily navigate the enchanted fog.

Gideon's awareness spread out as he raced through the magical barrier. The last remaining creature, another Ash demon, carried Dr. Carter to a dark blue van. Whoever held the puppet strings knew how to cook up major magic. Those kinds of creatures didn't work easy, or free. They were summoned with the darkest of arcane words and held to task with the strongest of wills, and still they demanded a king's ransom in payment and human slaves. He scanned the area for a Keeper, the war band leader that was a more powerful version of the Ash demon. He also looked for more of the foot soldiers. Lucky for him and the doc, the Keeper wasn't around, and neither were more troops.

Gideon reached the van as the demon dumped the doc inside. He shifted back into human form, the sword once more in his hand, and hamstrung the creature. As it dropped, he decapitated it with a single strike. His sword blazed blue like an angry moon as the evil was released. With the threat neutralized, he spoke the word, and the sword vanished. His tattoo tingled with a light burn then went dormant. Gideon pulled out a cell phone and hit a series of numbers.

A woman's throaty voice came across the connection. "Mammett's Cleaners."

"It's Sinclair. I have a level three spill."

"Do you require containment?"

"Yeah." He glanced around as the magical fog began to thin. This last demon must have been the key for the spell. "Make it quick. There's risk of seepage, and two vehicles involved."

The nameless woman took the pertinent details and disconnected.

Gideon looked down at the unconscious Meg. Her features were contorted in pain and she moaned softly. He could take her out of play here and now and the cleaners would do the rest. He removed the .22, watching the shallow rise and fall of her chest as she breathed. She shifted restlessly and turned on her side. He raised the .22. For a moment, the dark clouds in the sky cleared, and moonlight shone down upon her alabaster skin.

She had no significant contact with the artifact as far as he could tell. The mystics indicated it would be several days before key contact resulted. The creatures he'd killed were the servants of someone running a hell of a lot of magical juice, and they wanted her as bad as the Council of Wardens wanted her out of play. None of the mystics foresaw this attack according to the information contained in his briefing file, meaning the whole interpretation could be wrong. A mystic could be compromised, indicating the entire operation was at risk. Gideon sheathed the .22. The clouds slid soundlessly across the moonlight, leaving him in darkness once more.

An innocent shouldn't suffer because a group of fools thought they saw something in a scrap of fevered vision. He wasn't a Paladin, he didn't follow orders without question. He moved her gently to the edge of the van and picked her up.

Her scent surrounded him. Her body warmed his. Cradled in his arms she was soft and boneless against him. She wore a tissue-thin, copper-colored gypsy skirt that flowed silkily over her curves. Her heat burned him in ways he didn't want to admit. His groin tightened, a purely male reaction to the sultry female held so close. He was breaking all the rules. He knew this, even as he set off for his SUV. He was breaking the rules, and risking the world and his very life for a hunch, and a mortal woman.

He was a champion of justice, he reminded himself. He moved above the normal concerns, he worked by different rules. He knew his business enough to know there was something rotten at work. Tonight he'd take Meg Carter out of play, just not the way the Council believed. He'd find out what was really behind this convergence and he'd find out what the real deviation point was, if indeed there even was one. If he played his cards right he could score the artifact before she came into contact and stop the convergence that way. If a mystic was compromised, he'd find out who and why, and rain hell upon those involved.

He reached the vehicle, touched the door, and the enchantment released the locks. He set Meg gently into the passenger's seat and belted her in. Then he dipped the seat back a bit so it appeared she was nothing more than a sleeping woman. Her face was still strained. The gas attack of the Ash demons not only put victims into a state of suspended consciousness, it caused the average human body tremendous pain. He took out a small vial from a breast pocket, dabbed a little of the lily-scented fluid on his finger and rubbed it on her temples. Unable to stop himself, he traced her full, berry-colored lips with his thumb, marveling at the plush, silken feel. A man kissed by those lips was a lucky man indeed.

He shook off the crazy, errant thought, closed the vial and tucked it away. Most likely, she'd sleep soundly for the next hour or so. Any pain she felt would be diminished by the sacred healing oil he'd placed on her skin, and eventually pass. He could wake her easily enough once he got her to safety. Until then, it served his purposes for her to sleep.

As an afterthought, he returned to the lot and grabbed her backpack and missing sandal and tossed them into the backseat. As he secured the shotgun in a concealed compartment beneath the dash, a non-descript van, one of Mammett's many that dotted the globe, slid into the front lot. Gideon made a quick search of the demon's vehicle, the only thing left of the battle other than ash piles and zombie corpses. The van was scrubbed. It had no identification and nothing useful: another sign of a determined professional fronting this operation.

He returned to the SUV, climbed into the driver's side, gunned the engine and pulled out of the lot. Once safely lost in the anonymity of the city streets he risked a glance at Meg. Her head tilted towards him, her features now relaxed. Her chest rose and fell with long, deep drawn breaths. He could watch her for hours and never tire. A dangerous thing. Gideon turned away. He couldn't afford to think of her as a woman. She was a mission, a mystery, nothing more. He had to sort out this mess, get her off his hands and stash her someplace safe.

He left Troy and picked up the Northway, bound for Lake George. There was a safe house in an old motel built on consecrated ground just outside of the tourist trap. He could hole up there with her and know they'd escape even the most assiduous of magical searches.

The night was dark and moody. Meg's enticing scent filled the cab of the SUV, making it damned hard for him to concentrate. Her presence had power, so much so, it surprised and worried him. In mist form out in the parking lot, his body was incorporeal. It was easy to remain physically aloof from her charms even while he was drawn to her in other, less tangible ways. In human form, his body had the normal male reactions experienced in the company of a desirable female. Only he wasn't really a normal male, and he could never forget that fact. It was the reason he kept to his own kind when looking for company, or, kept to one night stands with women who had no interest in anything other than a good time on a first, or no name basis only. Meg Carter wasn't that kind, and never could be, not under the circumstances. His attraction could only lead to trouble for them both. He needed distance and objectivity, not complications.

Then again, he'd gone and complicated things beyond reason by changing plans. He figured he had time before the solstice. According to the information on the flash drive, the summer solstice was D-day. If he found the artifact before then, if he kept her clear of it and figured out who was really after it, he had a chance of correcting things prior to the convergence. And that was the way it needed to go down, wasn't it? *Keep the doc far away and the convergence doesn't happen.* Gideon smiled to himself. It was a sound plan. There was a more secure safe house by the Canadian border. He could stash Meg there while he worked things out.

Tonight, though, he needed to get information from her. He grimaced, knowing what was to come. As an innocent, she had no idea what was really out there going bump in the night. He'd seen the disbelief in her eyes during the fight. A part of her recognized she was dealing with forces beyond the mundane, but the rest of her fought that recognition. He knew her brain would continue to resist, he knew she would try to block out the truth. She would see him as just another enemy, a psycho killer and kidnapper.

He needed to show her irrefutable proof that the weird and the wild existed, that he was on her side, sent to help, and capable of dealing with what would come. And he needed to show her she was dealing with a situation that couldn't be fixed by a call to the local cops, or her lawyer. Dr. Carter was used to fighting, he didn't want her fighting him. Not tonight. Every second counted like never before.

His cell rang and he answered via the link to the vehicle's sound system.

"Sinclair."

"What are you doing, Gideon? I heard from the cleaner. The Carter woman wasn't in the pick up." Ramon Salazar's smooth as glass baritone vibrated into the quiet cab. "You know we don't condone coloring outside the lines."

"An unexpected event took place. Wasn't on the radar, but it changed the picture and the plan." Gideon wondered if he could count on Salazar's backing. No one played the game quite like the Spaniard. "I'll send you out a more detailed report. Right now I need to go dark."

"You're playing fast and loose. That's a risky thing."

"I have until the solstice."

"You're prolonging the inevitable and putting everyone into unnecessary danger."

"This whole op stinks, Ramon. We both know that. I'm not coloring out of the lines, I'm in a whole different book. And in that book I need more than the word of some strung out trancer to take the life of an innocent."

"She was attacked. She's not that innocent. Someone wants

her other than us. That should tell you something."

Gideon bit back a curse. Ramon would respond better to reason than threat. "Someone wanted her bad enough to send a team of zombies and Ash demons to do the job. That tells me they may want to prevent contact with the artifact just like us, and I'm pretty damn sure they're not working towards the same end as we are. That means we could be wrong about her role in the convergence. That means we need more facts before we risk the dimensional timeline and the rest of the world."

Salazar was silent for a moment. Then he cleared his throat. "I don't like what you're doing, Gideon, but I agree, there is something wrong with the picture. The mystics should have picked up such a powerful magical presence. Even now it's not registering. It bothers me when I don't know the other players in a game."

Gideon's body relaxed. He'd need a man on the inside if he was going to succeed at running a rogue op. No better ally than Ramon Salazar could be had. No more dangerous enemy. So far, Salazar was an ally. He'd need to keep that alliance running strong. For a man who hated politics, that would be a challenge all on its own. "I'll call you when I have more."

"I'll keep the line clear." Salazar let out a deep, tired breath. "You may be onto something, Gideon. You may also find out that in the end it doesn't matter. The outcome may remain unchanged. What will you do then, if the only way to make it right is follow through with the original protocol?"

Gideon's blood ran cold, at both the Spaniard's words and the truth. He could do all the digging in the world, and the deviation point, the critical measure of time and action that could doom or save the timeline, could still come down to one thing: Meg Carter's life. Or death.

He glanced at Meg resting beside him, blissfully unaware of

the torrent of events surrounding her or the powerful enemies aligning against her. And, against him, now that he'd decided to go rogue. Choices. So much came down to choices. The memories spilled forward into his consciousness, like an invading army. His choices had led to the destruction of others. A picture of the bloody past blurred his vision. He blinked hard, cleared his mind, and focused on the unbroken lines of the road ahead.

"Gideon?"

"I'll call you, Ramon. Until then, see what you can dig up on any local activity."

Gideon cut the connection and switched the phone off. He needed to get them to safety as fast as possible. He fought the urge to bury the gas pedal and unwind the engine to the max. Unfortunately, none of the quicker passages that slipped between the normal fabric of space were currently open. The few he could find didn't run near enough to the motel to make the risk worth taking. He had to make do with the mundane routes of travel. Hopefully, the enchantments worked into the vehicle would keep them safe enough until they reached the sanctified grounds of the motel. Magic. Always a crap shoot.

Gideon mulled over what he knew so far, which was far too little for his liking. Questioning Meg might bring him more information, give him some much-needed leads. He hated this kind of job, all cloak and dagger with murky objectives and invisible players with obscure and shifting agendas. They were never clear-cut, not like the normal ops run by the Tribunal forces. Tracking down offenders, bringing them back for justice or executing justice on the spot, that was his stock and trade. He consoled himself with the fact that he was still serving justice, that Meg deserved a fair shake before fate and the Council of Wardens wrote her off as an acceptable casualty of dimensional integrity preservation.

He reached the exit as the rain changed from a soft mist to a punishing downpour, and ten minutes later, he turned the SUV into the parking lot of The Pine Motor Lodge. The neon sign blinked on and off, announcing no vacancy, but that was standard fare to keep out the tourists and the straights. The Pine catered to the metaphysical set exclusively, and the signs for them read vacancy, any time they needed one.

He parked near the front office and checked one last time on Meg. She appeared comfortable and showed no signs of rousing. He wished idly he could settle this account without having to show her the darker side of life, the oily black shadow that trailed what passed for reality. Gideon stepped back from the car and the mortal. He'd wished many things in his life and none had come to pass except the opportunity to wreak vengeance through eternity. Meg would soon wake and he would threaten and destroy everything she thought she knew about her world, and her life.

An hour later, safely ensconced in the rear most unit from the road, Gideon finished securing the last knot in the ties that bound Doctor Megan Carter to the heavy desk chair. He'd gagged her as well. Not so much she couldn't breathe, just enough to muffle the screams he knew would come as soon as she woke and realized what was happening. He recalled the attack in the clinic's parking lot. She had a great set of lungs. If it wasn't for the enchantment, half of the city would have heard her cries for help. The memory made him check his knots again. She wasn't just a screamer, she was a fighter. She had suckered him in and sprayed him down with whatever it was she had in the little dispenser. It wasn't as caustic as pepper gas, or concentrated tear gas, but it had surprised him enough he let her go. The doc had fire beneath that angelic face and Mona Lisa smile. Fire and grit.

He took a last look at her and moved the chair away from the desk, putting it in the narrow space between the end of the king-sized bed and the beat-up dresser. If she managed to get loose she'd have no room to maneuver. A man needed to be prepared for anything when dealing with a woman as resourceful and unpredictable as Megan Carter.

Gideon glanced at the ammonia ampule that sat on the cheap, Formica dresser. Beside it was his Saxe dagger, made of the same enchanted steel as his sword. The mirror above reflected the absurd scene, Meg bound and gagged in the chair, him looming over her like some great beast of prey. It reaffirmed his choice of action tonight. There would be no other real way to convince her of the truth.

Gideon stripped off his shirt and tossed it on the bed next to his jacket. He crossed the small room, tested the locks, moved the gaudy orange curtains just enough to check the empty lot outside for trouble. Then, he got down to business.

He took the ammonia ampule and bent down so he was face to face with Meg. This close, her breath was warm against his skin. He touched her cheek, amazed at how silky it felt. The memories of the past pushed hard to break free, but the iron prison of his will held fast. Yet that will was not strong enough to resist the surge of longing that welled up. He almost gave in, almost kissed her, but at the last second, he held his move. A wave of guilt assaulted him and he jerked back.

"You're a perv, Gid." She was tied up, unconscious, helpless because of him, and he had no business touching her the way he did. He had no business wanting...what? Something indefinable and nebulous, something he half remembered from a long forgotten dream. He broke the ampule and the sharp tang of ammonia assaulted his senses. He held it under her nose until she showed signs of rousing.

Gideon discarded the broken ampule in the nearby wastebasket, stepped clear of Meg, crossed his arms before his chest and waited. Whatever idiocy was numbing his brain and plaguing his body would soon be driven out of him by the ordeal he was about to endure.

He watched intently as her eyelids fluttered, then opened. Her pupils were dilated, and she blinked several times before she tilted her head up and focused completely upon him. Awareness filled those wide green eyes with dark shadows of fear followed by blazing anger. She screamed into her gag and fought her bonds like a tigress, trying to unsettle the chair.

For a few minutes Gideon let her carry on. Talking now would do no good. She'd listen better once she realized there was no escape. Color flooded her cheeks, a dark pink the shade of summer roses. Gideon fisted his hands to keep from reaching for her. He held her gaze, enduring the heat until the fury subsided, until she stilled, until a single, fat tear welled up and slid silently down her cheek. It splashed onto the ropes binding her, and it burned him to his core. He felt like a prize ass. He needed her to believe, but to do that she had to see with her own eyes, and there was no way she'd sit by and witness what he was about to do without trying to either run for the hills, or, stay his hand.

"I wish I could do this the easy way, Doc. But we're short on time and I need you to understand that the world you think you know doesn't exist. You're in more trouble than you can imagine, and I'm the one man who can help you."

Her reaction was a few more weak screams and another tear.

"Sit back, try to relax. I'm not going to hurt you."

She broke the stare and looked down at the floor.

Mortals. They were never easy. "What I have to tell you will sound crazy, but I assure you, it's true. My name is Gideon Sinclair. I told you that already and it's the truth. I also told you the police can't help you, and that's true."

That got her attention. She glanced shyly back up at him.

"I've been sent to save you, Meg," he lied. "I can keep you safe but you need to trust me. You need to believe me. I'm an immortal soldier. I serve justice and nothing else."

She actually had the audacity to roll her eyes.

He smiled. "I know. Sounds nuts, right? You're a doctor. You believe in science. You believe what you see."

He picked up the dagger and she moaned, fear clouding out any sense of reason in her soft eyes. She thought the blade was meant for her.

"Don't worry. I'm not going to hurt you. I need you to believe so we can get on with business. I wasn't kidding when I told you we're short on time."

She settled down and he steeled himself for what was to come. He knew shapeshifting wouldn't be enough for her. It was too much like an illusionist's parlor trick. He had to go for blood with this one. He pointed to the space between two ribs and felt his heart pulse strong beneath his finger. Her eyes widened in question.

"You know what sits below these ribs, Doc. My heart. You know if I was mortal and this knife slipped between these two ribs it would pierce my heart and I'd be stone cold dead."

She nodded quickly, her movements panicked.

He had a feeling she got the drift of what he was about to do. He took a deep breath. "Good thing I'm not mortal."

Before he could think too hard he drove the blade deep into his chest, then jerked it free and let it drop to the floor. Pain flooded his senses, but as in the past, there was surprisingly little blood. He dimly heard Meg scream, then he fell to his knees and gave in to the agony.

Chapter Three

Meg screamed bloody murder as tall, dark and crazy drove a wicked looking knife directly into his heart. She pulled in vain at the ropes holding her fast to the chair. At first she'd wanted to kill him. Now that she was witness to his suicide she wanted to save him. He was deranged. No sane man thought he was immortal, no sane man kidnapped a woman and stabbed himself in the heart.

She yanked her wrists and legs until her skin rubbed raw, all to no avail. He was on all fours, blood dripping onto the hideous green shag carpet. She gave up fighting the ropes and tried to move the chair closer to him. With fits and jerks she was able to move so her knee touched his shoulder but the last jump tipped the chair too far and it toppled sideways. She knocked into him and he sprawled back on the floor.

From this position she could see his magnificent, injured chest. She watched it rise, then fall, as if he still breathed. She shook her head, and refocused. It wasn't as if he still breathed. He was actually breathing. Nice, slow, deep breaths. Not shallow gasps, not labored, hollow death rattles, but good, lusty lungfuls of oxygen that would feed his blood and nourish his brain. Certainly not the actions of a dead man.

Then he groaned.

Impossible. No one could survive that wound. Meg fought

the bonds some more but she was wedged between him and the end of the tacky dresser, leaving her little room to maneuver. Her struggle brought her close against his warm, solid body, and he gave another bear-like growl.

"Easy, Doc," he rumbled in that sexy, gravely voice. "Don't hurt yourself. I'm the immortal, not you."

He pushed himself up into a sitting position and slowly got to his feet. She turned her head and watched as he stood. The wound was already closed, the edges pink and well approximated. *Impossible.*

He grabbed her chair and righted her with a single move. His bare, muscled arms flexed with the action in a raw display of masculine power. He retrieved the knife and wiped the blood off on the edge of the yellow floral bedspread. She followed his every move, a study in sinuous grace.

He came close enough so his leather clad legs grazed hers and gazed down upon her with those inscrutable black eyes. "Do I need to show you a second time or do you believe?"

Believe what? That he was immortal. It was impossible. Yet he was living proof otherwise. She couldn't argue, gagged as she was. She couldn't believe, but she couldn't disbelieve.

"You think it's a trick." He half grinned, and for a moment the look in his eyes softened. "It's not. I'm the real deal."

Slowly, Meg nodded. A strange warmth spread throughout her body and as she analyzed it, a startling realization hit her. For the first time since walking out of the clinic, she didn't feel afraid. Perhaps her natural curiosity helped her overcome fear, perhaps it was because he could have hurt her at any time, and hadn't. Perhaps it was something deeper.

"This is no stage prop." He jammed the blade point down into the dresser and the blade held. "It's not retractable. And you already know how sharp it is, right, Doc?"

She bobbed her head in agreement. She tried to tell him "release me", but it came out sounding like a bunch of gibberish.

"So maybe I am what I say I am. Maybe you'll be quiet if I take off the gag."

What choice did she have? Meg knew she was in deep. At some point, just after leaving the sanctuary of the Russell Clinic building, she and reality parted ways. What if Gideon was an immortal? What if there were more of those sick, nightmarish things waiting beyond the walls of the outdated motel room? Now she knew how Alice felt falling down the rabbit hole. What if Gideon Sinclair was her only hope of finding her way back to her normal world?

The softness she'd seen earlier in him vanished in the blink of an eye. "Are you ready to listen to my story?"

She stayed very still as he judged her, that hot, black gaze burning deep into her soul. How sad to meet such an incredible looking man under such dubious circumstances. He was built like a god, with wide shoulders, a broad, deep chest, and a narrow, tapered waist. Corded, solid muscle stood out on every male inch of him. His skin was golden tanned and an ornate sword tattoo covered the inner right forearm.

She considered his words and her few options, then nodded in agreement. Maybe this was just a dream?

His long, calloused fingers grazed her cheeks as he released the gag. His touch sent shivers to her very core. No, Gideon Sinclair was no dream. He was a flesh and blood man, and he was all too real. She was crazy to be thinking of her kidnapper as some kind of sex god. Not only had she lost reality, she'd lost her mind as well.

"So, Doc, do you believe?"

Meg licked her dry lips. "You can't expect me to believe in

immortality."

"Take a moment, think of everything you've seen tonight. Does it add up to any reality you're aware of?" He sat down on the edge of the big bed and the mattress groaned beneath his bulk. "Have you ever seen the like? Of me, or them?"

The horrific scenes played through her mind, the macabre creatures, Gideon's stabbing and survival.

"I'm a doctor. A scientist." Her brain turned over the scenes again and again, and reason attempted and failed to supply answers. "There is no such thing as immortality."

"There is." He reached back onto the bed, grabbed his black T-shirt and shrugged into it, taking away the spectacular view. "There's magic. There's old Gods. There's feuds, wars, demons, creatures that go bump in the night. Boogey men exist. Nightmares are real. So am I, and I'm one of the guys who makes the dark a safer place. I'm one of the guys who works to keep the shadows to themselves, so the average mortal can go on with life and never worry too much about what's really lurking just one step behind and slightly out of focus."

"I can't accept that, Mr. Sinclair." If she did, it meant everything she thought she knew was suspect. It meant the anchor of science that kept her life from casting adrift was gone and that she was floating now in a storm she couldn't control or even begin to understand. There was nothing Meg hated more than being out of control. "Please, let me go. Let me go home, I'll forget all of this. I won't tell the authorities."

He cracked that half grin again, giving his harsh visage a suddenly boyish look. Then, before her very eyes, he faded into mist. The mist rose and swirled around her, carrying that scent she first experienced when she opened her balcony door to the sultry night. Every nerve in her body flared to life. Her skin electrified as the mist danced across her like a light, silken rain.

Heat pooled low in her belly and for a moment she forgot her situation and surrendered to the delicious, alien sensation.

When the air around her thinned, she opened her eyes. He stood before her, looking down at her with hooded, sleepy eyes. "Still don't believe?"

"You're impossible," she breathed, her throat tight and dry, her body hot and wet. "This is crazy."

"I couldn't agree more. But it's the truth." He reached out and brushed her cheek with his knuckle. "I'm immortal and I'm the only chance you have at staying alive in a very nasty, very deadly game."

Her body responded to his touch even as her mind recoiled. "Please. Let me go."

"I'll release you but I want your word you won't run. You're not safe out there."

I'm not safe in here. Not with a man like you. And yet, she did feel safe. On some strange, deep level, she'd never been safer. She was shocked by that thought. A part of her believed this insanity. How much more could she witness and not believe? She didn't feel drugged. He didn't appear to be a magician. He'd turned to mist, for God's sake. What if he was right? If there was magic, if there was someone, or something out to get her, no one she knew, not Bill Russell, not the police, no one could keep her safe but him. She'd need to trust this man Gideon Sinclair. She let out a deep breath. "Fine. I'll stay. I'll listen. But if I don't like what I hear, you need to promise to let me go."

He appeared about to reply when someone knocked on the door.

Gideon spoke a word that sounded like twelve consonants rushed together without the benefit of vowels, and the sword tattoo vanished from his forearm. In its stead, a sword appeared in his hand.

He walked cautiously to the door, every muscle tensed and ready for lethal action. “What?”

“It’s Roy. Got the food you ordered, Gid. Want me to leave it at the door?”

“Yeah. Thanks. Put it on the tab.”

“Will do, brother. I won’t forget to add my tip, either.”

Gideon waited a moment, spoke another one of those weird words, and the sword vanished. He brought in a pizza, an amber bottle of beer, and a couple of bottles of clear, sparkling spring water.

“That’s a fancy trick you do with the sword.” Meg wondered if he did it for safety, effect, or a combination of both.

“I’ve been with that blade since I was twenty-eight. We’re real comfortable with one another.” He grabbed the knife and made short work of her bonds, freeing her in seconds. Then he turned it over and handed it to her, hilt first. “Go ahead. Check it out. You’ll see. No tricks.”

She took the knife but she knew as she did he wasn’t lying. There were no tricks. A man didn’t stab himself in the heart, turn to mist, and bring a tattoo to life with tricks. The reality she thought she knew began to crumble to dust around her. And as the old world passed away, curiosity for the new world bloomed. She handed back the blade.

“How old are you now?” He appeared to be a rugged late thirties, but there was something ageless in the obsidian depths of his eyes. They reflected an old soul. “Or shouldn’t I ask?”

“Let’s just say I’ve been around the block a few times, and then some.” He slipped the knife into a sheath strapped to his calf and lowered the leg of his leather pants. “You’ve been through a lot tonight. Before we start, why don’t you have a drink and some food."

"I'm not hungry but I'll take a drink, thanks." She reached for one of the sparkling waters. Her hands shook as she opened it, betraying her anxiety. She wanted to brazen it out and she tried to summon as much courage as she could manage, but she found herself running close to empty. How did her patients manage? They faced off against death and the unknown everyday. They weren't adults, either. They were young kids who should be planning birthday parties and going to little league games, who instead spent hours taking in toxic chemicals trying to poison the poison and gain just a few more days, a few more weeks. The science was as much magic to them as what Gideon showed her tonight, and still they endured. Surely, she could do the same?

Meg took a deep drink of the cool water and felt it go down like ice. She couldn't fathom what she'd done to get mixed up in this madness. She never did anything out of the ordinary. She was a doctor with a very scant social life. Where had she gone wrong?

She stretched out her legs, crossed her arms, and gave her sexy captor what she hoped was a cold, hard stare. "So tell me, Mr. Sinclair, why exactly am I in such danger?"

She looked like a frightened kid one moment, an angry angel the next. Her hands grasped the bottle of sparkling water like a lifeline. She might still try to bolt. She was clearly still poised on the edge of panic.

He'd have to ease her into this, control the information in a way to get him what he needed without completely freaking her out. Or, letting her know the real truth of why he was sent for her. If she knew he'd come to kill her it would be hard to sell her the hero story.

Gideon twisted the cap off the lager bottle and sat on the edge of the bed. “There's a war going on, Doc, between good and evil. Right now, you're caught in the middle of one of the skirmishes.”

There. It was the truth. Kind of dressed down. He wasn't lying either, just not telling the whole story.

She frowned slightly and chewed on her bottom lip. He found the action completely fascinating and when she spoke it caught him by surprise. “Good and evil fighting? Does the good and evil have names? Anyone I know?”

There was the faintest tone of sarcasm. Better than hysteria, he reasoned. “Good and evil have many names. Take many forms.”

“Sounds very biblical.”

“Every religion and culture has their operating manual.”

She toyed with the bottle, her hands steadying at last. “And you work for good?”

“I work for justice. And, I work for balance.”

“You'll forgive me if it all seems a little esoteric.” She cocked her head slightly to one side and gave him a long, narrow-eyed stare. “I'm between good and evil?”

“You're in the middle of a fight for control of the balance between good and evil.”

“How will I affect this balance?” She sipped her drink. The droplets of spring water moistened her lips and when the tip of her pink tongue darted out to trace her top lip, Gideon couldn't suppress his groan, or stop the lightning fast rush of desire that stiffened his cock. He stood and turned his back to her, seeking composure that wouldn't come.

“How you affect the balance remains to be seen. I need some information from you.” Gideon forced his libido down like a misbehaving dog. What the hell was wrong with him? He wasn't a kid. He was over eight hundred years old for that matter. He mustered some self-control and turned back to face the red-headed siren. "Once I have some answers I'll have a better idea of what role you play in this game."

"Game?" She laughed lightly and shook her head. Some more silken curls slipped loose from the clip. "That's a nice, anesthetized term."

He longed to take the clip from her hair, to bury his hands deep into the curls. "It's the truth."

"The truth? Why do I get the feeling, Mr. Sinclair, you're telling me a highly edited version of the truth?"

Damn. Beautiful and smart. Just his luck. "Call me Gideon. Mr. Sinclair makes me feel old."

He took a swallow of lager and leaned against the ancient dresser. The best defense was a good offense. Time to take point and draw fire. "Have you come into contact with any Egyptian artifacts recently?"

The question caught her off-guard. She sat back in the chair, her look first surprised, then pensive. She licked her lips again. The soft knit fabric of her sweater pulled taut over her breasts as she took a deep breath and released it. Desire thickened his blood.

Meg swept the wild curls from her eyes. "I went to the Met two months ago, down in the city. Is that considered contact?"

So far so good. Maybe he grabbed her early enough. "This would be more hands on. It would have been a canopic jar, or a piece of jewelry resembling an ornate, woven metallic belt."

At the mention of the jar she went very still. His spirits crashed. He was too late. "What is it, Doc. What did you touch?"

"It wasn't an actual artifact." Her hands started to shake

again. She put down the bottle of water, laced her fingers together, and folded her hands in her lap. "Dr. Liebers, the other pediatric oncologist at the clinic, ordered a gag gift from a company that makes stage props and historical reproductions. He sent for a trocar and a few funerary implements to give the county coroner for his birthday."

"What other implements?" If she had contact with the artifact already it would speak to motive for the attack in the parking lot. His brain raced over possible next steps. He didn't want any of them to be completion of protocol. Gods, he hoped he had a choice. "Be specific, this is important."

"The company made a mistake and sent a canopic jar instead of the trocar." She frowned and looked up at him, guilt and fear clouding her eyes. "But it wasn't real."

Gideon put down the beer, retrieved his cell, and pulled up the pictures of the artifact. Okay, so maybe she touched it. That didn't mean she'd changed the timeline yet. He showed her the screen as he flashed through the photos. "Did the jar look similar to this one?"

He didn't need her to answer. Her face paled and she chewed on her bottom lip. She couldn't meet his gaze. "Where did you get those pictures? What is that jar? Why's it so important? It's a fake."

"The jar is real. It was one of five stolen from the newest dig at the Valley of the Tombs of the Kings in Egypt." He snapped the cell shut and shoved it into his pocket. She saw it, she touched it, that didn't mean she got her hands on the real deal inside: the woven silver belt known as the Buckle of Isis. According to his briefing materials, her contact with the Buckle of Isis was the driving event and the point where the timeline's negative convergence could be countered. Then again, all his info could be wrong if a mystic was compromised. Damn. The rock and the hard place. No worse spot to be stuck. "Did you see what was inside? Handle the contents in any way?"

"No. The jar was sealed tight. We passed it around for luck, rubbed it like you would a Buddha's belly. Everyone in the office had a good laugh. That's all. I swear."

Gideon released the breath he was holding. "That's good, Doc. One more thing in our favor."

"How is my touching something going to affect the balance between good and evil? It seems so random."

"Many things that look random are actually a result of fate, destiny, or outright interference."

"You make it sound as if there's a master plan being followed."

He couldn't help but laugh. Though untutored to the fine points of the game, Meg's comment was dead on. "Unfortunately, there are so many master plans being followed that the fate of the mortal world is always at risk during any given moment in time."

She smiled back at him, a small, wry twist of her luscious lips that made him hot all over. "The mortal world? So your kind protects my kind?"

"Something like that."

"How'd you become immortal?"

If she knew the real details she'd run screaming from him and never look back. "I did a favor for a Goddess, then I died. She offered me a job. Here I am."

"Goddess?" She furrowed her brow. "Well, I guess if you're going to be immortal, the old-fashioned gift from the Gods is as good as any way to get there. Of course, I imagined a fountain of youth, or some kind of vampire thing. More romantic."

"There's nothing romantic about vampires. They're soulless

parasites, most of them."

"Don't tell me vampires exist."

"Okay, I won't. But me not telling you doesn't change the fact." He could watch her for hours and never get tired. The woman who'd first seemed so plain in pictures was as seductive to him as a flame to a moth. What was it about this mortal? Why did she capture him so? And why did she threaten what he held so tight inside of him, those ghosts, the dead of his past? She didn't look like anyone he knew from his once mortal existence, and yet every moment he spent in her presence was another moment those ghosts gathered strength and pushed hard against his fortified walls. "You don't believe a Goddess would grant me immortality?"

She shrugged and her breasts moved in a languid, entrancing way. "No."

Gideon swallowed hard. "But you believe I'm immortal."

"I can't disprove it at the moment."

Ever the scientist. He only needed some more information, then he could lock her away at the safe house in Rouses Point and get on with this job. "Where's the jar now, Doc? I need to get it, and I need to get you to a safer place."

"Dr. Liebers still has it. The coroner's birthday is at the end of June."

"Call Liebers. Arrange a meeting tomorrow."

"It's after midnight. Are you crazy? No, wait, don't answer that. He's covering for me on my day off. He'll be in the office tomorrow at nine sharp. I can stop in and ask him about the jar. Then you can be on your way. Will that work for you?"

"Only if I go with you. I'm not sure I can trust you. I don't think you really get it yet. You can't go back to work, Doc. Can't go back to your old life. Not until this business is concluded, not until I've figured out who was trying to snatch you in that parking lot, and not until I'm sure that everything's nice and neat."

Color bloomed in her cheeks. Her eyes sparkled with fury. "What the hell does that mean?"

"I'm going to stick you in a safe house. It's a farm run by a Wiccan priestess. It's on consecrated, protected ground. Nothing can touch you while you're there."

She jumped to her feet and stormed over to him, standing toe to toe. "I don't know if you've realized this yet, but I'm a real doctor. Not a PhD. An MD. I don't only do research, I still have an active practice with live patients who need me to be there for them. I can't just run off and hide."

Gideon forced himself not to smile at her uproar. He'd pegged her right. Meg Carter was a fighter. She looked ready to take his head clean off. Her sultry heat washed over him in waves, despite the chill of the air conditioning cranked at full blast. He had to grab his beer with both hands to keep from reaching out and pulling Meg hard against him. She stirred the most primal of urges inside him in a way they'd not been touched since he was mortal. The effect was both terrifying and intoxicating. "What do you think those things in the parking lot were? Boy Scouts?"

"I can't explain what they were."

"I can. The greyish, yellow-skinned things were a species called Ash demons. The ones we fought were foot soldiers. They run in mercenary teams and sell out to high powered mages to do all kinds of nasty, evil things. They have a leader called a Keeper. He's ten times as tough as any of his soldiers. I didn't see him, but he'll be around soon with reinforcements, since the first wave of his boys failed to do their job."

"Demons?" She appeared confused. "No."

"Yes." He stood, set down the beer, and took a step closer. He wanted to wrap her in his arms and keep her safe, never let her go. He needed to get through her thick, scientist skull she was not only in danger, but a danger to everyone around her. "The other things were zombies. Again, servants of a powerful master. All of them out for you, Doc. They'll kill anything that gets in their way, and trust me, whoever this guy is that wants you, he'll send more. The Ash tend to travel in packs of twelve, and I only dusted three. You do the math. You want to help your patients? Your coworkers? Steer clear of them until I fix this mess."

She tilted her head up to look at him, her eyes misty, innocent, entrancing. "Why, Gideon. Why do they want me?"

He savored his name spoken by her. He brushed a stray curl back behind her delicate, shell-shaped ear. The strand was gossamer soft and burned him like a brand.

"I don't know." It was only half a lie, making it half the truth. "But I'll find out. And when I do, I'll put an end to it all. I swear this to you, Meg. I'll keep you safe."

"Did your Goddess send you to me?"

"She sent me." Another half truth.

She drew a ragged breath, and suddenly the stress and strain of the night showed. "Who is this Goddess, and why would she send you to me?"

Finally, something he could answer with complete honesty. He reached out for her, touching her shoulders lightly. She was so delicate, so feminine. The urge to protect Meg was as strong as the desire to possess her. "Her name is Bastet."

"The Egyptian Goddess of justice."

"And the patron of women and children. I'm her champion, Doc. I fight for justice, that's why she sent me."

"Justice wouldn't involve stopping me from my work, taking me from my life. I help children, I fight death. Don't lock me away. I'm needed."

"It won't be forever."

She pushed the hair from her face with a quick, impatient gesture. "How long?"

"One week. Maybe two."

His words renewed her ire. She pulled out of his grasp and planted her hands firmly on her shapely hips. "Two weeks? Not only do I have patients, but I'm scheduled to meet with a pharmaceutical company. The clinic is in the top three choices for staging a very important drug trial. Without me..."

"They'll survive."

Her shoulders slumped, and he felt like a total heel. Next he'd be kicking puppies. "It won't be easy, I'm sure," he added as consolation. "Maybe I'll get this taken care of sooner. If I can get the artifact, who knows?"

"What is the connection between me and that jar?" She shook her head in frustration. "I don't get it. I don't get any of this. How can a jar affect the balance of the universe?"

How much could he really tell her? How much should he tell her, about the timelines, the preservation effort, the games the Gods played. The convergences that hinted at the end of time, or worse. "The details don't matter. All that matters is you don't touch it, and lay low until the solstice passes."

She digested the information but she didn't back down. "But I touched it, Gideon. I told you I touched it."

"Did anything happen?"

Again, that dainty shrug.

He watched the rise and fall of her breasts and wished not for the first time he were mortal, a man who could meet her in her world, a man who could share a kiss, a touch, a normal life.

"You touched it, but not what's inside. Nothing happened, which means you're safe." He hoped. He wasn't exactly sure, and if the mystics were wrong as he suspected, it was really anyone's guess as to how her connection or lack thereof with the artifact would affect the timeline convergence.

Meg looked to him for answers, salvation, and he was fresh out of both. "You're tired. Stressed. Have something to eat. Try to relax."

She frowned and turned away from him. She paced to the far end of the room and stood by the small, beat-up desk in the shadows just beyond the pool of yellow light cast off from a cheap, dome-shaped overhead light. The unit was small, cramped, outdated. She looked around the room as if seeing it for the first time. "I've been attacked, kidnapped, held hostage in the worst decorating of the nineteen seventies, told all kinds of insane things, and you want me to eat pizza? Don't mind if I take a pass."

She appeared smaller, tired, like an elfin child abandoned in a strange place, with no hope of finding her way home. He would have given anything at that moment to change what happened, to change fate. "If you're not going to eat, then get some sleep. We need to leave early to be back in Troy by nine in the morning. It's already past midnight."

Meg wrapped her arms around herself, and shivered. "I'm scared, Gideon. Of you, of all you've told me. How am I supposed to sleep?"

"Lie down, Meg. You're exhausted."

She looked behind him at the bed, then back at him. "What about you?"

"I'm going to stay up a while. Eat. Think. Keep an eye out." He turned the dimmer switch, lowering the overhead light until it was nothing but a dull glow. Then he moved the chair and pizza, and took up guard by the door. "Go ahead. Clean up and get some shuteye. You're safe with me."

Meg took him up on the suggestion, and after a few minutes fussing in the bathroom, climbed onto the bed where she lay ramrod straight, staring at the ceiling. He moved the orange curtains enough that he could see the outside from his angle, but not be visible. As he sat, he ate and tried not to think about the captivating female in the bed. Time passed, and soon he heard the even, deep breaths of sleep. Despite the tension, she'd managed to drift off.

Gideon breathed in her unique scent and it played havoc with his self control. He couldn't recall a time in any of his centuries, mortal or immortal, when a woman had affected him so strongly in so short a time. Meg Carter was dangerous. She was a threat to his clear thinking. He couldn't dispose of her, not yet, nor did he want to. He figured at best he had another twenty-four hours in her company before he could dump her at the safe house.

He recalled the velvet feel of her skin, the sensuous texture of her lips, and he recalled his body's reaction to hers the instant she pressed against him in the heat of battle. Gideon had never lacked for female company. He'd never lived a monk's life like some of the other soldiers and players in the game. But he'd been careful and he had the added advantage of a heart that was less than whole. He remembered his ordeal, the trial of the Forty-Two Assessors when he died down in the sands just outside of Cairo so many, many years ago. They weighed his heart, those Egyptian Gods, because no other Gods came to claim him, because in life he'd denounced any faith in anything other than his sword and his lust for vengeance and battle. That heart came up wanting.

A man who could not be manipulated by the emotions

lodged in the heart, a man free from the complications of love and jealousy, was a rare prize. A man who was not beholden to any other Gods, a seasoned warrior not afraid to fight, was even rarer still. He was that man, and he was the right man for the job Bast had vacant. If it weren't for her, his wanting heart would have been devoured by the alligator-headed Goddess, and any hopes of afterlife, eternal rest, heaven, hell, or reincarnation, would have vanished. His existence would be nullified, his consciousness shredded, his body and blood an eternal feast for Sokar, the darkest Goddess of the Dead the Egyptians had to offer. So he counted himself lucky that sometimes, a wanting heart could be a valuable asset and that a mindless favor done to a four-legged creature would save him from an eternal nightmare.

It never mattered to him, not having a whole heart. Hell, it explained so much of his past in his mortal life and many of his mistakes. As he listened to the soft breathing of Meg Carter, as he watched her shadow, inhaled her scent, felt her essence in his blood, Gideon clung to that fact as a drowning man held fast to anything that would keep him afloat. Meg hit him on a far more visceral level. Hormones. Her presence stirred his hormones, stirred them hard into overload. No more. No less. She couldn't touch him any deeper, for there wasn't anything to touch. He was safe. And so was she.

She slept. She couldn't believe she managed it, but fatigue jumped her like a thief in the night and took her down. Gideon woke her at dawn and they had a hasty breakfast at a local diner, then they were on the road again.

She'd prodded him all morning for more answers, peppering him with questions, but his responses were measured, calculated and cautious. He was holding out on her. He told her nothing more than she'd heard last night except that she probably didn't know the person responsible for the attack. She found that hard to believe. Something so violent couldn't be random. Then again, what she thought she knew about everything was suspect. Last night's events had opened her eyes to another world, one that ran by different rules, one that cast a long dark shadow over her own. It would take time to know it all and to come to terms with it. It was easier to focus on the details and things close at hand than think too hard on the long term implications of dual realities and threats to timelines.

As she turned things over again and again in her mind, Meg stole glances at the lethal soldier seated beside her in the SUV. His stony face showed no hint of emotion nor any signs of fatigue from last night. She, on the other hand, looked like death warmed over. There were dark circles carved deep into her skin beneath her eyes and the rest of her face appeared completely devoid of color. Her eyes were bloodshot, and her hair a hornet's nest. She did her best to hold the curls back in a clip, but the humidity and the fitful sleep had turned it wild and nothing would keep it tame.

Gideon's black buzz cut looked perfect, every hair standing at attention, in neat, precise order. Sunglasses hid his dark eyes from her, but she imagined they held the same unblinking, intense stare behind the shades as they did with them off. That stare could burn a hole through ten tons of concrete. She'd seen it soften a few times, fleeting moments at best, and when it did, it made her melt.

He was a disconcerting package, her kidnapper turned hero. His body was built for war, and, she suspected for love. She vividly recalled how he looked without his shirt, all that golden skin covering taut, rippling muscle, begging to be touched. She wanted to run her hands over every inch of him, to linger over the sexy forearms, to trace the lines of each defined abdominal, to follow the line of crisp, dark curls that descended to a wondrous, mysterious place beneath his belt.

He wasn't immune to her either. She'd caught a glimpse of his growing interest as it tightened and pushed against the leather of his pants. At the time she'd dismissed it, giving her attention to more pressing matters like getting free or figuring out what the hell was going on. But he'd distracted her with his touch easily enough. His palms were wide, his fingers long, and the few times those hands had grazed her skin or held her body she felt power and restraint, and she felt a kindle of desire.

Conjuring up the delicious memories distracted her and gave her a strange sense of longing she couldn't quite define. She supposed thinking about Gideon in a simple, sexual way kept her mind off the other more disturbing events and facts of the night. She didn't want to believe in immortal soldiers and yellow-skinned boogey men, but it seemed she didn't have much of a choice. She didn't want to believe she had the hots for this enigmatic, deadly soldier. But she couldn't deny the attraction, nor could she rationalize it away. The feeling was too raw, too primal.

All night long she'd bordered on the verge of nightmares and each time it seemed the worst would happen, there he was, standing tall, sword out. *Come with me if you want to live.* She'd heard him say it a hundred times if she'd heard him say it once. His presence brought her peace, made her feel safe, and, at the same time, stoked the flames of her darkest desires. She knew on an instinctive level he would be a demanding lover, one who would take her to the edge and then push her beyond. In her dreams he'd touched her in ways that had her body writhing in ecstasy. When she thought she'd find release the darkness would come once more, and the nightmares begin. It was a terrifying cycle of death and sex, where every moment counted, where she never felt more alive, never felt more desired. When she finally woke, it was as if she'd had no sleep at all. And, no satisfaction.

She hungered for his touch and ached for release. The tension tightened into an unbearable knot of fire deep inside her core. She knew Gideon caused this, and she knew only he could cure her. Just as she knew she'd never have him, never find that satisfaction. She couldn't have found a more unattainable man in the world if she'd tried. He was a soldier on a mission. He may be attracted on a physical level but she could tell he was far too disciplined to let that get in the way. Mixing it up with her sexually would compromise his objective and Gideon Sinclair was not a man who compromised. He'd get his jar and then he'd dump her up at some farm and get on with saving the universe. She'd never see him again.

That thought cooled her desire and kicked her brain into gear. Maybe that explained this irrational desire. Maybe that explained why it came so fast, so devastatingly fast. Wanting the thing you know you can't have, only because you can't have it, was that the attraction? No. There was something more than the lure of the forbidden in Gideon. She gave it more consideration and by the time they pulled into Troy, Meg had what she believed to be a viable answer.

Scent. It had to be his scent. Not that the rest of his package wasn't worth a second or third look, or touch. Meg figured even the potent visuals weren't enough to trigger such a strong reaction in so short a time. As a doctor she knew human biology, knew the hardwiring. Gideon's pheromones spoke to hers and they said very wicked things. Her suffering was nothing but a case of nature asserting itself. Normal. Comforting in a way, since nothing else about him or their meeting was in any way, shape or form, normal. Unfortunately, not thinking about Gideon meant thinking about the other things she'd met yesterday.

He pulled the big SUV into the front lot of the clinic and she flinched as the memory of last night's attack replayed through her mind. "Are you sure about this, Gideon?"

"I need the artifact. Liebers has it. We can get it back, and you can tell Russell about the leave of absence." He turned off the motor. "You good with the cover?"

She nodded as butterflies took flight in her stomach. She hadn't been this nervous since her first surgical rotation as an intern. "You're the son of my mother's dearest friend Rita. Rita only has days to live and has elected to die at home with family and friends. I'm going to stay with her until she passes."

"Try not to be so robotic. You need to make it sound real."

"I thought it sounded fine."

"Just a suggestion. Where does Rita live?"

"Forestville, Pennsylvania. Her house is halfway down the mountain from the old coal mine where her father worked."

"Better." He flashed a quick grin. "What do I do for a living?"

"You're military. On leave from your unit." Very believable given his look. "What if we can't get the artifact back?"

"You said Liebers needs money all the time."

"He has a gambling addiction. He's in therapy for it, but he's always asking Bill for salary advances to pay off one shady loan or another."

"Liebers needs money. I need that jar. We'll make him an offer he can't refuse." He opened the car door, and stepped out. "Showtime, Doc. Remember, the sooner we get this done, the sooner you can get back to your normal routine."

Would anything be normal again? She climbed out of the

big vehicle and looked around half expecting to see the bodies from last night, but there was no trace. Even this early, the day was unseasonably hot and humid. A thick haze hung in the air. The scent of the surrounding vegetation was almost cloying. The parking lot held a few staff cars. The patients in the study would arrive in half an hour. The place was deceptively peaceful. It was hard to fathom that last night it was a scene straight from hell.

Meg looked around the lot a few times just to be sure. The creatures had appeared out of nowhere. They did it before, they could do it again. She clutched at the strap to her backpack, holding the bag tighter against her body. "Who's after me?"

"I don't know yet. Like I said at breakfast, it's probably no one you know."

"You don't know that for sure." She glanced over her shoulder, seeing nothing but her shadow. "What if it's someone I know, only I don't realize that? You said anyone could be a mage. You said the things that attacked me worked for one."

"Anyone could be a mage, but you can usually tell. Mages are obsessive, power hungry loners, and tend to devote all of their time to studying and using magic. That doesn't leave them much time for other things like day jobs." He stopped dead still and looked down at her. "I told you I'd keep you safe. I don't go back on my word."

She believed him. The way he spoke, so sure of himself, she believed he'd do what he could to keep her safe. But what if it wasn't enough? She didn't want to think beyond that. "Let's use the side entrance. We can take the staff elevator."

Gideon followed her lead, a silent, towering sentinel behind her. They passed few people on their way to the elevator, something Meg was grateful for. She was in the same clothes from yesterday. Her skirt was torn from when she fell, she looked all the worse for the wear, and she had the lone biker of the apocalypse in tow. Not a good picture.

She used her key to access the restricted fourth floor where all the physicians had their private offices. The elevator opened in a small dead end corridor just off the reception area. Meg peeked out and found the reception area empty. Lucy, the secretary, must have been making coffee in the small breakroom down the hall.

"Coast is clear." She came out from behind the elliptical reception desk, and motioned to Gideon. "Stan's office is this way."

She was halfway down the hall when Lucy came out of the breakroom, coffee mug in hand. The brassy-haired former trophy wife turned secretary stretched her plump scarlet lips into an artificially bright smile.

"Dr. Carter. Good morning." Her eyes lit upon Gideon, and the smile turned into a seductive grin. She lowered her gold-dusted lids. "Who's your friend? Don't tell me he's a doctor?"

Meg's butterflies turned to stomach acid. Lucy was always polite to Meg, but very solicitous to the male doctors in the practice. Meg tried to be sympathetic to her cause; it wasn't easy to be the cast-off first wife of the hottest plastic surgeon in town. Then again, Meg was fairly certain Lucy was the current mistress of Dr. Chang, the practice's pediatric neurologist. Chang was married. Small wonder she showed interest in Gideon as well. Fresh meat. No wedding band. "Lucy, this is my old friend, Gideon Sinclair. Gideon, our secretary, Lucy. Is Dr. Liebers in yet?"

"He came in about half an hour ago."

"Great, thanks." She swept past the woman, and Gideon followed.

"How do you take your coffee, Mr. Sinclair?"

"None for me, thanks." Gideon walked a little faster.

"I'm here if you change your mind."

Meg grit her teeth. To Gideon, she said low, "She's hooked up with one of the other doctors. If you're not careful, she'll try for you, too."

"She's not my type."

For some silly reason, his response pleased her. Most men found Lucy's bottle blond bombshell looks irresistible. Then again, Gideon Sinclair wasn't like most men. In fact, he wasn't like any man Meg had ever encountered before in her life. For one crazy moment she felt sad that they'd soon be parting ways. She shook it off and knocked on the door.

"Hey Stan, it's me, Meg. Can I come in?"

She took the muffled response to be an affirmative, and opened the door.

Stan Liebers came out of his small bathroom, freshly shaved, and buttoning up his shirt. "Hey, Meg. Don't you have a day off?" He caught sight of Gideon and scowled. "Who's this?"

Meg made introductions, spewing the long lost friend story.

"Geeze, for a second I thought you were some loan shark." He laughed nervously and fussed with the knot of his tie. "Guess that was in poor taste. So, what's up?"

"I need you to cover my patients for a week or so. There's only one in the Med Center right now."

Stan sat down behind his desk and leaned back in his chair. "Sure. Anything for you, Meg. Can I ask why?"

Meg laced her hands together to keep them steady. "I need to go to Pennsylvania. Gideon's mother is dying. She only has a few days left."

There. That didn't sound too robotic. It would help if Gideon showed some kind of emotion.

Stan looked up at Gideon. For a moment he studied him with a critical eye. Then he flashed his patented "sympathetic doctor" frown and donned his game face. "I'm sorry to hear that, Mr. Sinclair. It's never easy, is it? No matter what the age."

"No," Gideon rumbled. "It's not."

Great. Talk about robotic. Meg decided to jump tracks. She hated lying, and she hated being on the receiving end of Stan's phony caring doctor attitude. She knew he didn't give a crap about anything other than money. To him, medicine was a cash cow, and the clinic, a low stress way to keep the milk flowing. His saving grace was his undisputed skill, and that was the only reason Meg had him covering her patients.

"Listen, Stan, that's not all. This is going to sound weird coming on the heels of what I just told you, but, I got to thinking about that canopic jar. I really like it, so much, I want to buy it from you. There's time to get a replacement for Morty's party."

Stan smiled easily. "That was a sweet little piece, wasn't it? I'm more a modern art guy myself, but wow, it looked like the real deal. No wonder Bill gets all his stuff from that company. They're fakes but you'd never know to look at them."

Tension dug sharp claws into her shoulder blades. A sense of foreboding stole over her. "How much should I make the check out for?"

The mention of money set Stan's dull gray eyes to gleaming. "You know I'd love to sell it to you but I can't."

"Can't or won't." The tension increased, and panic uncoiled like a viper inside of her.

"Can't, Meg. I sent it back."

The panic tightened her chest and made it hard to breathe. "But you were going to give it to Morty."

"Sure, when I thought it didn't cost any more than the trocar. I told them I'd keep the jar, then I got their bill." Stan glanced up at Gideon. "You wouldn't believe how much they wanted. You'd have thought it was the friggin' Hope diamond. I called them up, told them to send me what I ordered, and had Lucy ship it back UPS on their dime."

"No!" Meg leaned over the desk. "Tell me you didn't!"

Stan sat back, surprised at her violent reaction. "I'm sorry, I didn't know you were interested."

She had the sudden urge to choke Stan. She felt Gideon loom up behind her and take her arm.

"You can contact the company direct, Meg." Gideon's voice was warm and steadying. "Thanks for your time, Dr. Liebers."

"Sure. Sure." Stan stood and shook hands with Gideon. "Sorry about your mother."

"Thank you."

"Hey, Meg, I'll need a number where I can reach you. Not your answering service, either."

"Right." In a haze, Meg scribbled her private cell number on a Post-it Note, and gave it to Stan. "I updated discharge charts last night. I'll sign the prints at the Med Center when I make rounds this morning and let my patients know you're picking up the slack."

She let Gideon lead her out of the room and when he shut the door, she gave in to a moment of panic. "The artifact's gone. That's bad, isn't it? I know it's bad."

"It's not good, Doc." He smiled down at her reassuringly. "But it's not terrible. I'll get the tracking number from Lucy while you tell your boss you need some time off."

"That's it?"

"That's it."

She took a deep breath and pulled herself together. God, he must think her a total weakling. She stiffened her spine. "Don't let Lucy take advantage of you."

She turned away, rounded the other corner, and found Bill just going into his office.

"Meg, good morning. I thought you were taking the day off."

"I need to talk to you, Bill."

He gave her the once over and pushed his glasses onto his forehead. "You're in the same clothes you wore yesterday." His eyes fixed on the tear in her skirt. He let go of his office door, came close to her and gently held her arms. His blue eyes filled with concern. "Are you injured? Did something happen, Meg? Are you okay?"

She nodded, feeling his warmth pour over her. Bill was like a teddy bear or a favorite blanket. You could sink into his safety net and never need to worry. So different, she realized, from Gideon. Gideon offered safety, not because he was comfortable, but because he was lethal. There was nothing warm and fuzzy about the immortal soldier. "I have an emergency, Bill. I need to take a brief leave of absence."

Bill's eyes widened slightly, but he didn't let her go. "When are you coming back?"

When, not why. No questions, he just understood. She was grateful for his friendship, for the way he seemed to know the right thing to do, the right thing to say. No matter how crazy her world got, Bill was there. One day, when he healed from his daughter's death, he'd make some lucky woman very happy. "A few days. A week maybe. A family friend's on hospice. She's in the last stretch. I'm going to stay with her, see her through."

Bill shifted, coming closer. He stepped into a shaft of golden morning light that slanted in through the office window, giving him an angelic aura. "I didn't realize someone so close was so sick. Take all the time you need. Will you be available by phone?"

"I'll have my private cell. You know the number." She felt a wave of guilt crash hard against her. She was letting Bill down, letting the kids down. Then she remembered Gideon's warning. What came for her last night wouldn't let things like doctors and sick kids stand in the way. She was a danger to others just by being around. "Stan's covering my patients. I'm sorry, I know we have the big meeting with Pharmetrica coming up and if this goes quick, I'll be there, I promise."

"As long as I know where to find you and how to reach you, everything's fine. I'll cover your end of the study, of course, but, if I have questions I'll need to call. I can also handle Pharmetrica. I'm the boss, remember?"

"I'll check in with you periodically as well."

His expression softened and he smiled down at her. Then, before she realized what was happening, he cupped her chin lightly and placed a tender kiss on her forehead.

"Take care of yourself, Meg." His voice was husky and low. His eyes mirrored both concern and desire. "You're very important to me. I don't think you realize how important."

The contact unnerved her. Here she was lying through her teeth to a man who very obviously cared a great deal about her. Meg knew Bill liked her as a colleague, but this was a new facet to their relationship. She should be flattered that someone like Bill had feelings for her, but instead, it left her with a strange, unpleasant feeling. It was just one more thing changing in the swirling maelstrom of her shattered reality. She couldn't think about what this meant, she couldn't think about anything clearly right now. "I'll call you."

Meg turned and all but fled around the corner and down the hall. She found Gideon leaning over the reception desk, chatting up Lucy. Lucy couldn't take her eyes off the man.

Meg linked her arm with his. "Are you ready?"

"Ready." He beamed a smile at Lucy that had her simpering in her seat. "Next time I'm in town, I'll take you up on that offer."

Meg was glad when they were finally out of the building. "Did you get what you need?"

"I have a tracking number. The package is in transit today. She only sent it out yesterday. I can take you to the safe house, then get to the city by night fall. I'll intercept it tomorrow morning."

She tried to swallow a growing sense of unease. She didn't believe in premonitions, but if she did, she'd guess that feeling she had was one of coming trouble. "I need to stop at the Med Center, then I want to go home. I need to pack a bag."

"It's not safe."

"I'll only be a few minutes. I want a toothbrush and some clothes. Let me grab my stuff, then you can take me to Tibet for all I care."

His mouth was a thin, straight line. She could tell from his rigid posture he didn't like what she wanted to do, but damn it all, if she had to do this she could at least have a change of clothes. And, a pair of sneakers. As she'd learned last night, sandals weren't ideal for making a quick getaway. "I need something normal with me, Gideon. Please try to understand. You can't leave me with nothing."

"Fine." He opened the door to the SUV for her. "I have to meet with a local anyway. You have twenty minutes at the Med Center. Ten at home. Then we hit the road."

"Who are you meeting?"

"A kind of cop."

"What kind?"

He slid in behind the wheel and gunned the engine. "The kind that locks up demons, zombies, mages, and the boogey man."

Chapter Four

Gideon hung back in the waiting area at the children's wing as Meg requested. He leaned against the wall beside a large, plastic potted plant and kept out of the main flow of traffic. The position gave him an excellent view of the nurses' station where Meg sat chatting with another physician, and he had a clear shot at the elevator bank.

They'd been in the Med Center less than ten minutes when the local contact he'd called from the joint task force that policed the shadows showed up. Matt Reichart looked every inch the special agent, complete with mirrored shades and a dark blue, boxy suit that sat uncomfortably on his wide-shouldered frame. Reichart spotted him, flashed a brief, humorless smile, and cut across the waiting area to join him.

"I have to say, Sinclair, this is the last place I'd expect you to pick for a meeting. You've always been the dark alley type." He shook hands with a firm, businesslike grip, then took off his shades. "Something happening in my patch I need to be aware of, or are you just visiting?"

"I'm on the clock." He nodded in the direction of Meg, and Matt followed his gaze.

"The redhead?"

"Yeah."

"Want to trade jobs?"

"She's complicated."

Matt continued to stare at Meg. "A little complication does a man good every once in a while."

"Not her type of complication." Gideon crossed his arms in front of his chest and lowered his voice. "Had a dust-up last night in Troy. Didn't know you guys had a demon problem in this neck of the woods."

Matt's mouth thinned into a tight line. "We don't. The local vampires don't like their kind. Too much competition for resources. Want to tell me about it? Maybe I can help."

Meg stopped talking with her colleague, an Indian man in his late thirties, set aside a clipboard and left the nurses' station.

Gideon gave her a moment to get distance, then motioned to the agent. "Let's take a walk."

He started out after her and Matt fell into step beside him. They followed Meg through a heavy set of double doors, and the change in scent and energy hit him like a fist to the gut. Death. He'd know the stink anywhere. It hung thick in the air, crowding the space and casting a gray aura of uncertainty over everything and everyone. It didn't matter that the sun streamed in through sparkling clear windows and artfully designed skylights. It didn't matter that bright-colored posters and paper flowers hung upon the walls, or that the laughter of small children echoed in the hall. Death was here, making its presence known in a subtle, unavoidable way, marking time, waiting like a hungry vulture to feed on its next victim.

Gideon's chest tightened inexplicably. How did she stand it? He couldn't imagine coming into this hall of death again, yet Meg fought daily in this arena. Now he understood how her vitality came through in a simple picture. She was life, she was hope, and that couldn't be concealed, or tempered.

Meg turned into a large playroom and walked over to a small boy seated in a large lounger. No less than three intravenous lines ran into his tiny, waif-thin body. He wore a blue baseball cap over a pale head devoid of any hair. In his hands he held the controls to a video game, which he played with more gusto and energy than Gideon thought possible given his fragile physical state. When Meg leaned over and spoke to him, the boy turned and beamed a mile wide smile. The doc sat down, picked up a second control set, and started to play the game.

"I get the feeling she's one of the good guys." Matt frowned deeply, cutting grooves into his smooth, tan skin. "No kid should have to live like this. You'd think your precious Gods could fix this kind of suffering."

Gideon did think that, but, there were other things to consider. "You can't screw too much with the natural order without causing major trouble. You know what's happened every time some God gets it in their head to 'alleviate' suffering."

"Genocide. Plagues. Natural disasters. Holy wars. Great group of folks, your employers."

"The universe is a tricky thing to keep running."

"Don't I know it. The butterfly effect's a bitch." Matt shoved his hands in the pockets of his dark blue trousers and turned away from the scene of the debilitated children. "About these demons."

"Right." Gideon kept a vigilant watch on Meg as he related the details of the attack to Matt. He made sure to keep the pertinent points of his mission to himself, and Matt was too much the professional to pry. When he finished, Matt took his hands from his pockets, pulled out a BlackBerry, and fussed some with the controls.

"Not even a blip on the radar, Gid." He punched a few final

buttons on the BlackBerry, then slipped it back into his pocket. “Something should have shown up. That means major magic’s in play. I’m going to have to open a formal inquiry.”

“That’s what I’m counting on.”

Gideon continued to keep his eyes front, watching every move she made. Meg finished playing the game and removed her stethoscope. The boy leaned forward, giving her access to his back. She warmed the listening device in her hands before placing it gently against his skin.

She was a good doctor, he realized, a doctor who cared about people, not just the practice of medicine. Taking her away for a week or two might keep her safe, but it would hurt others. Kids like that little guy in there, or any of the others, like the pig-tailed girl playing with blocks, her legs in bandages to the knees, or the boy painting by the window, his head covered in the black fuzzy return of hair, his eyes hollow and sunken like a hundred-year-old man in his last days of life. Taking her out of play, following protocol, would doom the kids she helped, not just her. Regret and guilt formed an unpleasant taste in his mouth. “Who do you like local for hiring out big guns like Ash demons?”

“Our usual suspects have their own personal entourages to do abductions and executions. You’re talking about someone who has the skill not only to summon a war band, but hire and bind them to the job until it’s done. I’ve got two locals that are out of the closet who could do that, but they’re so paranoid, they’d never take the risk. Ash demons have a nasty habit of turning on their employers. All it takes is one slip of will or focus, and it’s a blood bath.” Matt ran a hand nervously through his thick, blond hair. “I’m not sure any of my usual suspects are stupid enough, or crazy enough, to buy that kind of trouble. There are a few practitioners on the beat skilled enough, and demented enough, to make and run the kind of zombie you described. I'm more likely to get a hit there than with the demons. I can do some checking."

"I'd appreciate that, Matt."

"I appreciate the warning. The Council of Wardens isn't usually so cooperative with us locals. Think we're backward hillbillies."

"I work for the Tribunal."

"They're worse."

Gideon shrugged. Meg was talking to one of the nurses in the playroom. Her tiny patient had resumed his game.

"There's always a good chance your perp is local but off the grid. This could have been his first public appearance. It's not unusual for these magic types to stay hidden under a rock for any number of years before they come crawling out. Especially if your guy is ceremonial." Matt turned to him and leaned against the window, a thoughtful look on his youthful face. "Some of those clowns will wait twenty years or more for the right astrologic alignment and fortunate portents before taking a dump, let alone committing to some big magical money shot."

"So how do you find him?"

"He'll offend again, that's a given. From what you tell me, I'm guessing he wants your doctor. He failed, so he'll try till he gets her. We can put a tail on her. Use her as bait."

"No." Gideon's fists curled at the idea of putting Meg at risk. He took a deep breath and forced himself to relax. Matt's plan was sound. Under other circumstances, he'd suggest the very same thing. But these circumstances were different. Meg was different. "I'm sticking her in a safe house."

"Nothing's ever easy with you, is it, Gid." Matt narrowed his eyes and thought for a moment. "Okay, we work backward. The next major event is mid summer. That's always a fun time at the zoo, for a week before and after. The veil between the worlds is so damn thin it might as well be a dental floss thong. I can have one of my analysts take what you've given me, do an astrologic survey, work backward, and come up with some likely scenarios. Of course, you'll need to give me more solid details."

"I've given you as much as I can." Gideon's gaze followed Meg as she crossed the playroom and headed for the door. He was taking a tremendous risk telling Matt as much as he did, but, if there was a compromise in the mystics, or worse, the Warden's Council, then Gideon needed outside intel to get perspective. "Make do with what you have."

"Garbage in, garbage out. Whatever comes through will be high level at best."

"That'll have to do."

Meg opened the door, stepped out and glanced at Gideon and then Matt. She had a thick plastic binder in her hands. Her lips formed a disapproving frown, and her face hardened with a stern look. "You could have waited in reception. You don't need to follow me around like my bouncer. I'm safe here, Gideon."

"We've been over this ground, Doc. How much longer?"

Meg shook her head, and started walking back down the hall with a long, determined stride. "I need to chart my visit and check on some more lab results. Ten minutes at most."

Matt scooted around Gideon and intercepted her. "Dr. Carter, I'm Special Agent Reichart. I'd like to ask you some questions, follow up on what Gideon told me."

"You're the cop who locks up boogey men." She stepped by him and continued walking. "I'm sure Gideon told you everything you need to know."

Her answer warmed Gideon. He'd briefed her in the car about keeping things to herself if Matt asked her direct questions. He wasn't certain she'd play along, but she followed the party line, demonstrating her loyalty. She might be annoyed with him following her around, but, she at least believed him now, and, more important, listened to him. "You'll have to excuse Matt, Doc. He's ex-FBI. Rubber hose interrogation and bad cop/worse cop are the only tactics they know."

This drew a laugh from Matt. "Give me some credit, Gid. I like to think my time chasing monsters has polished me up some."

The light banter had a calming effect on Meg. Some of her earlier peevishness dissipated. Her face relaxed and the tight lines around her mouth vanished. She stopped at the entrance to a small room just before the double doors. "Ten minutes. I promise. There's only one way in and out of the chart room, I swear I'll be fine."

"Doorways aren't the only way in and out of rooms, Doc. Neither are windows. I'll wait here for you."

She rolled her eyes, went into the room, and shut the door. He could see clearly through the glass. He took up post just across the hall where he could monitor her and the double doors at the same time.

"She's a pistol," Matt observed. "How much does she know about our world?"

"Enough." *Too much.* What he wouldn't give for her to have continued her life untouched by the darkness of his shadowy world, safe from the machinations of vengeful Gods and madmen. "Don't try and reach me. I'm going dark. I'll check in when I can."

"I'm not making promises I can't keep, bro. Your info's skimpy at best. Don't expect any miracles."

Of all the things he did expect, that was never one he entertained. Not in his wildest dreams. No one better than him knew that things such as miracles didn't exist. Maybe they did for people like Meg, or for the kids she helped. But they didn't exist for guys like him. "I'll take what I can get."

Venice, Italy

"Signore." The lanky waiter handed Salazar the petal-shaped snifter of Macallan whiskey.

"Grazie."

Ramon set down the fine Havana cigar in the Lenox crystal ash tray, accepted the glass, and inhaled the complex aroma of citrus touched with the barest hint of sherry. Philistines used whiskey glasses, while the true connoisseur treated the waters of life with the appropriate level of dignity by drinking from the generous, curved snifter.

Macallan was Scottish in origin, but the finishing of this particular thirty-year-old whiskey took place in oak casks imported from Spain. Not only did the casks contribute to the rich, mahogany color of the drink, but Salazar liked to think the Spanish wood enhanced the overall sophistication and continental appeal. Smoothed out the rough, barbaric edges.

He sampled the beverage, and as always, the long finish came off virgin clean and warm as the Aegean sun. To think such nectar came from the brutal, barren wastes of Scotland. He took a second sip and placed the glass beside the ash tray. Around him, the pre-dinner bustle of the hotel Amici was evident. The elegant barroom was filled to near capacity with businessmen in fine tailored suits, some accompanied by stunning, expensively dressed women, others clustered in small male groups drinking the finest of liquors and talking loudly with both hand and mouth.

Ah, the Venetians, such a vital, friendly lot. Whenever in Venice, he felt welcome. The island, built upon a swamp, was more home to him than anywhere else he'd spent time. He glanced at the doorway, a mahogany arch bordered on either side by excellent frescos. His guest stood there looking surly as ever. Ian Campbell was a most unlikely mystic. Another product of the barbarous Scots, and yet a completely surprising package. Ramon had trained Ian himself in some of the ways of the game, he'd even tried to impart some refinement. Unlike the Spanish oak casks that held the Macallan, Ramon had been unable to take the edge off the Campbell.

Ian made his way through the growing crowd, towering over the smaller Italians, his golden blond hair and fair skin making him stand out even more than his height. He sat down opposite Ramon in one of the leather-covered wing chairs, grunted a hello, and motioned for a waiter.

"I'll have what he's having," he all but growled when the waiter appeared. "Only bring it in a real whiskey glass."

Ramon raised a brow. This was a change for his former student. He always drank the Springbank, insisting it was an insult to the Campbells who'd tried to burn him at the stake for witchcraft. They were all dead now and rotting in graves, while Ian lived eternal, enjoying their whiskey and cursing their name. "I thought you'd go for the Springbank."

Ian shifted nervously in the seat. His long fingers drummed the armrests of the chair. Dark shadows gathered around his gray eyes. "I'm branching out."

Ramon didn't like that answer. Nor did he like the shell of a man that sat before him today. "Studying this convergence has taken a toll on you, Ian. You look like hell."

The waiter returned with the whiskey and Ian shot half of it down his throat before speaking. "I've been over the vision ten thousand times, Ramon. I see it every time I close my eyes. I see it when I look in the mirror. It follows me everywhere. None of the others have this problem."

Not that they admitted. "You're imprinting. It's rare, but it's been known to happen."

"When was the last time it happened?" Ian's words held an accusatory tone. His accent was thicker, another sign of increasing stress.

"Two hundred and fifty-five years ago, give or take a day or two." Ramon picked up his own whiskey and swirled the dark fluid. The citrus aroma rose up and touched him like a lover's comforting hand. Ian was imprinting, running in the psychic equivalent of a rut. If he didn't find a way out, he'd go mad. Ian was one of the strongest mystics in the Warden's employ. Unshakable in his faith, a true believer in fighting for the balance, a favorite of his God. It was hard to imagine someone as potent as Ian Campbell getting stuck in a psychic imprint without some kind of sinister, outside intervention. Gideon's belief that a mystic could be compromised suddenly held more validity. "You don't know for sure if it's a true imprint, or just fatigue."

Ian shrugged then swallowed the remainder of his whiskey in one gulp. He motioned for more and sat back, a sullen look etched on his aristocratic face. Not for the first time, Salazar thought there was Roman blood mixed in with the Celt.

"I asked you here tonight because I'm wondering about the deviation point. We normally have choices. Why are we so restricted this time, Ian?" He'd asked the question of several other mystics today, and all of them demurred. Their answers resulted in the sum total of "you know how it is". Salazar found himself questioning, just as Gideon did, and was glad that the Tribunal had thrown its weight around and assigned a champion to this job. If a Paladin had taken it on, the mortal woman would be dead, and none of them would know the real truth. He sipped the whiskey, savoring the smooth descent it made.

"I asked myself the same thing, Ramon. I always question, I always probe." Ian's fine brows arched in surprise. He sat forward. "Maybe that's why I'm stuck? Maybe that's why I'm imprinting? I keep forcing myself into the same thread, the same detail. Maybe I've created the groove myself."

"It's possible." Possible, but improbable. The mystics were one force in the army that fought for balance. They could trance the timeline, traveling all the worlds and realms linked to that dimensional thread, see the breaks in continuity that threatened dimensional and timeline integrity, see the machinations of the supposedly docile Gods as they played cold war games of cloak and dagger with the mortals, see the dangers posed by followers of the Gods acting on their own. They were also adept at locating trouble caused by the multitude of magic users ever seeking power, always tampering with things better left alone. And, they could discern when a timeline threat risked dimensional breach, putting all the realms, including those of the Gods, at severe risk.

But, they could be fooled, too. They could be compromised, tampered with, and tricked. It was rare, and exceedingly difficult, but if an enemy was cunning enough, daring enough, powerful enough, they could succeed. When the mystics were compromised, everything under the sun, quite literally, was at risk. Salazar held his glass a little tighter. "Tell me, how have you been feeling lately, other than the recurring vision?"

"Tired," Ian answered without hesitation. His look turned to one of disgust. "Used up. Dry. Confused. I keep forgetting things, like where I left my watch before trancing. I've missed a few dates with friends, and mixed up a few phone numbers. I told the doctors. I've been checked out three times. Complete work up."

"And?" He made a mental note to collect the findings of the examinations. There were things that might be significant to him another set of eyes would miss.

"And nothing. I'm not compromised, if that's what you're thinking. I'm clean. I'm just off my bleeding rocker." When the waiter handed him the second glass of scotch, Ian held onto it with both hands. He leaned over the small drinks table and glanced around nervously. "Elsa took me out of rotation. I'm going on mandatory holiday as soon as I'm done here."

"I must admit, I've been worried about you lately." At least, since Gideon's call. "You haven't seemed yourself. I thought coming out to talk, in a safe place, maybe I could be of some assistance. Perhaps if you tell me how you felt leading up to your first vision, the one that identified the break in continuity? Maybe there's something contributing to the imprinting, something you've not considered."

Ian took a long swallow of whisky and shut his eyes as it went down. When he opened them again, the pupils were fine points, and the irises a troubled, stormy gray.

He's checking me out, thought Ramon. It was almost amusing, this young boy thinking he could ferret out the intent of an elder Warden who'd lived for countless centuries. Oh, they thought him a mere thousand years old, and he let them. Only a few of the Gods knew the truth of his heritage, knew how many ages he'd lived through. In a way, he wasn't really lying. One thousand years ago, he had become Ramon Salazar, the Spaniard. He just didn't tell them that the years prior, he'd been many other people, gone by many other names. Everyone in the game had their secrets, even him.

Ian's eyes dimmed and returned to the placid, mirror-like

gray. He relaxed into the chair and rolled the glass between his hands. "Where do you want me to start?"

So, he'd passed the test. Excellent. "Take me through the days leading up to the vision. Did anything strike you out of the ordinary?"

Ian talked for a good two hours, and Ramon listened. The bar patrons emptied out, went to their dinners, and a new set filtered in. Ian drank several more glasses of the whisky, but like a true Scot, it did little to him. In the end, Ramon couldn't find anything that spoke to compromise or tampering. But it was early in this particular game yet. Even with the short timeline and the risk of keeping the mortal alive, Ramon had to agree with Gideon. The op stank.

Finally, Ian had no more to say. "Thanks, Ramon. For listening. I know I didn't tell you what you wanted to hear, but, I feel better, if only because of the whisky."

"Why do you think I wanted to hear anything in particular?" Ramon stood and they shook hands like civilized men, even though they'd both come from most uncivilized roots. "I've no agenda."

"Everyone in the game has an agenda."

Ramon conceded with a small nod of his head. "Where are you going on holiday? Someplace with beautiful women, I hope?"

"Monte Carlo. Between the beaches and casinos, I'll find something mindless to lose myself in until my head returns to normal."

A dead zone. He should have expected as much. When a psychic needed a rest, they went to a place where visions were hard to come by, where magic had a tough run. Monte Carlo was on a cross of energetic forces that deadened a psychic's ability, almost to the point of non-existence. It was one of the reasons the city functioned as a gambling Mecca. Luck actually had a chance to work. "An excellent choice."

They shared a few more parting comments and Ian left. Ramon took his seat and relit his cigar. He puffed thoughtfully as he sifted through the details provided by his former student. The waiter returned, silent like a ghost, and refilled his glass. The lights dimmed, signaling that the true evening had begun. He let the ambiance of the Amici's elegant continental décor take him back to earlier ages as he searched his ancient memory and compared the past with the present. Several links formed and developed into possibilities. In the end he knew he had little choice but to roll up his sleeves and get dirty. It had been a while since he'd worked a rouge op. If he was going to do the job, he'd need to start out right. For that, he'd need more than Gideon and the champion's "instincts".

Salazar finished his whisky and cigar and went out onto the balcony that overlooked the Amici's private canal and launch. He strolled round the building, enjoying the evening air, until he reached the side that faced the lagoon in front of St. Martin's square. He went to a corner of the balcony, far from the ears of the hotel patrons and staff, yet close enough not to stand out as anything other than a man taking in the Venetian air. From his inside jacket pocket he removed a razor thin cell phone and called a number known only to ten beings in the entire mortal, and immortal world.

It rang three times and then connected.

Salazar spoke using his birth language. It felt hard on his tongue and sounded foreign to his ears. "It's me. I need a favor."

"Make a left on Clearview Drive. My place is the last one in the cul-de-sac." Meg fidgeted in her seat as Gideon slowly drove up the long block to her house. Her head was killing her again, and a few times since leaving the Med Center she'd experienced vertigo. She had a sense of finality now. Once she packed her bag, Gideon would take her to this safe house up north and then she'd have nothing to do but sit and wait.

Meg couldn't stand having time on her hands. She had a few medical journals she could take to catch up on her reading. Gideon said the safe house had Internet access. That would help pass the time. Maybe she could talk him into stopping at a bookstore before leaving town? One glance at the impassive, chiseled face, and she dismissed the idea. He was dead set on dumping her up near Canada with no time for side trips. She'd have to find something other than the latest Tess Gerritsen to fill her hours. She suspected no matter what diversion she tried her hand at, her mind would linger over memories of the enigmatic soldier who burst into her life last night. Gideon was a man who left an impression, one that was hard to forget. Or ignore.

"I want to check the place out first." His deep voice rumbled into the silence. "You stay in the car. I'll fix it so nothing can get in. But no matter what, don't leave. You open the door from the inside, you break the enchantment."

"Magical keyless entry?"

"I'm serious, Doc." He backed the car into her drive, and left it so the front end lined up with the edge of the road. Then he took off the shades and stared at her with a penetrating, unblinking gaze that made her hot all over and scared her senseless.

"I know, Gideon. It was a joke."

He furrowed his brow, the concept of jokes obviously foreign to him. "Something makes a big play for you and I'm not around, you take off. Don't look back. I'm leaving you my cell. Matt's on speed dial, just hit two, and he'll take care of you."

"Nothing's going to happen to you." The idea didn't sit well at all with her, and brought on another spate of vertigo. She gripped the door handle, bit down on her lower lip and tried to steady herself.

"Are you okay?" He undid the seat belt and moved into her personal space. "You've gone all pale on me."

That much man so close made her want to lean into his strength. She was afraid once she touched him she wouldn't stop. "I'm fine. I have migraines lately. Sometimes I get a little dizzy. It will pass."

He didn't look convinced.

"Really, Gideon, I'll take two aspirins and be fine. I'm a doctor. I know what I'm talking about." He didn't need to know she had no idea what was causing the headaches. Nor did he need to know that nothing relieved them. They came and went on their own schedule. Meg was beginning to wonder if fear drove them off. She'd had a killer one walking out of the clinic last night, but the attack had cleared her head in an instant. "Go. Satisfy your curiosity that my little three bedroom cape is safe. I'll wait here."

He slipped out of the car without another word, shut the door, and then did the strangest thing she'd seen so far. He took a tiny, green, velvet drawstring pouch from a pocket inside his biker jacket, and sprinkled what appeared to be pixie dust on the hood of the SUV. She watched the golden sparkles float free, and then as one, the locks in the car engaged. She jumped at the sound. Gideon put the bag away and stalked up her driveway. She smiled as she watched him in the rear-view mirror. The man had a nice ass for an immortal.

Her headache began to dull. Meg turned up the AC then

fooled around with the high tech radio until she found a classical station playing something soothing in strings. Normally she liked classic rock and a little bit of dance, but today, she wanted something that would soothe her savage nerves. Meg moved her seat back a little and closed her eyes, letting the comfort of the soft music and the even softer leather seat ease the tension out of her.

Time passed, the piece ended, and the next track featuring French horns startled her out of her relaxed state. She sat up and shut the radio off, then wondered what was taking her soldier so long. She craned around to see her house, but it sat, placid as always, the bricks sun dappled, the rhododendrons shifting in the light breeze. A feeling of warmth stole over her. She loved the little cape, in the unpretentious neighborhood in central Troy. On an early summer afternoon, the block was deserted. But on the evenings and weekends, it was alive with people. Most of the families were in their backyard pools, out on the municipal golf course, or, walking dogs and children around the maze of blocks. Everyone knew everyone else, and everyone had a friendly smile and a wave.

Her house was one of a line of post-war capes, distinguished from the others only by the number of flowers she'd planted in the front yard. It was so like the place she grew up in, right down to the attic turned master bedroom. She remembered how it felt like home the moment she first walked across the threshold with the realtor. With her parents gone, their old house bulldozed to make way for a new development, this little cape offered her a much needed sense of security, and nostalgia. All it needed was the carpet of perennials and annuals, which she'd added her first year, and it was like walking back into the past every time she came home.

Meg was about to turn around again when her quaint, whiteboard door splintered into a million pieces as Gideon's black clad body came sailing outside. He skidded down her brick walkway and his head thumped against the painted rock that identified her house as number twenty-five. Blood covered one side of his face, coming from a deep, nasty gash in his forehead. She couldn't see much else of his body, but she could tell from the way he slumped that he'd lost consciousness. And she could tell that he was in trouble. He'd lost his sword in the tumble. But what was worse was the thing coming through her entry from the interior of her home.

The demon was easily seven foot and had to hunch and turn sideways to get through the door. It was dressed like a man, in blue jeans, and a white T-shirt that stretched across a broad, well-muscled chest. But the similarity ended there. The creature was a dull jaundice shade, with hideous red tribal-like markings covering exposed skin. Two massive horns protruded from its wide forehead. Yellow blood oozed from a split dead center on its skull. Like the others, it had no real nose, and long, pointy ears. It held a curved sword clutched in a massive fist. The worst thing, though: it was headed for Gideon.

Meg was out of the car and moving, any thoughts of her own safety gone from her mind. Gideon started to come round as she ran up her walk. The demon moved slower, as if in pain. She trampled the pansies and pulled the sword from the marigolds. The creature took note of her, snorted, and kept walking towards the immortal.

Gideon got to his knees, saw the demon coming down with a vicious swing, and lurched to the side. He rolled into the spill and came up on his feet just in time to sidestep another strike. This close Meg could see the other wounds. His shirt was sliced in a few spots, and blood poured freely. His cheekbone was bruised, and he was favoring his right leg.

The blade felt incredibly light in her hands. Her heart rammed hard against her ribs. She couldn't breathe. She couldn't move. But she managed. She put one foot in front of the other, and reached him just before the demon.

"Run. Meg. Run," he ground out between clenched teeth. He grabbed the sword from her and lunged.

Meg stepped clear and started to back away as the two engaged in a series of traded strikes. The demon pivoted on the last salvo, changed gears, and made a run towards her. Before it could connect, Gideon leapt in between them, blade gripped with both hands, poised up in a defensive position. The creature's sword connected, and Gideon's sword severed the curved blade in two. A brilliant burst of light accompanied the shearing of steel, and the demon lurched back with an ungodly hiss.

Gideon pressed his advantage, taking a series of offensive strikes that connected more than they missed. He fought the creature back into the little house and disappeared around the corner of the vestibule. Meg knew she should go back to the car, every part of her sane mind told her to run away, but instead, she ran into the house, following her immortal. She didn't know the rules, didn't know the physiology of an immortal, but Gideon was a mess. She dearly hoped immortals couldn't be killed. But if they couldn't, why would he have so many weapons?

She hit her living room and froze in her tracks. Red blood and yellow gore covered her walls. Ash littered her furniture. What was left of it, at least. Her books were out of the built-in shelves and scattered in piles. Everything remotely breakable was in pieces. Even the floorboards fell victim. They were torn down to the joists in several spots. Gideon and the creature fought in her kitchen. She moved fully into the room and saw them as they traded blows. The demon had some kind of dagger now, but it was no match for Gideon's superior weapon.

Meg worried a creature like that would fight dirtier, have more tricks. And she worried about Gideon. He was hurt, bad, and showing signs of fatigue. Meg swallowed the panic threatening to consume her and walked into her kitchen. Her kitchen, her house, her immortal soldier. He needed an advantage. He needed help. He needed her.

She was a mortal, but she wasn't an idiot. However mythical the creature in her kitchen, it still had the same rise and fall of the thoracic region, demonstrating it still had to breathe. The first thing they taught in emergency responder class was to clear the airway. No airway, everything else was a wash. The exposed nasal passage presented an excellent point of entry. As calmly as she might grab a mug from the bakers rack near the south facing window and pour herself morning coffee, she pulled the fire extinguisher from the wall holder, moved into position, and opened up on the face of the demon.

The white foam shot out in a single stream and she angled it towards the wide nose holes. It was sucking wind already from the fight and couldn't stop from inhaling the chemical antidote for fire. The foam was designed to expand on contact and that's exactly what it did. The demon's features seized, it grabbed for its throat and lurched back, coughing and choking. It banged into her stove and pushed it through the dry wall. Gideon used the momentary diversion and drove his sword through its exposed flank. As he pulled back his blade, a brilliant white light flared through the kitchen, its epicenter the demon's rapidly disintegrating body. Then, a second later, everything returned to normal. All that remained was the destruction and a scattering of dark gray ash.

Gideon lowered his sword and it vanished. He staggered back hard into her refrigerator, braced his hands on his knees and slid to the floor. He looked up at her, a mixture of confusion, and something she couldn't quite identify in his eyes. Then his visage shifted. His lips formed a hard frown, and his burning coal black eyes pinned her with an incendiary glare. "I told you to...wait...in...the...car."

"Save the thanks." She found herself finally able to breathe now that he was safe. Now that they were safe. "I don't know much about immortals, but I'm willing to bet you could use a few Band-Aids right now. I'll be right back with my med kit."

Gideon wiped the sweat and blood from his forehead. His lungs burned from breathing in all the ash and from the taxing battle. He couldn't seem to get enough air. He briefly considered moving and started to push up to a standing position, but his body screamed in pain, so he decided instead to sit and wait for the doc. He was pissed at her for risking her pretty little neck, and he was damned impressed that she'd wade into battle with demons without a second thought. She was a red-headed Valkyrie, and a genius. Spraying the Keeper in the face with the extinguisher gave Gideon the edge he'd desperately needed to turn the battle. Even without the sword, the Keeper was an ass kicker. Only one thing bothered him. The Keeper shouldn't have died. Not from a flank wound.

Gideon had skewered the thing to help immobilize it, choosing the sweet spot: the nexus points of nerves that clustered on either flank of a demon. The thing's hands blocked the neck, preventing beheading, but a shot to the sweet spot would result in momentary paralysis, giving him a chance to fell a killing blow. Except the strike finished the thing as effectively as beheading. It made no sense. And things that made no sense bothered him.

He heard Meg's approach as she muttered curses to herself. She carried a little black bag, like something a country doctor might have. She scowled at him and knelt by his side.

“Take your jacket off, and your shirt.”

He smiled and shrugged out of his leathers. “Whatever you say, Doc.”

“Don’t get too excited. This is a professional visit, not a social call.”

The T-shirt was shredded and useless to him, so he pulled the tatters from his body. Meg might think this was a professional visit, but, judging by the way her pupils dilated and she licked her lips with that delicate pink tongue, he’d bet she was enjoying the view anyway. He felt a sharp stab of masculine pride. The doc liked him. He started grinning like an idiot, even though he felt like hell. “I have a small kit in the jacket pocket. I heal fast. That will help me heal faster if it’s applied to the wounds.”

Wordlessly, she grabbed the jacket, removed the small, hard-shelled kit and opened it up. “Which one?”

“The cobalt-blue bottle.”

She opened it and sniffed, then wrinkled her nose. “It smells like raw sewage. What’s it made of?”

“This and that.”

“Let’s start with some cleaning. We can use this later.” She sealed it up, opened her own bag, and set up shop.

Gideon watched as she ripped the seal off a small plastic tray, dropped in several gauze pads, and filled the tray with saline. Her movements were smooth, practiced, economical. He found himself both dreading and longing for her touch.

“This may hurt.” Much to his disappointment, she donned a pair of latex gloves. “I want to clean the wound on your head first.”

She repositioned, leaning over him so she could better assess the wound. It gave him a spectacular view of her breasts and brought her body so close she ignited him with a slow, dangerous flame. She touched his forehead lightly, and her lips formed a slight, delectable pout. "The blood flow appears to have stopped. Amazing."

If he straightened just a bit, moved an inch or so to the right, he could capture those juicy lips and kiss away any frowns. "You have no idea."

She changed gears and moved back on her heels so she could give his chest and abdomen a better look. Her hand feathered across his bare skin and he shivered at her touch.

The corners of her lips tilted up. "You're ticklish?"

"What can I say, Doc. You have the touch."

She colored slightly and turned away, keeping her eyes solidly focused on his naked torso. He had to suppress the urge to grab her and roll her beneath him. He had a vivid image of how she would look, how she would feel. He felt himself start to harden and pushed away the tantalizing thoughts of her soft body, pliable and hot beneath his own. She'd taste sweet as cotton candy, melt in the mouth sweet. He knew it. He craved it. He realized as she poked and prodded with that skimming, gentle touch that he felt better. Instantly better. He'd had none of the wound gel, nothing other than her touch, and his pain was fading.

All thoughts of sensual delight fled, replaced by a rising sense of unease. Gideon stared down at the gashes that cut across his body and realized that since she'd started her examination, the healing process increased. Rapidly increased, to a frantic, impossible pace.

Meg reached for some gauze. "The torso lacerations looked much worse from far away. They're far more superficial than I thought."

"My kind heal quick." *But not that quick*. Especially when

the wounds were made by enchanted and poisoned weapons. Those always took a few days to really go on the mend. If you managed to survive them. Something was wrong. Just like the Keeper dying from a single non-killing strike.

"You're not kidding." She shook her head, a look of disbelief in her eyes. "The wound's closing even as I'm cleaning it. Just like it did last night."

Last night was different. The blade wasn't contaminated with dark magic. Something changed. Not in him, he realized, panic surging into his blood. She'd changed. Meg was different. Very different. Her touch healed. He shut his eyes for a moment as a powerful realization hit him like a kick to the gut.

He was too late. She'd touched the artifact's case, the jar, but it didn't matter. She'd changed. She'd changed, and there was no turning back. He couldn't take her to the safe house while he ran after the artifact. If he didn't fix this, fix her...

"Gideon, what's wrong? Are you in pain?"

He opened his eyes. Her face was very close to his, so close he could feel her breath warm against his cheek. Her eyes were clouded with concern. Concern for him. She shouldn't worry for him. She should worry for herself. Gods damn him, he was too late. He reached out and caressed her cheek. "I'm sorry."

"Sorry?" She cocked her head to the side, confused. "For what? You saved my life. Again, I might add."

She felt so real, so alive beneath his hand. So normal. But the evidence of his healing was damning. She'd absorbed the magic in the artifact. It gave her a healing touch. This much he was sure of, but past that, he had no clue what else it had done. The briefing warned against something like this happening, but considered it a remote possibility. "You're a fighter, Meg. I like that. Brave."

"I'm a chicken, Gideon. You're the one slugging it out

with—well, you know." She moved her attentions to the wounds on his belly, cleaning them with the same meticulous, loving touch. "Are you sure you're okay? You seem worse since I've started doctoring you."

"It's not you." *It's the magic.* How to fix this one, Gid?

Salazar's warning sounded like a death knell in his head. What if, in the end, he had to implement protocol? As he watched her care for him, dabbing his skin so carefully, her every action focused on him and him alone, he knew there was no way at this point he'd follow protocol. To hell with all of that trash. She'd absorbed the spell energy from the Buckle of Isis, all that meant was a change of plan. He'd need to find a way to get the magic out of her before getting the artifact. In a way, this was helpful. If she had the energy, it meant that the artifact was most likely inert. It also meant the perp wouldn't stop trying to grab her. He couldn't use the artifact as bait.

"I'm not taking you to the safe house, Doc." It wasn't really a lie, he told himself. The latest attack revealed the truth of the situation to him. But she didn't need to know that. Not yet. Not until he fully understood what it meant, and knew how to get her back to normal. The way he saw it, he had no other option. "This attack means we need to change plans."

She glanced sideways at him, then changed the wet gauze for a dry one. "Why?"

"You're too hot a property right now." He hedged the truth again. Better to play it cool. "I need to figure out why."

"What does that mean for me, Gideon?" She stared at him full on, her innocent eyes boring a hole through his black soul. "You're giving me part of the story again, aren't you."

"Trust me, Doc, you don't want the whole thing right now."

She pulled away. "You should let me judge for myself."

Gideon used the opportunity to get distance and stand. His

body responded immediately. There wasn't an ache or pain to be found. They were screwed. They were so screwed.

"I don't know the whole thing, Meg. I'm a soldier, nothing more. I'm going to take you to an expert in the field of magic. One I know I can trust. Right now you're a walking beacon for trouble, I need to know why."

Meg cleaned up quickly and dumped the used supplies in her trash. She stepped gingerly over the debris and picked her way to the arched entry into the living room. She paused and looked back at him. "When will this really end, Gideon? Is it really a week or two? Or will it go on longer?"

They both had until the solstice. He didn't want to consider the consequences of failure. He'd fix it, he'd find the real truth, he'd save the fair maid. Like a battering ram, the memory that threatened him since he first laid eyes on Meg's picture burst into his consciousness. He'd failed a fair maid once. Failed the woman he should have protected above all others. He wouldn't fail this time. This time, the fair maid would get the fair shake and the dragon slayer she needed. This time, he'd be there.

"It will end by the solstice." One way, or the other, it would end, in that he had no choice. He grabbed the biker jacket and donned it like his old suit of armor. "Don't worry, Meg. I gave you my word I'd keep you safe. I don't go back on my word."

"I've delivered a similar line before, Gideon. I know how important it is to help keep someone's spirits up in the face of overwhelming odds." She let out a deep breath, and shook her head. "I'm in trouble, aren't I? I'm going to die."

He plowed through the mess and grabbed her arms, pulling her tight against his chest. She was boneless, unresisting. "Not on my watch, Doc."

She tilted her head up and her misty, fey eyes locked with his. "Tell me the truth, for once, Gideon. The whole truth. I need to know. If you want me to run off with you, be straight with me. Am I going to die?"

"I think you've absorbed the magic of the artifact. Honestly, I don't know what that means for you or me, but I know it's not good. This guy we're going to see is just outside of Vegas. He can help." He searched her eyes looking for a sign, praying this was enough. It was as much truth as he was prepared to speak aloud. "The stakes are high in this game, Doc. Right now both of us are at mortal risk. Every second, every step of the way."

"I thought you were immortal."

"I am, but it doesn't mean I can't be dusted. The correct weapon used a certain way, or, the right kind and amount of corporeal damage, and I'm toast." Gods, he wanted to kiss her. Amidst all this madness, that one thought plagued him, that one savage need drove him to the very edge. He felt his control fray, his desire mount. She was so close. He angled his head lower so they almost touched. "I'm immortal, but like everything else under the sun, I have my weaknesses."

She lifted her hands and placed them against the lapels of his jacket. Even through the layers of leather, her heat scorched him. "If I'm going to play this game, as you call it, I need to know the rules."

The pressure of her hands parted the biker jacket, and the tips of her breasts skimmed his bare skin. He sucked in a hard breath, felt himself go tight in all the wrong places. If she kept it up, he'd take her here, now, in the middle of hell, consequences be damned. He released her and stepped clear of temptation. Her scent followed him, his blood on fire from her touch. "Some things are better left alone. I know the rules, that's enough."

"No, Gideon, it's not enough." Color rose high in her cheeks. "I'm going to pack a bag. Vegas is a long way, that will give you plenty of time to catch me up. If I'm going to play this game, I'm damn well going to play to win."

Chapter Five

Atlantis, the Border Realm

Seth gazed out upon the serene waters of the Aegean Sea. The aquamarine waves were gentle, gilded by the touch of everlasting sun that illuminated this part of the immortal realm. He turned his face up to the pristine, blue sky, and let the heat fill his soul. He was a God of Upper Egypt, but he rarely visited the sands of his former domain these days. When he needed the sun to soothe his black heart, he came here, to this mystical island, and walked along the mythical shores. Atlantis had a way about it and he could understand why it inspired so much legend. He found it funny that the mortals considered it a given the island sank into the sea, and lately, they'd decided it was located somewhere near Santorini.

This made him smile as he strolled. He owned a villa on Santorini. It was a nice island, despite the increased tourism, but it was certainly not the compass arrow that pointed the way to paradise. Atlantis was central to everywhere since it existed in a different realm along the dimensional thread. So in theory, yes, it was off the shore of Santorini. And, off the shore of Rhode Island, or Borneo, if need be. Atlantis bordered on everywhere, and nowhere, but to get to any of the infinite places it touched, you needed to use one of the many arches to find your border. While the portals led to the magical edge of the island, the physical portion of Atlantis resided in the Aegean, undetected, unnoticed, ever waiting. Only once had the protective barriers failed. But once was enough in the minds and the myths of the mortals. One glimpse of paradise was not easily forgotten by those consigned to a mediocrity bordering on hell.

Seth felt the approach of another deity. Felt it like a dark cloud blotting out his sun. His favored clerics trailed behind him at a discreete and obsequious distance, an ever present shadow. He had so few followers in this age. Lucky for him the ones he had were very devout, giving him the energy he needed to keep his existence at an acceptable level. When he faced front again, there she stood, the other deity, in all her bitchy feline glory. Bastet, the meddler. "Funny, I thought you favored the dark. A cat thing, right?"

She was in human form today, but her eyes she could never quite get right. They were tawny with the signature feline elliptical, iridescent irises that reflected the world back upon itself, never revealing a hint of what went on behind their mysterious surface. She nodded politely at him and joined him without invite in his stroll. "I've been looking for you, Seth."

"I've been right here. On the beach. Taking the air." He angled a bit so his steps brought him into contact with the rolling tide. The water washed over his sandaled feet, feeling like a sensual bath of warm honeyed wine. "Don't you know? Walking is good for your health."

"Abiding the rules is better for your health, or have you forgotten the terms of the Covenant?"

Forgotten? Never. The eternal stalemate of the Covenant meant he and Horus would never know who was the best in battle. He could never fight his war to a satisfactory end. He had to trade off souls with the other God, the son of his cursed brother Osirus. The brother he killed.

Seth smiled to himself. The memories warmed him even more than the heated, Mediterranean waters. So Bast was here to remind him of the rules of the game, that no overt action may be taken to upset the balance and threaten timeline integrity. Interesting. He, least of all, wanted the dimension at risk. Put the dimension at risk, you put the Gods at risk, including him. That put what little power and influence he did wield at risk. He didn't care for that, but, nothing ventured, nothing gained. Whenever he believed he could score a gain in power and still preserve dimensional integrity, he was willing to throw down. "I believe I know better than most how far I can bend the rules before they snap back at me."

"How far have you bent them this time?"

Bast had a way of speaking that few others could duplicate. Her words, when she chose, were hissed, a sound that grated on his nerves and made his ears ache.

"I like my life, Bastet." He used her full name, putting condescending emphasis on it as a father might when speaking to a wayward and difficult child. "Yes, our wars and petty conflicts are cold. We have minor intrigues at best. Most of the fun is had by our mortal followers, and they're few and far between in this age. It's not in my best interest to upset the game. You, better than most, know I always act in my best interest. Now, Horus, on the other hand, he has a nasty habit of acting in what he passes off as the 'greater' good. You know what happens when Gods get savior complexes. Suddenly, the rules don't apply."

"Save your lies and half truths. I'm here to warn you. Respect the rules we play by, Seth, or you both may be judged. Once in action, the sword of justice does not stop until the job is complete." Her tip-tilted nose twitched in annoyance, as if she could smell his real intent. "You say you're compliant and complacent. Are you sure you're ready to stand the test of judgment?"

Atlantis and its splendorous, unspoiled beauty kept him relatively calm. But Bast's prodding and imperious behavior scraped away that calm. He held his anger in check. It wouldn't do to stir her up. He knew on some level she wanted him mad, because when he was mad, he made mistakes. It was early yet in this game. He'd only taken a few cautious actions to see where they led. Too early to make mistakes, especially when a fresh soul was promised to him. Fresh, unsullied, one Horus did not know of, one Seth didn't need to barter or share. Better yet, it was the soul of an innocent. All he had to do was grant a small favor here and there. Not so much to ask of a God when promising such a plum prize in return. Yes, one did not need many followers, if one had followers of such quality who knew how real tribute and commerce with the Gods worked.

"You ask me if I'm ready?" Seth took a steadying breath and stilled his body. She was so smug in the role of a Tribunal God, so conceited as commander of the creatures that policed the deities of the Covenant and their followers. It bothered him, yes, but, it was something he could throw back at her. "You should be asking yourself a similar question. Is your dog soldier ready for judgment? Can your favored Gideon stand up to the scrutiny, handle the double-edged blade? He's broken the protocol, I hear. He's one step away from going rogue."

Instead of angering her, Seth's words had the opposite effect. She seemed pleased by his response, in some unfathomable way. Her eyes glowed like molten gold, and she smiled enigmatically. She linked her sinewy, bare arms behind her and gave him the barest nod of her head. Her jet black, blunt-cut hair swung down like a sharp blade, hiding half of her arrestingly beautiful face. "Don't worry, Seth. He has until the solstice. Gideon is the thinking man's soldier. He always gets the job done, and always serves justice in the process."

Her visage turned to a brilliant, gilded mist, and she was gone, leaving him alone with his now disturbed thoughts. He had no real idea where this convergence was heading. He was merely dabbling in one aspect of it, assisting a follower. He'd heard it could start up the war again, and he wasn't certain if he cared. Then again, he didn't want to sacrifice the comfort he had either. He walked on, plodding now, missing the scenery as he focused on his internal landscape.

They'd never believe him, of course. The sanctimonious prigs that comprised the Tribunal of Justice always looked on the dark side, always thought the worst. Given the history of Gods and their methods of conflict resolution, he couldn't really fault them. He knew he was treading on dangerous ground. Ah, but he could taste the freshness of that unsullied young soul: his for the taking, costing him such small, meaningless favors.

He wasn't responsible for the actions of a crazed Dedicant, was he? He could make the Tribunal see that, if things went bad. Then again, perhaps things going bad would put him back in a position of true power. What would it be like to live the old days again? To feel so alive, to feel truly Godlike and dispense no mercy nor succor, to be no longer a eunuch relegated to passing out indulgences like sugar candies to grasping, grubby, thankless little children? The forbidden fantasy made his blood thick and hot with desire, with longing. Perhaps he would tread this dangerous ground a little longer and see what he might gain. All he had to do was avoid dirtying his robes.

He rounded a spit of land and changed course, heading inland to a small outcropping of rock that held a shallow cave. The rock face was arranged with a blind that blocked out the sunlight, and the stone itself was of a mineral that minimized release of magical energy. Atlantis, like all other spots in the realm of the Gods, held many such alcoves, and he knew where most of them were located.

Before he reached the spot, he dismissed his priests. They were like beacons, and he wanted no one to know where he was, or what he was doing. The cave interior was cool and moist. The shadows closed in around him like old friends, embracing him with a knowing touch. The Atlantean beaches had bleach white sand that blinded the eyes at times, but in the cave, the sand was night black, and an ideal medium for scrying.

Seth got on bended knee and waved a bejeweled hand over a spot of sand. It swirled beneath his palm, rising like a tiny desert storm, then settled again in a spiral pattern that turned in upon itself like a labyrinth without end. The black color changed, became mirror like, then clear. Seth could see the acolyte at his practice. He fought down a sense of giddiness when he realized the mage was scrying. Such fortuitous timing! It was a good omen, one that told him he was wise to continue with his chosen role in this game.

He furrowed his brow as he struggled to make sense of what information the mage sought. Though this mortal had a great store of power, he'd been using much of it lately. The loss of vital energy took its toll. The message was garbled. Seth used his powers to see into the mind of the mage. It was easier this way. At once the reason for depletion was evident. The mage was binding demons, sending them off to do his bidding. In such a modern age, there were easier ways of accomplishing one's ends, if that end was a simple abduction.

Seth smiled to himself as he sent back a message to the mage. It was one couched in suitably cryptic terms. Should it be discovered, it could be taken many ways. At the same time, he planted a seed in the mage, a hint on how to proceed. *No more demons. Don't use your magical energy; use cold, hard cash.*

He wasn't certain the mage completely understood but the mortal was intelligent. He would figure it out. Seth moved his hand over the sand once more and it reverted back to its former state. He stood and brushed off his robes. He'd stayed within the bounds. He answered the call of a follower, no more, no less. It would be hard to prove his hand guided this next round. Hard, if not impossible.

Satisfied he was safe, Seth left the cave and abandoned the beach in favor of a visit to his concubines. The lusty thoughts of the old days made him hard and ready. Since he could no longer level cities with his legions to satisfy that particular itch, he'd need to content himself with more visceral, sanctioned pursuits. Perhaps one day soon he'd be able to slip his leash and run free. Only time would tell if this convergence was as dangerous and real as the mystics perceived. Seth had his doubts about their vision and interpretation, though he couldn't say why. Something didn't sit right, but, he was getting his fresh soul so he dismissed the troubling thoughts the way one swatted gnats. No matter what transpired, he was confident he would come out ahead of the game.

Meg changed quickly into a comfortable pair of worn denim capris, her favorite green T-shirt, and running shoes. Not that she did much running. She was more the leisurely walk in the park kind of girl. As she laced them up, she supposed that was about to change. Gideon forbade a shower, so she made do with a quick five in the bathroom, shoved an assortment of clothes and personal items into a gym bag, and met him downstairs.

He was still bare-chested, still wearing the biker jacket. He looked rough, sexy, entirely masculine the way he prowled around her living room. She vividly recalled the sensation of his rippling muscles beneath her hands as she tended his wounds. The adrenaline rush of the fear and the fight turned into something far more devastating from that contact. Her need for him rubbed like a burr just beneath her skin. It was an itch she couldn't seem to scratch, an ache she couldn't ease.

Of course, he'd killed her carnal buzz when he informed her about the change. His face had gone all stony, his eyes darkened to void black as she tended his wounds. She was worried she'd hurt him at first. Then he broke the news to her, and it was like someone dipped her in an ice bath. She'd touched the artifact, and was no longer herself. She'd changed. Her touch, not her skills, healed. No more safe house. Now they were off to see some wizard, who maybe could help. Or, maybe not. He said it would be okay, but she'd delivered enough similar speeches to recognize the hollow ring. It was sobering to her to be on the receiving end of a platitude, and humbling to face mortality in such an up close and personal way. She'd never realized how much she insulated herself from death, and life.

Meg's steps slowed as she entered the living room. He told her things would be wrapped up in a week or two. What if that was all the time she had left? Every doctor heard stories about patients, that when given terminal news, took what life they had left and lived it to the hilt, sucking the marrow out of every second they still breathed. She'd become one of them. Just like her patients, she had no control over what was happening to her. Just like her patients, she was facing death. Gideon turned in her direction, his intense gaze sweeping over her like a summer heat wave. She knew then, what she was going to do in those two weeks. She was going to live, embrace the edge and dance on its razor sharp line for all she was worth. If she went down, it would be fighting to her last breath.

He hooked his thumbs into the front pockets of his leather

pants. The movement caused his powerful chest to flex and opened the jacket more, treating her to a glorious display of hard body and washboard abs. “You ready, Doc?”

She felt a thrill spark through her body followed by a sense of purpose and an eerie dead calm. “Ready.”

She stepped out of her ruined home into the sunlight, and squinted at the glare. A white panel van was pulling up curbside. The signage read Mammett’s Cleaning Service. “Gideon?”

He loomed up behind her. “They’ll take care of the mess. Fix the door. When they’re done, no one will know what went down here.”

“My house is trashed, right down to the floorboards.”

“When we get back, it will be just fine.”

It might look fine, she thought, but it wouldn’t be the same. The safety she thought she had was all an illusion, and now that she knew it, she had a different view on life and reality. She couldn’t close her eyes, she couldn’t click her heels and return home.

Gideon took her bag and tossed it in the back of the SUV. From a duffle, he removed another black T-shirt and took a moment to put it on. Instead of turning away, Meg watched every movement he made. When he held the door for her, she brushed against him and didn’t pull back from the electric contact. Instead she let it run through her and enjoyed the moment of stolen pleasure.

“Tell me about the game, Gideon,” she said, the minute they hit the interstate. “I want to know everything.”

“Everything, Doc?” He gunned the accelerator and moved into the fast lane, passing the flow of normal traffic. “The game’s been going on for ages. That’s a lot of ground to cover.”

"We're driving to Vegas. We have time." He'd put his dark glasses on again, but she could tell without seeing his eyes that her questions made him uncomfortable. His square jaw tightened imperceptibly, his wide hands held the steering wheel a little tighter. She realized she was using her doctor voice with him, that imperious MD-means-Most-Divine approach designed to communicate her authority. She usually reserved it for dealing with difficult, corporate bean counters involved in the pharmaceutical studies. She shifted gears, and dialed down the personality a bit. "Start with the highlights."

"You sure you want to know? It may make you feel worse."

"I'm a doctor, Gideon. We're control freaks. We need to know things, and when we don't it drives us crazy." If she could understand, get the facts, maybe she could find a way to help, instead of sitting idly like Rapunzel in a tower, waiting for rescue. "Please. I can't stand being in the dark, helpless."

"You didn't look too helpless back in the kitchen hosing down the Keeper. How'd you come up with the idea to use the fire extinguisher?"

"Ash made me think of fire which made me think of the extinguisher. Then I figured even though it's something magical, it's still breathing. If it can't breathe, it can't fight. The foam expands. It was a no brainer."

"See." He glanced her way and flashed a quick, heart-stopping grin. "You're a fighter, Doc. Most men would be wetting their pants and crying for mama in the middle of that kind of dust-up. You walk in, kicking ass, taking names, like you've been doing it your whole life. You're not helpless."

His words were sincere, and they made her feel a little better. But she needed more. And he was changing the topic. "The more I know, the better I can fight."

He took a deep breath and let it out as a hard sigh. "Fine.

You know mythology?"

"Some. Which myth system?"

"Any. All. Doesn't matter." He eased the big SUV into a sharp turn. "They're true. All those different Gods and Goddesses really are running around, screwing with the mortal world."

Not a comforting thought. "How does that impact the game?"

"It's the thing that started the game. The Gods were fooling with the natural order so much, between wars, plagues, and backward time travel, they started to fragment the integrity of the dimensional timeline."

She heard the words but the sense of them eluded her. "Time travel?"

"Time is fairly linear for a dimension. You can go back and rewrite it, but you can't move forward beyond your start point." He pulled out into the middle lane and passed a slower vehicle on the right. "Picture a long, straight branch from a flexible bush. That's your dimensional line. Off of that you have leaves and berries, and those are all different realms. A dimension can have any number, some you can access off the line, others are closed, but, they all belong to that one line. If you start monkeying around too much with the branch, keep bending it the wrong way or pull too much stuff off, it can break."

He was being so matter of fact about such outrageous things. Meg told herself she was prepared for the truth of this expanded reality, but now she wasn't so sure. "And breaking is bad."

"Very bad. All the realms ride the dimensional line. There are an infinite number of alternate dimensions all with their own lines. If you crack one, fracture the integrity, you can open it to an alternate. That invites potential encroachment, or invasion. And, you risk collapse. Collapse a line, and all the realms, including those of the Gods, disappear. No more. That's all she wrote. The end."

Meg digested this for a few minutes. "So the actions of these Gods risked fracture."

"Once some of them realized what was at stake, they gathered together and formed the Eternity Covenant. The Gods that joined agreed to ease up on the throttle and play by a unified set of rules that limited power. For the most part they corralled their actions on the mortal plane, and they made a stab at keeping followers in line. Only, mankind has free will, so that makes things messy."

It was weird, but making more sense. All she had to do was accept possibilities and then it all sort of hung together with unified principles. Meg felt herself getting sea legs, using her scientific reasoning skills to reframe the reality change. "This Covenant sounds like a league of nations."

Gideon nodded. "The Covenant also set up a branch to deal with infractions. The Tribunal of Justice. Only a few Gods hold places on the Tribunal. I work for one of them. Operative word is work. If you're on the Tribunal, you can't follow the Gods because you need to police them."

"If you police the Gods, why are you here with me? I'm just a mortal."

He chuckled at her comment. "You're a deviation point, Meg. In addition to the Tribunal, there's a group called the Council of Wardens. Their mystics spend time in meditation studying all activity along our dimensional timeline. The Gods still get out of line, only they have some latitude and they always test the boundaries. The real troublemakers are often the followers. The mystics watch for negative convergences that can lead to fracture, then they find a deviation point that can be used to divert destiny prior to the negative event. The Wardens determine how best to exploit the deviation point."

"And that deviation point would be me?" She mulled this over for a moment. "Isn't there another one, or do they all boil down to a single point?"

"Most times, there are a series of points where you can disrupt a convergence. Sometimes it appears the universe has a certain destiny in mind and that's harder to disrupt. Sometimes, there is only one point to jump the track. Right now, you're the one point. If we don't jump tracks, the mystics have seen an old war between Seth and Horus waking back up. That leads to massive fracture, and directly to collapse."

It was just like the human body, striving to maintain homeostasis. Any threat to that would result in the body's reaction, and sometimes, that could be a series of negative reactions that drove the body into deeper trouble, and often death. She understood, now. Heaven help her she understood. "I know a bit about Egyptian myth. I learned it when I was in Cairo helping with a humanitarian aide project. Don't Seth and Horus fight for the souls of man in some kind of apocalyptic battle?"

Again, the curt nod. "You can see why everyone's all hot and bothered over this vision."

They may be hot and bothered but right now her blood ran cold as an ice floe. She shivered as she considered the consequences. A world at war with itself, good and evil destroying everything they touched in a battle for supremacy. "This goes on all the time? Throughout the centuries?"

"In one form or another, yes. It helped that for a long time, only a few Gods had die-hard followers. The less in number, or the less dedicated, the less power a God can wield. Of course, sometimes that makes them desperate and stupid. Usually, though, they play things on a much smaller scale. No one benefits from a line collapse. Even the Gods get that."

Meg considered what her options might be as the sole point to avert universal destruction. Talk about checkmate. Only one thing came to mind. "Why not just kill me? If I'm out of the picture, the line is safe."

Gideon's lips tightened into a thin frown. "You're assuming the vision is accurate."

"You're not?"

"Not this time, no."

Come with me if you want to live. His words echoed through her brain. It was more than the demons he saved her from. "You're telling me that the Gods are out to get me?"

He didn't respond.

"Why are you helping me, Gideon?" Her initial shock turned to anger. What had she done to deserve this? "It sounds like you're violating one of the major rules of this precious game. You should be making sure I don't start the apocalypse, not driving me to Vegas."

"You're not the problem, Meg. The vision is inaccurate. That means I need to find the real truth if I want to maintain the integrity of the line. You were in the wrong place at the wrong time. Nothing more." He sighed audibly, a sound mixed with both frustration and resignation. "I didn't want to tell you this much because I need you focused. I don't want you in a state of panic. The Gods are not out to get you. You've been caught up in something by accident. I'm here to keep you safe, and remove you from risk as soon as I can figure out how. Once I do that, I'll figure out what's really behind the vision, just like I'll figure out how to find the real deviation point and exploit it to our advantage."

"You still haven't answered my question. Why are you

helping me?"

"Because I work for the Goddess Bast, and I serve justice. Justice doesn't mete out punishment upon innocents. That fate is reserved for the guilty."

She wanted to take comfort in his words. They were so forthright, so noble. They were also very final, a confirmation of all her fears. She was on borrowed time. "Why does Bast care if I live or die?"

"I've worked with the Gods for centuries, Meg, and I'm still confounded by their capriciousness and callousness." He shrugged. "Bast watches over women and children. You help children. Perhaps it's as simple as that. She picked me for immortality because I did her an unknowing favor when I stopped two soldiers from beating an alley cat to death with sticks. Gods are big on whims. That's why they've come so close to destroying the line so many times. The universe craves order, the Gods incite disorder. The mortals get caught in the middle."

"Oh." She couldn't think of anything else to say. She was so confident once she knew the general ground rules she'd be able to find a way to win. She was used to cheating death, to finding new and inventive ways to forestall it in her patients, she assumed she'd do the same here. To know there was such randomness around her, to know that disaster lurked around every corner, that was worse than knowing things like demons and vampires and magic existed in her world.

They fell into tense silence as the miles rolled by and she struggled to accept everything she'd learned. She kept trying to push the boundaries in her mind, but they resisted and the struggle wore her out. After a while the landscape blurred together in one swirling mass of green, and she must have fallen asleep.

Next thing she knew, Gideon was shaking her awake, and

the sky was dark and full of stars.

Her neck hurt and her body ached. She had no clue how long she was out. She rubbed her eyes and looked at her wrist watch. Nine thirty p.m. "Where are we?"

"Right near the Ohio border." He pulled his hand from her shoulder and she felt the air cool the spot where it had rested so gently. "We're at a truck stop. It's a neutral spot. We'll be safe here. I need to make some calls. We can grab a bite to eat. We have one more stop to make, and then I'll get us a room and we can let up for the night."

Meg got out of the car and shivered in the cool, damp night air. They must be in the mountains, in a higher elevation. Western Pennsylvania had a ton of them. She'd need her sweater from her bag. Before she could say a word Gideon shrugged out of his jacket and draped it over her shoulders.

"This will keep you warm. Come on, let's go inside."

The leather enveloped her like armor. It smelled like him, radiating heat and comfort in an equal mix. She felt safe and secure, as if nothing in the universe could touch her. She gazed up into his eyes and a brilliant flare of carnal hunger sparked up from their fathomless depths. It spoke to her on a visceral gut level. All she wanted to do was touch him, tell him she shared that hunger, that gnawing primal need that could only be sated one way. Unable or unwilling to stop herself, she gave in to her urge.

As she reached for him, Gideon stepped aside and the look vanished. A blast of chill mountain air gusted between them. Meg lowered her arm and snuggled further into the protective cocoon of the jacket. She might want, and he might want, but together they couldn't be more wrong. Then again... Meg banished the fantastic thought, mentally chiding herself for her silliness. "Thanks."

"Don't thank me yet, Doc." He put his arm around her in a companionable way. "You haven't tasted the food."

His touch baited her, teasing her body, promising all kinds of unimaginable pleasure. She found herself wondering if perhaps she wasn't being premature, or puritanical, dismissing the potential of a liaison with Gideon so quickly. Plenty of people had sex without strings, every day, every night. There'd been a time, back in her college days, when that kind of careless abandon was a way to break up the boredom, to learn about sexuality, to have fun, if only for a night. When had she become so closed off? She shifted closer to him, settling into the warmth of his rock solid body, while she let her mind drift over the delicious fantasy of a wild night of abandon with a sexy immortal all to herself. It would be an excellent, if only temporary, antidote to the anxiety created by being number one on the hit list of the Gods. Something to block out the cold, harsh reality that she was in it, and in it deep.

He was a fool for touching her. A damned fool. He couldn't have her, even if she did look at him with desire transparent in her misty green eyes. He noticed that the silvery hue was brighter when he was near, and that stroked his masculine pride. She trusted him, and more, she wanted him. He wanted her. No one woman, however, could be more out of reach. Her scent enveloped him, filled him, teased him like a wicked lover playing bedroom games. He should be ten feet away or more, whatever the safe distance was to keep his libido under control and his mind on anything other than making love to her until she screamed his name again, and again and again. He was torturing himself. Touching Meg like he did, holding her against his side as they walked into Ray's Truckstop, that was all he'd get. All he'd allow himself to have. Anything more was only a fevered dream at best. A dangerous indulgence that could cost them both the ultimate price.

The traffic was heavy tonight. Many of the booths were filled, blood-sworn enemies sitting side by side at times, all abiding the rules of neutral ground. A few of them gave him a hard, long stare, but no one was stupid or crazy enough to start trouble. He'd had enough trouble to last him a century or two. It wasn't just fighting the remaining demons, either. It was Meg, and her questions, and conclusions. She was too damn smart for her own good. She'd almost figured out he was there to kill her, not save her. He'd been lucky to turn that one around.

Gideon found them an empty booth not too far from the entrance to the gift shop and, more importantly, the phone banks. He got Meg seated, ordered up some food, then excused himself to make some calls. He checked in with Ramon first. The Spaniard answered the dedicated line on the first ring.

"You're racking up a substantial bill with Mammett's."

"Don't worry, Salazar. The Tribunal's good for it."

"Speaking of the Tribunal, Seth put in a discreet request to investigate your actions. He knows you've gone rogue."

Shit. The Egyptian God of chaos was always a royal pain in the ass. "Didn't take him long to jump into the mix. Makes him look good for this. Has an official warrant been issued?"

"I was able to redirect the involved parties. For the moment. As troublesome as he is, I can't imagine Seth has the raw skill to compromise a mystic, or plant a false vision."

So, his gut was right. The vision was wrong. Relief spread in a warm rush through his body. "What did you find out?"

"Not as much as I like, but enough to think you're on to something. I need to leave shortly for Monte Carlo. I may be out of touch for a day."

"So will I."

As Salazar briefed him, Gideon debated telling him about Meg's newfound talent. In the end, he decided to keep it to himself until he knew more. "I'm following up a lead at my end, I'll check in midday tomorrow, my time. That work for you?"

"Yes. And, Gideon, be careful. If Seth is directly involved, he'll come for you as well as the mortal. You two don't exactly have the best history."

"I've got the same track record with Seth as I do with any ten Gods. I'll watch my back."

He rang up Matt next, but the shadow ops agent had nothing new to offer other than the theory that the mage could be a tourist and not a resident to the area. If the theory proved true, it would make it more difficult to track him down.

Disappointed, Gideon returned to the table. He considered contacting Bast, but he needed more before he checked in with her. So far, they had no breaks. No leads. He hoped like hell Jack could help him out. The crazy sorcerer seemed certain after hearing the preliminaries over the phone, but wouldn't commit until he got his hands on Meg.

Gideon made some attempts at small talk with Meg, keeping it light, but she was still keyed up. He could tell, because her eyes were shadowed, her movements jerky. She picked at her steak and potatoes, more moving the food around on the plate than anything. He couldn't blame her, knowing what she did. They didn't bother with dessert, so he settled up, and they hit the road again. She was surprised when he didn't turn onto the interstate.

"Where are we going next?"

"I need to get some supplies. A little extra protection. There's no safe house available tonight, so we need to make do with a regular motel." He took another blind turn. "The motel is run by friendlies, so if we run into trouble and raise the roof, they won't call the cops. But we're on our own when it comes to magical cover."

She nodded and drew the lapels of his jacket closer to her. He wished her hands would hold him with the same possessive touch.

The silence between them was tight and uneasy. Gideon concentrated on the terrain until he found the dirt road turn-off he needed. Meg continued to stare out the window, but her interest piqued when he pulled up in front of an old farm house.

"This looks like the house from *The Waltons.*"

"Don't let the picket fence fool you. The guy who owns this place is an ancient who deals in magical supplies and covers all systems from Santeria to Runic spells." He shut off the engine. "I'll only be a minute. Please, Meg, stay in the car. There are things that keep the peace here, things you don't want to screw with."

She gave him a wan smile. "Don't worry. I'm too tired to fight."

"So am I."

Gideon ventured into the farmhouse and for once, luck was on his side. He managed to score everything he needed to set up a protective barrier, and the proprietor made a few additional recommendations that would come in handy. He had more than enough to shield them from undue magical probing. Back at the truck, he found Meg, staring up at the sky through the rolled down window. Her skin glittered like moon dust in the dark. His breath stuck in his chest, and for a moment, all he could do was stare.

Meg noticed him after a moment, leaned back in the SUV, and rolled up the window. He got into the SUV, and pulled back out onto the dirt road.

"There aren't this many stars where I live."

"You can't see them because of the city lights. They're still there, though."

"A lot is there you can't see. But my eyes are opening, Gideon. I'm seeing a lot more, now, in a very different way."

Her voice was low, throaty, and laced with a sugar coating that screamed sexy to his ears. The sound played havoc with his senses. If she could do this to him with her voice, her nearness, what might her touch do?

"The motel's just up ahead." He kept his eyes glued to the road, his mind on task, but his body had thoughts of its own. His cock grew harder, stretching against the bounds of his pants, making it difficult to sit still. His blood raced inside his body, and his pulse quickened. By the time he pulled into the motel, he had a raging hard-on that was trying to short-circuit his brain.

The units were small cabin-like structures, with a kitchenette and two double beds. He was able to get them one set back from the road, which afforded them some privacy. They were the motel's only occupants, another plus. The minute he dropped the bags, he locked the door, and got down to business. He hoped the arcane rites might take some of the starch out of his dick, otherwise he was facing a long and difficult night.

"I'm going to shower." Meg's announcement had a defiant tone.

"Enjoy."

She grabbed her bag, and disappeared into the small side room, shutting the door with a forceful bang.

Gideon was glad for the break away from her. The intensity of the attraction he felt gnawed at him like an insatiable hunger. Tasting her was the only way he'd fill that empty spot in his gut, and she wasn't on tonight's menu.

He pulled out the stuff he'd purchased and got to work. He fired up one of the hot plates, filled a deep pot with the holy water from the half gallon milk jug supplied by the magic dealer and poured the requisite three cylinders of sacred sea salts into the mix. The water hissed, then settled down as the joining process began. While that merged energies via heat, he moved on to the more complex part of the working. He opened a Mason jar of what smelled and looked like moonshine, and dipped in a hand-carved bone and horsetail stylus. Then, starting with the low ceiling, he began to paint protective sigils.

The shower hummed as he worked, and fragrant steam seeped out from beneath the bathroom door. He remembered how it felt to wrap himself in mist around Meg's body, to slide against her skin and envelope her inside of him. The thought did little to ease the tight, desperate ache in his groin. That ache only got worse when she emerged, freshly bathed, her copper-colored hair curling around her angelic, heart-shaped face. She wore a simple pale blue T-shirt and thin gray jersey pants. The cold air from the AC in the main room caused her nipples to harden and press insistently against the thin, clingy fabric of the shirt. Gideon groaned and turned away from the delectable, damning sight. He finished with the back wall and repeated the procedure on the wall over the first of the two beds. He caught Meg's scent as she neared and he shut his eyes and prayed to no one in particular to help him keep control.

"What are you doing?"

He opened his eyes. She was right next to him, half-turned, displaying a tempting profile of her ripe breast. He swallowed hard. "I'm trying to keep you safe."

"How?"

"This stuff is magically charged to create a protective

barrier, and I'm using it to create a series of sigils that will enhance the protection."

She sniffed, wrinkling her nose. "Smells like cheap liquor."

He continued to paint, moving to the other bed. She followed. "What can I do to help?"

Stay far away from me. "Nothing. Sit down. Watch TV. I have it under control." Yeah. Right.

She wandered into the kitchenette, treating him to an excellent view of her round bottom as it swayed invitingly. "What's cooking?"

His core temperature rose another notch. At this rate, he'd spontaneously combust if he wasn't careful. "More protection. It should be ready. Can you turn off the burner?"

"Sure." She turned the dial down, sat in the plastic chair at the Formica café table, and tapped her foot nervously against the black and white linoleum. "I can't stand being so useless. There must be something I can do to help you."

Touch me. Feel me. Let me make love to you until we both drop, too exhausted to move. "Nope. I'm fine."

He paused at the threshold to the bathroom. He needed to inscribe a few markers in there, but he dreaded entering the confined space. It smelled too much of her, of her perfume, her musk. It would kill him. But he couldn't avoid it without compromising the spell. He steeled himself and stepped inside the sweet hell. For a moment, all he did was breathe, and then he thought he'd die. His erection pulled heavily at his hips, begging for release. She came up behind him and touched his back. He jumped and spun around.

"How will that work in here?" She chewed her plump lower lip, her look earnest and trusting. "Aren't the walls too slick?"

Gods she was a powerful package. Her mix of vulnerability

and sensual appeal pushed him over the edge. He gripped the stylus so hard it cracked in his fist. "You know what you can do? Grab that pot from the hot plate, go around to the doors and windows, and sprinkle the water across each. There's a thing that looks like a miniature whisk broom on the end table. Use that to spread the water."

She gave him a quizzical look as if he were some kind of test-finding she couldn't understand. Then the look passed, and she shrugged. "Okay."

Gideon returned to the job at hand but he couldn't get her out of his mind. The bathroom had only two exterior walls, and no window, so within a few minutes he was back in the main room of the tiny cabin and she was back in his orbit, a fiery sun burning him and his resistance to ash.

She'd made fast work and was finishing the main window and door on the wall he still needed to inscribe. He had to complete marks beside the window and over the doorway for the spell energy to knit properly. He focused every ounce of his attention on the task, slowly painting the ancient symbols with the clear, noxious fluid. When he finished the last he stepped back with relief, turned, and knocked into Meg. She'd crept up behind him waiting to finish the door. The hot water splashed from her pot onto his hand and burned the exposed flesh of his hand.

He jerked back and dropped the stylus and the Mason jar.

"Oh my God! Gideon, I'm sorry!" Meg stuck the pot on the air conditioning unit and grabbed his hand in hers.

The contact ran through him like a bolt of pure lightning. Something inside of him snapped. "Meg, no."

"Let me see. I'm a doctor." The words died on her lips as she watched the burn fade, and his skin heal. "I guess you don't need me after all."

She released his hand, but it was too late. The last frayed thread holding him together came undone.

"I need you, Doc."

He took her hand and pulled her hard against him. His cock pressed against her soft belly. The peaked tips of her breasts teased him. He slanted his head down, shifted his hold so he could hold her around her waist with one hand, and bury the other in the damp, silken mass of her curls. Then he captured her sweet, honeyed lips, kissing her as he'd fantasized a thousand times.

Chapter Six

Gideon took her mouth softly, savoring the taste. He skimmed the plush surface with a feather-light pressure, holding her gently, as if she were a treasure that should he squeeze too hard, would break in his hands. His cock was rock hard and ready, standing at attention, waiting for the call. She was a drug that made his heart race and his blood thrum. Her body sparked him like no other, setting loose a wild, needy desire that refused to be contained. He didn't want to rush, he wanted to live every second touching her like a man who had lived a thousand good years. He wanted to cherish her, to show her skill and patience. And he wanted to devour her whole. He wanted to throw her down and let loose, take her to the edge of madness with him, bury himself inside her slick vault and forget anything but them and the moment that they shared.

The desire was so pure, so white hot and intense, it went well beyond simple lust, or anything he'd felt with a woman in both mortal and immortal life. The fury frightened him and exhilarated him, taking him into dangerous, uncharted territory. He forced himself to stay in control, forced himself to slow down, but every second spent tasting her, touching her, wanting her, brought him closer and closer to the treacherous cliffs bordering the abyss of abandon. Somewhere, in the far distance of his mind, a small voice screamed a warning into the growing storm of passion, a warning that went unheard.

Meg's eyes drifted closed as he intensified the kiss. She parted her lips, granting him entry, and he dove from the edge heedless of the rocks below. He swept his tongue inside of her, tasting her essence, savoring her. She responded, melting against him, boneless, yet wanting. Her tongue met his with gentle, teasing sweeps that inflamed him. Every nerve ending in his body flared to life. His senses were on fire, his body caught up in a maelstrom of sweet agony. He lowered his hand, tracing her spine as he skimmed across her body. She shivered at his touch, and he went lower still, marveling at the thrill Meg woke inside of him.

His hand followed the sweet curve of her hip, found the soft flesh of her rounded bottom and roamed the delectable mounds. His cock strained, desperate to be free. She moaned low in her throat, and he deepened the kiss, cupping her bottom, holding her so she knew how much he desired her, so there could be no question of his intent or his need. His skin ached as she ran her hands up his chest. She didn't pull back. Instead she moved her hips in a sultry, subtle rhythm, pressing against him then shifting imperceptibly away, then moving back again for more torment. Through all the centuries no one woman had wielded such absolute control over him. He had to regain sanity, take back some measure of his own power, resist her and what he so desperately wanted from her.

He pulled back, drew in a ragged breath. They had to stop. He had to stop. If he didn't, there would be no turning back. "I need you, Meg. More than is safe for both of us."

Meg caressed his cheek with a loving touch, but her eyes held wicked promises of trouble to come. "I don't want to be safe."

She pulled him down to her once more, returning his kiss with a blistering one of her own that pushed him past all reason. She danced her hips closer, as she nibbled on his lower lip. The dueling sensations were a sweet torment. She was fire in his hands, liquid honey in his mouth, a siren singing him to his death. A dim part of him knew this had to stop, but the rest of him moved on pure, primal instinct. He wanted to lose himself in her and never find his way back.

This is what heaven is like.

Meg surrendered to the blissful sensations Gideon's skilled kisses aroused. He showed her no mercy as he claimed her mouth with aggressive, bruising need. She knew he'd be a demanding lover, but he was a man crazed, and she loved every reckless moment. To be completely possessed, desired beyond reason, was as new to her as it was to desire beyond such reason.

She breathed in his heady scent instead of air as every masculine inch of him moved against her. He was a heart-jolting thrill that kept amping up higher and higher with no signs of stopping. Her pulse raced as a delicious heat built low in her belly. She moved hard against him now, seeking his swollen ridge. She wanted him to know the torment as she did, wanted him as mad and reckless as herself and she didn't care what she had to do to bring him with her over that edge.

He made a sound between a growl and a groan, cupped both her buttocks and lifted her up from the floor. She spread her legs so she could get closer to him, while he moved her against him. He never stopped kissing, plundering her mouth as he teased her with the lure of satisfaction. An insistent, restless need plagued her, building with each subtle stroke his rigid, contained cock made. She held on to his broad shoulders and tilted her pelvis forward. The promise and the longing were tearing her apart in the most wonderful way.

She didn't care that twenty-four hours ago she'd never met

this incredible man. She didn't care about the consequences of her lusty actions. Tonight all she cared about was living in the moment, giving in to the wild desires without regret. Artificial taboos of propriety and decorum turned to ash in the blazing realization that there were no more guaranteed tomorrows, no promised future, and no need to pretend otherwise. To hesitate now was to lose everything she never knew she wanted, or could have.

Gideon turned and settled her on the bed. He abandoned her mouth and moved to the sensitive flesh of her neck, raising goose bumps as he trailed low to her collar bone. Shifting his weight, he dipped his head lower still, nuzzling one breast, then the other with his mouth, teasing the hardened nipples through the shirt fabric. A line of white hot flame torched through her and she arched her back, inviting more of his sweet, sinful torture. She eased back, giving him open access to her body, encouraging him with her touch to give her more, to give her all. She couldn't seem to draw breath, but it didn't matter. She was alive, all her nerves awake and poised on the razor's edge.

Gideon settled beside her, watching her with fevered eyes as he slipped his hand beneath her shirt to caress her breast. His thumb abraded her sensitized nipple, coaxing it to tighten even more. Closing her eyes, she tilted her head back, and focused on the sublime feeling of his masterful touch. As he shifted his attention to her other breast, her final tether stretched and snapped. Meg moaned and reached for him, needing to feel all of him against all of her, skin to skin with nothing more to stand between them. She succeeded in grabbing a portion of his shirt, and he stopped briefly to help in its removal.

He rose over her, kissed her hotly, then moved down so he was poised over her torso. Her hands rode over him, feeling every rigid cord of muscle and sinew that tightened beneath the heated golden skin. A shudder worked through him, and she smiled. He felt the same pain, the same need. Good. It served him right for turning her world inside out and upside down. For turning her inside out and upside down.

He mastered control, and flashed her a wicked grin. Then he lowered his head, nudged up her already rumpled shirt, used his mouth on the ridge of her tight nipple. He was hot silk sliding over her. She gasped as a jolt rocked her very core. No man's touch had ever brought her so close to orgasm. He was more than a man, though, and he was hers. She laced her fingers through his thick, spiky hair. She needed release, God she needed it so bad. He knew. He had to know. She was a moaning, panting mess, for God's sake, but he kept up the sensual punishment, forcing her higher and higher but never giving that fatal push. "Please." Her voice was raw, harsh, breathless. "No more."

"If some is good, more is better." He sucked and nipped, then increased the pressure as he captured the nub between his teeth. There was a moment of sharp pain followed by a flood of pleasure as he tongued it with a stiff, thrusting motion. The smell of sex filled the air like a lethal, drugging incense. She bucked against him, moving now without the guidance of her mind, following an ancient instinct for satisfaction on the most primal and basic of levels.

Despite his brave words, he couldn't hold out any more than she. Gideon returned to capture her mouth with a kiss that stole her breath as he slipped off her jersey pants with a swift move she barely noticed. His next move, however, had all of her attention. His hand ventured to the apex of her thighs and she parted for him. The simple contact forced all the air from her lungs, and curled her toes. She ached for him in ways she couldn't even comprehend. He stroked her inner thighs first, using the heel of his palm to rub against her mound with alternating pressure. "Now, Gideon. I want you now. No more games."

Her crazy words scared her and thrilled her as she swirled in the torrent of his relentless attack. Gideon gave her what she desired, burying two fingers deep inside her slick core, fingering her expertly until she was dizzy and senseless.

"Come for me, Meg." His deep voice penetrated the manic haze of pleasure. He increased the pace, pushing her beyond her limits, taking her to a dark, dangerous place. "Come for me."

The combination of his magic touch and his deep, alluring voice shattered the last defenses, triggering an endless orgasm that swallowed her whole. She was only dimly aware of her own voice, calling out to him. She'd lost her mind. Fully lost her mind. And she'd never cared less in her life.

A loud horn blew caustically outside, shattering the silence of the night. As her tremors subsided, a cold breeze moved across her, chilling her.

"Gods, what am I doing?" Gideon rolled off her and stood. "This can't happen. I'm sorry, Meg."

Chill air swept across her bare skin, turning her sweat to ice. The afterglow of orgasm vanished in an instant. She regained some of her wits, and sat up. "Sorry for what? Did I seem upset?"

His eyes were hollow, his face held a haunted look. He stepped back from the bed, from her, as if she had the plague. The muscles of his neck were strained, as if he were in great pain. She could see his swollen cock rigidly outlined in his pants. He wanted her, as much if not more than she wanted him. She could see the inner war play out in his darkened eyes. "What's wrong? We're both adults here—"

"I'm an immortal, Meg. You're mortal. I'm supposed to

protect you. I can't do this, and keep you safe."

She could tell he was serious, that he really believed his words. There was underlying terror in his voice, mixed with no small dose of disgust. It made no sense. "Is it the spell? Is that why you don't want this to happen?"

He ran a hand through his hair, took a haggard breath. "I'm going to take a shower. A long, cold shower. After that, we've both got a night to get through. We need to forget what's between us. We can't let this happen again."

His body shimmered before her eyes and faded into a mist that filtered rapidly into the bathroom. The door slammed shut and the lock engaged. Meg sat in stunned silence, unable to understand or comprehend what just happened.

He'd played her body like she was meant for his hands, brought her pleasure like she'd never known. Then he stormed out on her like she'd attacked him. All she did was touch him. He was the one who started ravishing her, kissing away her breath. Meg collected herself and went to the kitchenette where she made herself a cup of decaf in the microwave.

What was wrong with her, she wondered angrily as she drank the tepid, weak brew. So she wasn't one of his kind. What did it matter? What did one night of meaningless sex matter? People had one-night stands all the time. She eyed the barrier of the locked bathroom door. Her body recalled his touch all too readily, and she frowned. She was willing to bet tall, dark and insane had more than a few one nighters himself. A man didn't get to know how to work a woman's body that fast without a load of practice. She sipped some of the dishwater decaf, then dumped the rest down the drain and cleaned the cup with fast, angry motions.

Frustrated, she climbed into the bed and hit the remote for the TV. She was too keyed up to sleep now, but she had no way to work it off, or deal with the embarrassment. She'd called out for him, came for him, and then when she wanted to return the favor, he walked away. What kind of normal man did that?

She pushed her hair from her eyes and let out a deep breath. Boy, she really was an idiot, wasn't she. An idiot, and totally out of her depth. Apparently these immortals must have some kind of code. Maybe he had to say no, maybe he couldn't give in to what she knew he desired until the mission was complete. Some of her earlier fury and confusion subsided. Yes. That was reasonable. He did say he couldn't keep her safe if his mind was on other things. Gideon was a man who took his job seriously. Too seriously.

She flipped through channels, and settled on one running an uncut *Phantom of the Opera*. As she watched the crazed phantom struggle with madness, passion, pain and obsession, she was reminded of the moment where Gideon changed from confident to terrified in the blink of an eye. That haunted, pained look made her thoughtful, took some of the focus off her own issues. She wanted to have sex with him, screw him senseless. She knew he wanted the same. He was ready, she knew he was, up until that one strange moment. It was startling, revealing, showing her another side that lurked beneath that stony, hard-ass exterior. It made her wonder about him as a man, not just a buff soldier out to protect her from the big bad evil. It made her sit back and consider the person. What happened to Gideon to make him so cautious, to cause him such worry that he'd abandon his own pleasure?

The movie continued to play, and the bathroom door stayed locked. The shower ran like heavy rain, the only sound besides the TV in the small, rented cabin. She couldn't get him out of her mind, couldn't stop wondering about his past. Something happened way back when, she was certain of it, something that made him afraid of himself, afraid of his passions. But what?

A yawn stretched through her, then another. Meg shivered and got beneath the covers, arranging the pillows so she could see the last of the movie from a reclining position. She fell asleep to the ending credits, the eerie soundtrack lulling her into twisted, vicious dreams.

Gideon came out of his self-imposed prison first as mist, the non-corporeal form that didn't feel the normal sensations of the body. Meg was deep in sleep. The TV played a Technicolor test pattern. He materialized to form, picked the remote up from the floor beside her bed, and shut down the tube for the night. He stood over her for a long moment, his body recalling in vivid detail the taste and feel of her. She was made for him. He knew it as well as he knew his own rotten soul. She was so responsive, so uninhibited. He could love her through a million nights and it wouldn't be enough.

Gideon shut out the light on the nightstand and finished fortifying the room. He'd cleaned up in the shower, but the cold water did little to help his need. In the end he'd given in, masturbating to memories of her moaning beneath him as he brought her over the edge. Even now, after emptying himself, he grew thick with need watching her sleep in the shadows. Gods, they could be so good together.

He could have taken her. She was ready for him, she wanted him. She told him as much. Her body was his for the asking, and he'd almost gone through with it. Almost shucked his clothes, stripped her bare, and shown her the true extent of his hunger.

Then sanity returned, in one dark, crystalline, eminently painful moment. Thank the Gods he'd had the strength to stop. He wasn't sure he could if it happened again. He told himself he needed to be the sane one. Meg was under far more stress than him. No doubt her desire was a reaction to that stress. He'd seen it before in other mortals when they learned the truth about reality, when they found themselves facing down death. They got extreme. They took risks they normally wouldn't take on pain of death. Placid, safe Dr. Meg gave in to her libido because she thought her days were numbered. She wanted him, but he told himself she'd probably take any port in this storm.

She was vulnerable and he was pig enough to take advantage of her, letting sexual arousal cloud his judgment. He was a jackass, and he knew it. At least he'd managed to pull back at the last moment. She didn't realize it, but if they'd made love, she'd hate him, and she'd hate herself more in the morning. He'd rather do without her than endure her loathing. A woman's thoughts about him never mattered before, but no woman was ever like Megan Carter. Everything about her mattered, and he couldn't stomach disappointing her.

He cleaned up the remainder of the magical supplies and finished off the wards by crossing the entryways to the room with the last of the sea salt. His body was taxed. Between the battles with demons and the battle with desire, it was spent. Gideon didn't look forward to another night in a chair, then again, he'd had worse beds. He was a soldier, could sleep anywhere, under any conditions, always with one eye open.

He pulled over one of the yellow plastic chairs, stuck a bed pillow against the back, and settled in for a long night. He had the shotgun handy along with the rest of his weapons. The tattoo was active. All he had to do was speak the word and his sword would materialize in his hands. He kicked his legs up on the bed, stared long into the darkness, and eventually the memories of the past captured him in dreams.

He walked a barren landscape in the charcoal grey light that characterized predawn. In the distance, upon a hill, were the remains of a dwelling. Smoke belched up like chimney spit, darkening the sky above. A burning pain erupted in his chest, buried on the left side beneath his ribs. It felt like his insides were cooking at an infernal, unbearable temperature. His mouth was dry and tasted of ash. He walked on towards the burning ruin, his steps slow and heavy. A mist enshrouded the rising hills before him, and when he entered its thickest part, he realized he was in some sort of military encampment.

Soldiers meandered about, setting up cookfires, drinking from horns and skins, joking with one another. Whores mixed in with them, sharing drink, sliding like snakes against them. It wasn't long before the soldiers openly fucked them in the camp, bending them over piles of gear, tossing up their filthy skirts and taking them like animals. The smoke of the fires burned his eyes and they began to tear. He moved on through the grotesque orgy, walking a path that led him to a red tent with parted door panels. Two soldiers, probably the only sober ones in camp, stood guard. He walked by them unseen.

The tent's interior was warm, the air thick with the musky stench of cheap sex. Two whores were sprawled on the thick, carpeted floor. They were naked, asleep near the central brazier. On the pallet, beneath skins, a muscular man sported with a third. She was on her knees, spread before him. He slammed into her again and again, disgusting invectives spilling from him in slurred, drunken sentences. The girl's forearms were braced as she absorbed the force of his savage attack. She smiled broadly, her teeth black and in other spots, completely gone. The man grabbed her knotted hair and pulled her head back as he drove into her one last time, then he collapsed upon her and rolled off to his side. His eyes closed, and he passed into a drunken slumber from which he would not wake. Not until it was too late.

Gideon stared at the man's familiar face. Even with the long hair, and thick beard, he recognized the fiend. He saw that face every time he gazed upon a mirror, or polished surface. Gideon recoiled, the pain in his chest searing him until he thought he would burst. He shut his eyes and when he opened them again he was inside the remains of a bailey. Bodies rotted as carrion birds feasted on the flesh. The acrid scent of smoke hung in the thick, moist air. He stumbled around seeking a way out, tripping over the dead, knowing all the while there was only one way out. There was only one way for this to end.

"No!" He held his hands over his eyes, unwilling to see what came next, even as his body moved on. "Wake up, you fool. Wake up!"

He'd not had this dream since he was mortal. Centuries had passed silently without reliving this nightmare. Now he was trapped in the horrific memories, stark reminders of his failure as a man, as a husband, and a father. Gideon opened his eyes once more and he stood before the ramshackle stables, their charred remains sticking up like burnt bones half buried in a muddy, ravaged earth.

He was dreaming about the past he buried. His dead were rising. And they were coming for him. There was no avoiding it, so he forced himself to walk around and finish what he'd started. The woman's body waited, curled on its side, hands bound, stripped bare. Flesh was torn from the bones, maggots writhed upon the corpse. Gideon fought his rising bile, and toughed it out. Until he buried her, he would not escape to consciousness. He stepped closer and a cloud of smoke billowed up from nowhere, obscuring his vision. He rubbed hard at his eyes, and when the smoke cleared, something had changed in a nightmare that never wavered.

The corpse should have yellow hair, like a field of corn or the glow of the summer sun. She always had yellow hair. This time the hair was red like fire, a molten mass of tangled curls. He rushed to it now, knelt at it, unable to breathe. When he touched the silken strands of hair, the thing came to life, turned and faced him. Near all flesh was gone from the face, and it smiled a death's head grin. Fey eyes stared at him accusingly. A fatal pain stabbed him through the chest, stealing away his life, destroying all hope, and he knew without a doubt he'd failed her too. Or would, if he wasn't careful.

"Gideon..." Meg's voice floated on the putrefied air, a specter's call damning him for eternity. "Gideon."

Meg sat up straight in the bed, her head and heart pounding an insistent tattoo like an out of control alarm. Grey light filtered in through the gaps in the curtains, casting the room in uncertain, tentative shadows. She reoriented, and the disturbing dream she'd been having faded into the mist. She still smelled fire and ash, still felt the sorrow of the man she'd watch bury his dead.

She rubbed her temples and tried to recall her dream. Where had she been? Hell? Purgatory? The land was barren, burned to a crisp. She remembered tending wounded soldiers, then things became blurry. She thought there were corpses involved, and soldiers in a disorganized camp. The taste of fear was bitter in her mouth throughout the dream, but the worst part had been the man. He was dressed like some kind of medieval warrior but she couldn't recall a coat of arms or anything she could use to identify him. She'd watched from the distance as he and other soldiers gathered the bodies one by one, stacking them in a pyre, burning them. It was hard to see his face with all the smoke and the thick fog, but she could feel his anguish deep in her soul.

And when he collected the two small bodies that lay near a stone well, and then the woman's from behind a stable, she'd felt his rage thick and hot, consuming her soul. A haze of fury clouded her own vision as she listened to him curse his God, and then fall to his knees and weep openly. Meg struggled to reach him, to console him, but her steps were mired and slow. When she got close enough to touch him, the scene faded before her eyes, replaced by the sight of her living room, torn to shreds, her personal items destroyed. The safety she once knew, the sanctuary she'd created, was gone.

No sooner had she admitted that to herself than the walls around her burst into fire. Flames surrounded her in an instant and she couldn't breathe. She held her hand before her nose and mouth as she searched the inferno for a way out, but it was no use. The fire was a solid, impenetrable wall. She shivered recalling how instead of hot, the flames were ice cold, like the skin of a corpse. Thankfully, the dream ended. Or at least, what she could consciously recall clearly stopped. Meg didn't want to imagine what came next. It sucked when your dreams were as frightening as your reality. Somehow there should be some relief in slumber, she thought, some escape when your waking world had turned into its own brand of nightmare.

She took a deep breath, climbed out of bed and headed for the aspirins she kept in her purse. Life wasn't fair. She knew that in the abstract sense, watching her kids get sicker and sicker and most often die. Now she knew it intimately. Last night the thoughts of no tomorrow had set a part of her free, giving her the courage to explore her wanton desires without any guilt or second guesses. Today, the thoughts of no tomorrow made her more sober, more thoughtful. Anger lingered, perhaps part of last night's dream, perhaps her own over Gideon's reluctance to let himself go. And there was a curious restlessness inside of her, as if she no longer fit in the skin of her life, but didn't know what life she would fit. The uncertain state no doubt contributed to her headache. She itched to do something, to rage against the man, to fight the machine, maybe even do what that soldier in her dream did—curse the Gods. Meg pulled out a travel packet of aspirins and tore it open, eagerly anticipating relief. Luckily, this pain wasn't like the earlier migraines. She was sure this time the simple application of medicine would provide some much needed help.

She chewed the aspirins and sucked on the acrid mash until it dissolved in her mouth. It was the quickest way to get them to work even if it did taste like crap. Gideon mumbled in his sleep, and she padded over to where he slept fitfully in one of the uncomfortable plastic chairs. His burly body overflowed the confines of the tiny retro seat. The muscles in his powerful shoulders and neck bunched and corded with tension. Sweat beaded his brow and soaked the front of his shirt. His face was drawn and tense.

"No!"

His shout startled her.

"No! No! No!" He cried out like a wounded animal.

"Gideon." She put her hand on his broad shoulder and pushed gently. "Gideon, wake up. You're dreaming."

He stilled beneath her touch, then he roused.

"Meg?" He sat back and shook off his sleepiness. His black eyes went on instant alert. He cursed and jumped from the chair. "Did something happen?"

"You were having a nightmare."

"Oh." He looked confused, then embarrassed. "Sorry. Did I wake you?"

"No. I had a bad dream myself. But I think the headache is what woke me." She put some distance between them now that she knew he was okay. She was unsure of how to talk to him after last night, of how to act. Yesterday she'd wanted him so badly she'd tasted it like a drug. This morning, she wanted to feel comfortable around him again, but she couldn't. The restlessness increased tenfold now that he was awake, alert, looking at her. He was in her blood, making it pound, and she didn't know how to get him out. Then again, she really didn't want him out. Even after his rejection last night, she still wanted him, and she knew she wouldn't stop wanting him. If she had the chance again, Meg knew with dead certainty, she'd seduce him with every ounce of her being until he was too weak with passion to care about consequence or whatever soldier rules held him back. They shared a potent, undeniable attraction. It was unlike anything she'd ever felt in her life, something she never imagined could exist. And, it was one she wanted to know more fully before they parted ways.

She went to the cabinet, pulled out two chipped mugs and packets of freeze-dried instant coffee. When she turned to face him, the haunted look in his eyes stabbed her. A timeless, unending pain pierced her soul. And, she tasted fear, the same fear she'd tasted in last night's dream. Meg wanted to rush to him, to hold him, to drive out the pain and the sorrow. Then he blinked, the wall came up, and he was the stone cold soldier again. Meg clutched the mugs like a lifeline and told herself to get a grip. She forced a smile. "How about some java to take off the night's edge?"

"Meg, about last night—"

"I told you I wasn't complaining."

"Neither was I, and that's the problem. I need to be alert, ready to protect you at a moment's notice. I don't want to lose you, Meg. You know the stakes in this game. Life and death. I'm immortal, so I don't matter. But you're not. You've only got one life, and if something happens, there's no turning back."

"You're not a morning person, are you, Gideon? I get it, the whole immortal protector gig. Really, I do. And I get the mortality thing too." She filled the mugs and stuck them in the microwave. The headache made her crabby as did thoughts of last night. "I know how fragile life is and I know I may not have much in the way of tomorrows, which is why I did what I did. Under any other circumstances, do you think I'd have let you touch me that way, that quickly? You're not the only one in the room with principles."

He stared at her for a long, hot, uncomfortable moment, then nodded curtly. "It's just physical between us, Doc. If we're both careful, we won't get caught up in it again. Right?"

Wrong. Let the big oaf think what he would. They had chemistry that set the world around them on fire. Short of donning asbestos suits and staying on opposite corners of the earth, she doubted there'd be any other way to avoid getting caught up. He looked so uncertain at this moment it made a part of her wonder what he really feared. Was it loss of his precious discipline, or was it something else? A vision of last night's horror flashed before her eyes. Fear raced through her, making the room close in too tight, making his presence too large, too close. Meg grabbed the heated mugs from the microwave and set them on the round café table. "I'm going to brush my teeth and clean up. Afterwards, maybe we can see about breakfast?"

"Sure. Breakfast." He appeared shaken by her quick change of subjects, but he made a fast recovery. "There's an all-night diner just down the road. They make great mushroom omelets."

Meg shut the door, grateful for the barrier the bathroom offered her from the immortal. She splashed cold water on her face and mentally cursed Gideon for being a man of principle. He was right, of course, he did need to be alert, and on his guard. Sure, she'd fought the creatures who came after her, but they'd caught her the first time, and could catch her again. He did stand between her and an early grave. Still there seemed something more holding him back, something that lured her, dared her to chase it down through the shadowed maze and expose it to the light.

She sighed and used the rough motel towel to dry off. She was losing it. Life down the rabbit hole was making her nuts. She was just a tourist here, while Gideon was a card carrying resident of crazy town. He was probably used to this whole life and death hanging in thc balance thing. He was used to the rush where every second could be your last. She was still too new, too fresh. Maybe she needed to put her own desires in check for a moment and listen to his logic. Maybe it wasn't a bad thing to leave the embers alone, avoid the deadly blaze. She finished up her morning routine, stepped out into the main room of the cabin, and all hell broke loose.

There was a loud crash and before she could react, Gideon was on her, taking her to the ground, covering her with his body.

He was off her the next instant, sword in hand. He blocked her from any attack as he faced the door. "Take cover!"

Chapter Seven

Three men struggled to get through the open space of the door but couldn't pass some invisible barrier. Meg swallowed hard. The magic must be holding them. As Gideon rushed to attack, she got to all fours and started to crawl behind the bed. Almost instantly, there was a loud pop like a dull gunshot. The three rushed into the room and Gideon met them head-on. The moment they crossed the threshold, there was a burst of blinding light, and when it cleared, three of the largest wolves she'd ever seen were in their place. Gideon gutted the biggest as it launched at him from a crouch. The force of the strike sent the carcass flying across the room. Blood sprayed into the air. The creature fell next to her, intestines pouring from its split belly like spilled spaghetti. Meg cried out and backed up against the wall, drawing her knees tight against her.

The other two wolves charged at Gideon. He shifted to mist and they leapt right through him, then turned to charge again. As she blinked, he became the sleek panther she'd first seen. He growled furiously, and launched himself at them, claws out and gleaming. They engaged, and rolled together in a brawling tangle of beast, growling, hissing, biting. The wolves were powerful, but no match for the certain death of the panther. Gideon as beast moved at a blinding speed, a swirling black shadow of doom tangling with the creatures. Gore spattered in a macabre pattern across the walls, the TV, the mirror, as the wolves were shredded.

Then, as quick as the attack started, it was over. The panther was gone. Gideon stood, bloody, in the center of the room.

"Are you okay, Doc?"

He was breathing heavily, and his eyes glowed with a strange, animal light.

She nodded mutely.

"Good." He walked across the room and kicked the door shut. Then he grabbed his cell and called in the cleaners.

The wolves began to shift, the hair receding, the bodies contorting as they changed back into human form. Meg suppressed a shudder. These were humans. Not demons. They were real people. So much more real.

"Meg?"

She looked up at Gideon. He reached down and gathered her up, holding her close. "It's all over, Doc. Don't worry." He smoothed her hair as she buried her head against him.

"They're real, Gideon. Real people."

"They're shapeshifters. Mortal, but fast-healing and long-lived. Bounty hunters if I'm not mistaken."

"They look like me and you."

"I know. I know."

Cold shock stole over her. She kept thinking she had a grasp on the madness, and then it slipped her hold, reached out and sucker punched her. "How'd they find us?"

"A good shifter can track a target through multiple realms. Magic protected us in here, but it didn't conceal our scents. They run in a gang, not a clan. They're outcasts paid to hunt, which means someone is picking up the tab." He released her with obvious reluctance and methodically searched the bodies.

On the last one he appeared to find something. He held up a small scroll for her to see. "Looks like the mage decided to hire out. This is a marker. It will have some link back to the guy who's after you. We just got our first break."

"Can you find him?"

"We'll see. Since he hired these guys, there will be a money trail. My people can track that back, though it will take time. The mage mark is distinctive, unique to every mage. Jack may be able to pick something up. Either way, we've got something to work with at last."

He picked up his cell and made a second call that consisted only of entering a string of numbers, then he hung up.

Meg stared at the bodies for a moment as a morbid thought took shape in her mind. "If they're fast healing, how come they won't heal now?"

"Shapeshifter attacks, if brutal enough, are fatal to them. Even though Bast gives me the magic to shift, I still pack the same punch as one of the home grown kind. The trick is to deal out heavy damage as fast as possible. It circumvents the rapid healing ability."

More of the rules. One day, when she wasn't being hounded by demons, werewolves, and angry Gods, she would need to study this rapid healing thing they all seemed to have. If magic existed, could it be mixed with the science of medicine to do good for mankind?

"You don't happen to have a guidebook for this version of reality, do you?"

"There are thousands. From fairy tales to grimoires."

"Nothing abridged."

"The mythic world likes to keep things sketchy."

"Figures." Meg picked her way around the worst of the

blood, grabbed some clothes, and changed in the bathroom. When she emerged, Gideon had the rest of their belongings packed and stood waiting at the door.

"Let's go, Doc. Mammett will be here in a few minutes."

The cleaners. No matter what the trouble, they were always one phone call away. So neat, it was maddening. "Do you always have someone to clean up your mess?"

His jaw tightened, and he slipped on his shades. "I try to run a clean operation. No strings."

"Oh." She followed him to the car, leaving the horrific scene behind her. "Am I a string?"

He threw the bags in the back of the SUV and shut the door. "Meg, listen to me very carefully. I want you. So bad it makes me crazy, so bad it's all I can do to keep my hands to myself. Every second I'm fighting myself to keep off of you. Trust me, you're not a string."

She liked the sound of her name from him. "Then why hold back? Don't give me that nonsense about needing to protect me. You do a decent job of that no matter the circumstance."

He leaned in close, kept his voice very soft, but it carried a strange edge. "You came for me, Meg. How'd that make you feel this morning, when you woke up and remembered? What were you thinking?"

A lot of things, all jumbled, none making sense. Her mind cleared as an irrational anger swirled inside of her. He was twisting things, just like a regular man. She wouldn't be played, not like that.

She closed the miniscule distance between them and stabbed an accusatory finger at his broad chest. "Don't put this on me, Gideon. You're afraid of me. Admit it. Me, mere mortal, Doctor Meg, I scare you and you don't like that."

He jammed his hands in his pockets. "Maybe I'm afraid of me. Of what I can do. Of what I've done. Maybe I don't want you hurt like I've hurt others."

His voice was raw now, laced with a palpable pain.

She stopped pointing, pulled back her hand and considered his words. She could swear she felt his ache, deep inside herself. It was a curious, unsettling sensation, but she didn't shy from it. Or from him. "I'm not afraid of you, Gideon. You shouldn't be either."

"You've known me two nights, Doc. You don't get to decide that. If you had any idea..."

"Tell me, Gideon. Tell me what you're running from. What you're afraid of. Is it what you dreamed of last night? What made you cry out in your sleep?"

Silence stretched between them. He appeared ready to say something when the howl of a lone wolf pierced the quiet morning. Several more answered the call in an eerie chorus that echoed off the surrounding hills.

Fear pricked her spine, raised the hairs on the nape of her neck.

He glanced over his shoulder, and pulled out a nasty looking pistol from his holster. "We need to hustle, Doc. It's not safe here anymore."

Monte Carlo

Salazar gave the keys to his Mercedes to the valet and buttoned up his favorite Armani blazer. The Hotel Solei was bustling, even though it was still early evening by continental standards. He ascended the carpeted stairs and emerged in the sumptuous lobby. Beautiful people, members of the elite European jet set, as well as moneyed sheiks, mixed with *nouveau riche* and even a few Americans. For a moment he stood still, soaking it all in: the costal air, the cosmopolitan feel, the thrum of excitement and energy that flowed like strong ocean currents through the swarming crowd. Venice was a provincial cousin compared to this glittering socialite city.

The last time he'd visited Monte Carlo he'd come to bring an operative in from the cold. In the end, there was no salvaging the woman. He'd followed protocol, taken her out of play, called the cleaners, and moved on. Ramon straightened his cuffs and jacket. The woman had been close. A lover. But she'd got caught up in playing the game. Surprisingly, he still felt the same tightness in his chest, the same sense of absence and longing as clear and sharp as he did the night he was forced to end their liaison. And her life.

He shrugged off the unpleasant memory and moved deeper into the casino. Ian was here, at a blackjack table, drinking champagne and losing obscenely large sums of money. Ramon stayed near a fluted column, ordered a Limoncella, and observed. He blended well with the crowd and surroundings, and was hard to pick out standing amongst the other olive-skinned, dark-haired, well-dressed males of a certain age that congregated in places such as these. And Ian's senses were deadened due to the void that was Monte Carlo. Ramon wasn't sure what he expected to find. Even knowing what he did. Perhaps he hoped the truth would not be proved out. The last truth proved out in Monte Carlo killed him, as well as the woman he thought he loved. He sipped the soothing aperitif as Ian accepted another card from the dealer.

From the throng, a woman of distinction separated herself. She moved like a billion-dollar yacht amongst freighters and barges, slipping easily through the traffic, seeming so far above the cut. She was polished to a shine, her golden blonde hair pulled back into an elegant bun, her white, haute couture gown a sleek cloud wrapped around her statuesque, heavenly body. Ramon's muscles went rigid, like a cat ready to spring into battle. He'd not seen this one's like in two thousand years. Not since their kind was locked down by the Aesir into a sealed realm. And this one in particular, she'd been a casualty of that war and peace accord. She should be dead. But here she was, alive, in someone else's skin. Wonderful. His day was getting better and better by the moment. Thank providence Bast had put Gideon on this job. Ramon couldn't imagine what would have happened if the champion's instincts had not brought conspiracy and ruin to light.

Ramon finished his drink and set it down on a nearby table as he moved closer to observe. Skathi, as he had known her then, laid a milky, elegant arm around Ian's broad shoulders and whispered something in his ear that made the drunken mystic smile devilishly. It wasn't hard to guess what she offered. Certainly something better than the losing streak at the table.

Ah, Ian, you're safer playing odds against the house than mixing with her kind. Frost Giants were a dangerous, shifty lot. They thrived on chaos, and held grudges to the end of time and beyond. And this one, an Enchantress, she was the most dangerous of the lot. They were not evil, not in the true sense, and they were not good either, which made them even more problematic.

Ian finished his hand and his drink and departed with the creature. Ramon sighed softly to himself. How unfortunate that his information was correct. More unfortunate was Ian's choice. Better to lose at the table, than to play this loser's game. Either the Enchantress would kill him, or Ramon would be forced to do the same. A compromised mystic was not tolerated. Ever.

He trailed them at a safe distance as the couple went out into the early night. They kissed on the stairs, a gauche, frantic affair, and called for a vehicle. It was hers, a sleek, ice white Lamborghini. How she fit her tall frame inside, Ramon had no clue. He considered summoning his Mercedes, then changed his mind. Instead he ducked into a corner and let one of his forms assert itself. Moments later, he was Raven, spreading dark black wings and taking flight. Below, the Lamborghini raced through the twists and turns of the treacherous Monte Carlo streets, driving far out into the costal hillside.

The car finally stopped in the manicured courtyard of a secluded, modern styled villa that cut back into the rocks and overlooked the ocean. Ramon crested down upon the ground for a moment to get his bearings. Then he flew round the house, peering into the windows, seeking the couple. The place was well furnished, expensively decorated, and exclusively white, relieved only by silver, chrome and the diamond iridescence of highly polished glass.

He found a suitable balcony to gain entry but realized it was alarmed: both magically and mundanely. They were now beyond the barriers of Monte Carlo's magic dead zone, so he needed to apply more caution. Ramon flew to the rear by the alarm junction box, returned to human form, and pulled out a small kit from the inside blazer pocket. His talent for burglary came in handy every now and again, allowing him to bypass the alarm with ease. The modern ages had such helpful devices to assist the well-schooled thief. In raven form, he returned to the balcony, shifted back to man, and finessed entry into the unused bedroom with a mixture of modern technology and ancient sorcery. It was almost too easy, he thought, and that put him on edge.

Ian and Skathi were downstairs, mixing drinks, and talking. Her laughter reminded him of the splitting of icebergs. He used the time to wander the second floor, exploring, testing the boundaries of the magic, discerning the energy's origin and make. As well as the maker. As he reached out with his honed senses, he learned that the make was ancient indeed, and intricate. It was all protective, more to keep energy seekers out and contain the truth of the creature that dwelled here than to provide offensive action.

He found several mage marks but they were obscure to him, just as the strings of sigils he found in an upstairs office, carved beneath the desk that held a computer and fax. It put him in mind of demonic magic, which was at odds with the Frost Giantess downstairs. He also found it strange for an Enchantress to shop out her magical protections. Perhaps it wasn't her home? That would make more sense.

As Ian and Skathi came up the stairs now, he blended into the shadows. They passed him without notice, went into one of the rooms at the end of the hall, and as soon as the door was shut, he went to listen. He'd not taken three steps when the distinct sound of gunshots rang out. Salazar abandoned caution and threw open the door. Ian and Skathi were on the bed. Each had a thick dart protruding from the neck and sightless eyes that stared into the oblivion of unconsciousness.

Two men in black tactical gear and balaclavas turned to face him, each holding the signature modified immortal suppression rifles issued to the troops that served the Covenant. A sudden jolt of pain ripped through his side as electricity fried his nerves. Enraged, he spun on his attacker, and was hit point blank with a deadly dart loaded with just the right amount of titrated vampiric acid to take a creature like him down. His vision clouded, his body seized, and he collapsed into the darkness.

Gideon swore to himself as the phone line continued to ring. "Where the hell are you, Ramon?" After another ten rings he hung up and sat for a moment as a bad feeling spread like fast-acting poison through his blood.

He'd tried all the numbers the Spaniard had when the dedicated line wasn't answered. He left cryptic messages on each, except this last. This was the final resort number, and didn't have a machine. It was Salazar's special line, and other than Gideon, only a handful of beings knew of its existence.

This was bad. Very bad. Gideon swore again and dialed another number. After two rings, a woman's rich voice purred across the line.

"Gideon, I wondered when you'd check in."

"Salazar's in trouble, Bast. I can't reach him."

She chuckled, a low, deceptively sweet sound. "Salazar is always into some kind of trouble. How goes the job, Champion?"

Gideon paused, confused by the subtle humor in her voice. If he didn't know better he'd think she was baiting him. "I've changed the op."

"I gathered."

"I thought something felt wrong."

"And?"

"And I was right." He took a moment and caught up his boss, careful to leave out the part about Meg manifesting healing powers.

"You were right to check in with me, Gideon. I need to be very careful in how I handle this, you understand. You've gone rogue, and while your reasons are good, you still don't have enough proof to buy your way out of this. If someone calls for censure, I won't be able to bend the rules far enough to prevent dispatch of a rogue hunter."

That was Bast. She knew how to walk the line, and she knew enough never to cross. "I'm working on the proof."

"Work faster."

Meg passed by the closed booth, on her way back to the SUV from the ladies' room of the rest stop. She neared the front window where the brilliant afternoon sun turned her hair to fire and surrounded her in a lustrous halo of light. Gideon's chest tightened. "Don't worry, I'm on it. You need to worry about the Spaniard. He was working in deep with me. Last contact I had was yesterday. He was on his way to Monte Carlo."

Bast cursed. "Ian Campbell was sent there on mandatory holiday after a breakdown."

"So I hear."

"Don't worry about Salazar, I'll take care of him. You find the mage, and fix the difficulties at your end."

Gideon hung up and considered placing a call in to Jack. They'd be arriving early. After this morning, he didn't want to risk traveling any more than necessary. That meant cutting through the mists, using the nebulous passages that shifted somewhere between time and space. To do that safely and reach Jack's, he'd have to hire a guide from one of the motor clans. He made a few more calls, finally called in a marker, and set up a meeting with a local rider, but he didn't feel any better. Traveling the mists, particularly the shifting mists, was dicey. Passages were always in motion, and today's road could easily turn into eternity's grave if you took a wrong turn, or, if the road's temporal position began to drift.

He tried the emergency number one last time, then left the booth. Salazar was a tough bastard. For him to drop out of sight meant big trouble. Conspiracy at the Warden's Council was a bad scene. If one vision of convergence was compromised, there could be more. Bad intel led to wrong actions which completely compromised the timeline. And if that wasn't enough to keep him on edge, that damn dream replayed again and again in his head on some kind of horrific loop. It was as if his past kept smacking him in the head, telling him to wise up and watch his step, or he'd be responsible for yet another colossal failure.

The burning pain in his chest started up again, kind of like a cross between indigestion and what he felt when he stabbed himself there a few nights back. Maybe he still had some internal trauma to his heart? Yeah, that was it. Sure, he healed fast, and the doc's touch helped, but some wounds had a way of lingering no matter what you did to patch them up.

He met up with Meg out by the SUV. She'd taken a seat at a picnic table, and was munching on chips and drinking a soda. She had a serene air about her today, a thoughtful look, and to all the world, appeared no different from any of the other travelers stopping at the rest facility.

"I got you a soda." She motioned for him to join her.

"Thanks." Gideon sat on the edge of the seat and opened the plastic bottle. "We're going to take a short cut to Jack's. I don't want to risk another night in this realm, even in a safe house."

Meg arched a fine brow. "This realm? You make it sound like Jack lives in Never-Never Land. I thought you said he had a place in Vegas."

"Jack lives in what he calls his fortress of solitude. It borders on the mortal realm in the desert outside of Las Vegas, but it's about half a step behind the normal reality stream. It kind of sits on the edge of the line in the between space. He can merge with this realm, but usually keeps to himself."

"He sounds like a fairy prince, complete with his own

castle."

Gideon laughed, surprising himself. "His mother was a fey witch. I suppose in one sense he could be considered royalty."

"You keep interesting company." She pulled a ridged chip from the bag, popped it into her mouth and followed with a sip of soda.

Her lips glistened with salt crystals, shining like diamond chips in the light. He wanted to lick them clean. He wanted to lick all of her, he thought, remembering how good she tasted last night. "Jack cooks up some serious magic. The place really is a fortress. He has this thing about feeling safe. He has a lot of things that need protecting, including himself."

"Couldn't we just stay there until this is all over?"

"You might be able to. I still need to do some outside work."

She played with the soda bottle, tearing at the edge of the wrapper. "I feel safer staying with you."

Gideon went warm all over. It was foolish, he knew, but a part of him liked being her protector, her champion. He really had it bad for this one. He stood and jammed his hands into his pockets. "We need to meet a guide. She'll take us through the passage to reach Jack's."

She finished off the last chip, crumpled the bag, and tossed it into the nearby can. The light summer breeze teased her curls as she stood. "Passage?"

He swallowed hard, his throat hot and dry. "I'll explain on the way."

Meg peppered him with questions for the twenty or so miles it took to reach the meeting point. He was constantly surprised at her ability to take in the information. Each question built on the last, drawing facts out in a nice, linear procession until they formed a cohesive picture. Normally he didn't care for interrogations, but the sound of her voice enchanted him and her natural curiosity was good-natured and enjoyable. It made him feel like a regular guy, talking with her as the miles rolled by, even if they were discussing topics from the theater bizarre.

"That's our guide?" Meg stared at the lanky, leather clad blonde woman standing beside the silver Harley-Davidson. "She's an Amazon."

"No, she's a North American werewolf." Gideon pulled up along side, and rolled down the window. "Hey, Kara. Good to see you again."

"I was surprised to get your call, Gid. Thought you'd be dead by now for sure." Kara's voice was dark and husky, and once was able to stir his blood to a fast and wicked boil. Now he found himself immune to her, and all else, except Meg. "I wired you the usual fee."

"I know. I wouldn't be here otherwise." She came close to the car, rested her arms on the edge of the open window and leaned in. "I'm Kara Blake, with Clan Stormshadow."

Meg nodded at Kara. "Meg Carter."

"Nice to meet you, Meg Carter. Ever traveled the mists before?"

"I told you she didn't," Gideon said.

Kara glanced at him. "I like to ask on my own, just to be sure. I'm not much for casualties." She reached into a pocket and produced a small, silvery stone which she handed in through the cab to Meg. "Take this, keep it on you while we ride the passage. It's a clan talisman. It will help prevent the sickness."

Kara watched as Meg put it into her pocket. When she was done, Kara tapped the car and stepped back. "Okay, folks. Showtime. Keep the windows up. This is a shifting passage. We'll need to run fast and hard but we'll get to Jack's in time for dinner."

She climbed on the hog, fired it up, and started out on the small rural route. Gideon followed on her six and as they drove. The surrounding trees and rolling farmland faded out as dense, pewter mists surrounded the vehicles. He kept the accelerator floored in an attempt to stay within line of sight of his guide. His blood tingled as they left the safety of a formed reality and ventured into the uncertain paths that drifted between realms.

"I feel itchy." Meg's voice startled him. "Is that normal?"

"You have a small amount of magic in you right now. It's reacting to the aura of the mists. Kara's talisman should keep the worst of the travel sickness down. If you feel you need to vomit, there's a bag in the glove box."

"Other than the itch, I feel fine." She shifted in her seat and stretched her long legs out. "You two were lovers."

The statement surprised him. Damn, she was perceptive. "A while back. What gave it away?"

"The way she looked at you. Like you were a prime piece of steak she'd love to tear into."

He cleared his throat, uncomfortable with this new line of discussion. "It was brief. Very brief. I ended it with her ten years ago."

She turned to stare out into the endless, silvery clouds of mist. Her face was reflected in the window glass. "You don't stick around much, do you?"

"Not really." He pressed harder on the gas pedal, but it had no place to go. "Why do you ask?"

She turned back to him and studied him with a frank, assessing gaze. "I'm wondering what you'll be doing once you're done protecting me. That's what's holding you back now. Will it hold you back later, when all this is over? What then?"

"I don't know." And honestly, he didn't. He'd still want her, there was no disputing that. But she was mortal, and could enjoy a real life. He was nothing more than a shadow in her world. And a dark one at that. She'd want more than a night. So would he. In the end, he knew he'd bring her ruin. He was no good. All he had to do was look to his mortal past, and the evidence was there, screaming at him like the Banshee come for her dead. "You deserve better than me, Meg."

"You've only known me for two nights. You don't get to say what I do and don't deserve."

She turned her eyes forward and fell silent.

Gideon was both relieved at the silence and maddened by it. Talking with her was as close as he could come to doing what he wanted—touching her, tasting her, loving her. There were two men inside of him, at constant war, and he wondered who would ultimately win: the knight who wanted her safe in an ivory tower, or the beast who wanted her naked beneath him. Her scent tantalized him, and her body heat branded him like a blazing sun. The minutes passed as hours of torment. When she leaned down to grab a notebook from her backpack, her hair spilled forward in a sexy cascade of silken fire and Gideon knew that if given the slightest opportunity, the beast would devour the knight and claim his woman in the most carnal of ways.

She opened the book and wrote in it for a while, filling several pages before he screwed up the courage to talk to her.

"You look busy, Doc. What are you writing?"

The edges of her wide mouth tilted up into a smile. "I'm taking notes, making my own instruction manual. If I can see things down in black and white, I can make better sense of them."

Some things defied sense, but he didn't tell her that. He

knew she hated being out of control. If this made her feel better he was all for it. “So what are you covering now?”

“You. Everything about you, from your healing, to your ability to shift matter and mass at will.” Her grin widened. “You really are quite fascinating, Gideon.”

A cold chill crept up his spine. He didn’t mind her probing, but he didn’t want her probing him. A picture of her corpse from the dream flashed through his mind. He gripped the steering wheel tighter. “I’m just an ordinary guy in my world. Nothing worth knowing that you don’t already know.”

“There’s a lot I don’t know. You told me as much outside the last motel. We have time, so maybe you can fill me in.” She half turned in the seat so she could look at him, the notebook perched in her lap, the pen poised like a sword in her hand. “So how old are you, Gideon, and where’d you come from? You had to be mortal once, right? What was your life like before the change?”

The chill froze into a cold anger. Not at her, but at himself. There wasn’t anything good he could tell her about that creature he was back in the mortal days. *Vermin. I was vermin, a pox on those I knew. A scourge.* “I’m not some lab rat in one of your experiments.”

Her pretty smile faded. “I want to know you better. Is that so wrong?”

“There’s nothing to know. I was a guy once. Just like every other guy of my day. Trying to get ahead, pass the time the best way I knew how.” She wouldn’t let up. He knew that as sure as he knew his own dark past. Somehow she’d get it out of him, strip him bare to the bone. Strangely enough, there was a part of him that wanted to be free, to let out the shame, to release the ghosts that plagued him.

“When was your day? And where? You sound American.”

He eased his grip on the wheel. Maybe if he gave her a little bit, a controlled dose, she'd leave off. "I've been living here for the last three hundred years, that's why."

She jotted this down. "Where?"

"All around. Lately, I keep a place in Virginia. It's a cabin tucked away in the Blue Ridge mountains."

"You're older than three hundred years?"

He nodded. "I kind of lost count." On purpose.

"Your body is so well-preserved," she muttered as she wrote. "You must have phenomenal cellular regeneration. So where was home, initially?"

Home. There was a good one. Home was wherever the lust for battle took him. But he doubted she'd be happy to know that. "Britton. A little before William of Normandy's time, back in 1066."

The ache in his chest spread throughout his body. The discussion was painful in a way he'd never experienced. He had to stop this. He wasn't ready. Not now. Not ever. "Listen, Doc, my past is just that. Mine. I don't share. You want to know about my world, I'll tell you. You want to know what I know about magic, we can talk all night. You want to know about me as a mortal, forget it. I buried my dead a long time ago. I have no intention of digging them up again to satisfy anyone's curiosity. Even yours."

Chapter Eight

Gideon's response was laced with acid emotion. Meg drew back, shocked at the intense words coming from the stoic soldier. So his mortal life was a raw nerve? She'd suspected that his old life might be the source of the pain she glimpsed those few times when he was not in complete, iron clad control of himself. She never guessed at the depth of those feelings.

"Okay, your mortal past is off-limits. No problem. I guess what really interests me is the change in physiology afterwards." Not so much a lie, she thought. She did have interest in that. But more she wanted to know him as he once was, when he was human. He was closed to her now, however, she'd have to wait for another time to draw out his truths. "What happened to you after Bast staked her claim?"

His deep chest rose and fell with a long breath. "I don't age. I can't die. Not by normal, or even most extraordinary means. I don't get sick. I'm immune to all mortal diseases, and most magical ones. And, I can't reproduce."

"Immortals are sterile?"

He nodded.

She made a note. If he knew he was sterile, that meant prior to his change, he knew he wasn't. Which meant he probably had children in his mortal life. The thought saddened her. Did he outlive his children? Watch them grow old and wither with age? A scrap of her nightmare resurfaced, a man burying his young ones. Perhaps that had happened? He could live while they could die? Either possibility was horrible. How did these immortals manage to stay sane? That thought had her scribbling again. The brain must change as well as the hormones influencing mood. Cellular regeneration, massive endocrine reprogramming, it boggled the mind. "And this is done through magic?"

He shrugged. "Yeah, I guess. I think there's an aspect of the divine involved in some way. Maybe it just takes that much juice to turn a mortal into one of my kind."

"So the Gods have access to powers beyond magic."

"Some more than others. Depends."

He seemed to relax again, so Meg decided to pursue this new avenue. She'd filled twenty more pages of the small spiral bound notebook by the time the thick silver mist faded and the desert outside of Las Vegas came into view. She didn't even feel the change, so subtle it was, moving from a channel between worlds to entering terra firma again.

The sun was still high in the sky, and the clock on the dash indicated only two hours had passed since the midday break at the rest stop. Meg jotted down the time, a few last notes on how she felt leaving the passage, and shoved the book back into her backpack.

"Jack's place is a few minutes down the road." Gideon waved out the window at the blonde biker Amazon, then pulled past her and took a turnoff that led them to a dirt road. "We were lucky to find a passage, and a guide. Maybe things are turning in our favor."

Judging by the grim look on his face, Meg had her doubts but she kept them to herself. The red and gold desert was a stark contrast to the lush, almost oppressive green of upstate

New York and the mountains. Heat rose in waves and dust swirled off the road in granular clouds, giving the landscape a surreal, desolate look.

Gideon took one last turn that led him into the hills, and ended at a set of ornate, two story wrought iron gates. From either end of the gates stretched a wall of hand-fitted stone just as high, and a few feet thick. Iron spikes topped the wall, giving it a sinister appearance. Beyond, the road ran through the saddle of two high flats and vanished in a turn.

Gideon rolled down the window and jammed a finger against the call buzzer. The intercom connected and static erupted into the quiet desert air.

"Jack, it's me. Open up."

Gideon sat back. There was a grinding sound from outside, and the gates slowly parted.

He drove through, following the road into the shadows of the saddle, and when he took the final blind turn, a whitewashed Moroccan-style mansion appeared, sprawling languidly across the rough landscape.

A man waited placidly for them, standing beside a graceful, three-tiered fountain tiled in cobalt and turquoise mosaic mixed with gilded flecks. He was tall, rangy, with long silver hair that ran past his shoulders and trailed down his back. His skin was pale like moonlight and his face was exotic with high cheekbones, almond-shaped cobalt eyes, dark slashing brows, and vaguely oriental features. He was wearing tight fitting black velvet pants and a flowing white poet's shirt open to the waist, over which he had a crimson velvet frock coat. Knee-high motocross boots with no less than twelve buckle closures each finished the outfit.

He wasn't to her taste; that ran more to tall, broody immortals with sketchy pasts, but still, Jack Madden was a strange, sweet kind of eye candy. He reminded her of one of those animated tragic anti-heroes that decorated the covers of computer video games: all angles, impossible grace, and elegant, sensual looks.

"You're early," Jack drawled in a smooth baritone as they emerged from the car. "I haven't completed my research."

"You need to work faster, Jack. We're on a schedule here."

Jack nodded, and his hair swung forward, revealing the pointed tips of his very inhuman ears.

"So I hear." He flashed a devilish smile and gave Meg the once over. "You must be the woman who made Gideon break the rules. I'm impressed. Even I couldn't get him to go back on his precious oaths."

"Shut the hell up, Jack." Gideon's body tensed as if ready for battle.

"I'm Meg Carter." She held out her hand to shake, but Jack took it, and breathed a light kiss across her knuckles. His lips were deceptively cool, as if he were devoid of life or blood, or any kind of human warmth. She drew her hand back and suppressed a shiver. Up close, she sensed an underlying malevolence lurking just beneath the beautiful façade.

Gideon's jaw tightened. "I should have warned you, Meg. In addition to being crazy, Jack's a perv."

Jack pulled his lips into a mock pout. "Rake, Gideon. Roué. Cad. Perv is far too post-modern a description for a relic like me." He started for the arched door, the tails of the ridiculous frock coat swirling at his knees. "Let's get started, shall we? Havers has an early supper cooking. She'll skin us if we're late."

They moved into the cool interior of the house and Meg had impressions of understated wealth and great antiquity as they wound through the seemingly endless corridors and key-shaped doorways. The level of authenticity of décor made her wonder if this wasn't transported lock, stock and barrel from *A Thousand and One Arabian Nights.*

The hall they were in dead-ended. Jack threw open a thick wooden door revealing a wide sunken room filled to the rafters with everything and anything a self-respecting mad scientist or crazed wizard might need. Floor to ceiling shelves lined one wall, filled with jars of unidentifiable and no doubt dangerous substances. The opposite wall contained more modern amenities, and could have easily fit in at her clinic.

Meg's legs went weak. She stepped back, suddenly afraid to cross into the lair. "What's going on? What are you planning to do to me?"

"Nothing I'd like to, Meg. Gideon would try to kill me, and that would eat up all our precious time." Jack locked eyes with her, and they changed from cobalt to a deep, stormy midnight blue that made her blood chill. "I'm going to give you a brief exam. Draw some blood. Ask you some questions. If you're lucky, I can help. If you're not, well, we'll deal with that later."

Gideon put his arm around her shoulders, sending her strength and support. "It will be okay, Doc. Trust me."

"I trust you." *Not him.* She swallowed hard, realizing she had no other choice. "I guess I'm used to being the doctor, not the patient."

Jack had her sit in a comfortable, scarlet leather wingback, while he assembled a few vaccutainers and his draw kit. Gideon stood beside her, his wide hand covering her shoulder, his heat warming her. His strength was a flow of life pouring into her.

"So you touched the canopic jar, Meg, not the artifact. Yet you've experienced some changes." Jack pulled up a stool on rollers, so like the ones the clinic had in every exam room. He reached for her left arm and expertly tied tubing just above the elbow. He smiled reassuringly as he palpated for a good vein.

She'd done the same herself a thousand times in her old life. Her stomach churned.

"How've you been feeling since?" Jack's fingers were cool against her skin. He found a vein he liked, and before she knew it, slid in the tip of the butterfly needle and accessed the flow. Her blood ran into the thin tubing and filled the first stoppered vial. "Any physical issues? Nausea and vomiting? Rashes? Headaches? Vision changes?"

Everything fell disturbingly into place, dropping into her mind like a guillotine. "I've had migraines. I was going to see a neurologist. I don't normally get them."

"Nothing you took relieved them, am I correct?"

"Yes." The room appeared to tilt and Meg was glad she was seated, else she might pass out. He finished with one vial and proceeded to fill another one. She turned away, unable to look or acknowledge what was happening.

"Anything else you can think of?"

"I can heal Gideon when I touch him."

"Go on." He started on a third vial. "Last one, I promise."

"My glasses give me headaches when I wear them. And my asthma's been in remission. I haven't had an attack since that day."

"That's it?"

"Isn't that enough?"

Jack removed the thin needle of the butterfly and covered the draw site with gauze and paper tape. "There might be other changes we don't immediately see. I think the tests might reveal some of them."

Tests? A fine sheen of perspiration beaded up like ice water on her skin. Her blood tingled and her stomach recoiled. "I don't feel so good."

"It's the magic inside of you." Jack stored the vials in a small refrigerator located beneath a shelving unit full of assorted colored quartz crystals, and vials of vibrant purple dust. "This room is designed to enhance magical energy."

"How long do I need to stay here?"

"I need to complete a full exam. That means physical and metaphysical. If you could take off your clothes—"

Gideon stepped between her and Jack. "The clothes stay on."

"No, they don't." Jack crossed his arms and the previous hint of malevolence darkened his features with full threat. "I need to see if she's marked in any way. It's a significant and likely finding under these circumstances."

"Trust me, she's not marked."

The men talked around her and their words blended into a buzzing sound. Her stomach went into full rebellion, and she clutched the armrests of the chair to keep from falling. Vertigo seized her and the room began to spin.

"Gideon, I can't help you if you get in my way." The buzzing stopped abruptly and suddenly all sounds were too loud to manage. Jack's voice boomed inside of Meg's skull. "Meg, you're a doctor. You understand these things. Will you please talk your overprotective boyfriend off the ledge?"

Meg managed to glance up at Jack, even opened her mouth to speak, but ended up heaving her guts and her lunch all over his very expensive velvet pants, and decorative leather boots. "Water," she croaked, her throat burning, "please."

She was dimly aware of someone handing her a glass. She drank the contents down, and leaned back in the chair, spent. Exhaustion seeped into her bones. "Can we do this somewhere else? I don't know if I can stay conscious in here."

Jack's pale face loomed into view. "I've prepared the Oasis suite for you. We can finish there, then you can rest."

Meg nodded, too tired now to even speak.

Gideon's strong arms scooped her up from the seat, and she rested her head against his broad, muscled shoulder. His warmth cocooned her in a safety net she knew was only temporary.

"It's okay, Doc. Breathe. That's right. You'll be fine in a few minutes. Then I'll kill Jack for doing this to you."

"I had to be sure." This from the man with pointed ears.

Movement seemed much quicker this time. They passed through a doorway and emerged outside into an endless garden filled with fountains and pools and all manner of exotic plants. Meg might have enjoyed it if she didn't feel so awful. They reached a small outbuilding which held a suite of sumptuous rooms. They went directly to the bedroom where Gideon laid her back on a canopy bed filled with silken pillows. Meg drew in deep gulps of cinnamon and vanilla-scented air and the worst of the malaise receded. Her body was plagued with a lassitude she couldn't seem to shake.

Jack followed through with a quick physical exam that employed a stethoscope, aural thermometer, and an assortment of crystals, some of which were suspended and used like a pendulum over different parts of her body.

The mage's placid features never hinted or betrayed any of his thoughts, and he didn't share any conclusions or findings. Occasionally, he'd flash a smile that never reached his stormy eyes. He'd have made an excellent physician, she thought. He had the dance down to the very last move. At least she got to keep her clothes on. Jack decided wisely to take Gideon's statement about her "markings" at face value, and for that, Meg was heartily glad. She hated being on this side of the exam table, despised being the patient, the one to be treated as opposed to the one treating. And at the same time, she was morbidly fascinated by Jack's mix of magic and medicine. Under other circumstances, she'd have asked a thousand questions. As it was, when he was finished, she only had the strength for one.

"Can I rest now?"

Gideon sat beside her on the bed, his burly body cutting a deep groove in the feather soft mattress. He touched her brow with a loving hand and smoothed back her hair. His black eyes were dark with concern. "I'll stay with you."

"No. Go with Jack. I'll be fine. I just want to sleep." *And I can't do it with you around.* Even with the fatigue, desire rippled through her from his touch.

He smiled. "I'll check in on you in a few hours."

She nodded, and burrowed deep into the pillows, finding a comfortable position. Gideon and Jack left her, and she was asleep before the door even closed. But her dreams offered her no escape, as the nightmare from the hotel played once more through her mind.

Jack debriefed him until the sun lowered and continued all through supper. All the while, worry ate away at Gideon. Jack was his last hope for fixing Meg, and judging by his friend's cagey behavior, things weren't looking good.

"My turn for questions, Jack." Gideon poured himself a fresh brandy after the long dining table was cleared, and pushed back his chair. "Can you help us?"

"You know I'd do anything to screw the Gods, Gideon. And I'd do anything to help you. In this case, I know what I can do, I just don't know if it will get you the results you're looking for." Jack regarded him with a strange expression as he finished his own brandy. The enchanted snifter refilled the instant he set it back to rest upon the linen-covered table. "She's farther along than I thought, and far worse."

The words were like a physical blow. He stood so fast, the high-backed chair fell to the floor. "Gods damn it. I hate this fucking game."

"So do I, Gid. It's why I left the playing field."

"You got kicked off the field."

"Because I burned the rule book. I hate it when the house always wins. That's a sucker's game."

"No shit." Gideon stalked around the table, feeling caged. He wanted to lash out, but he knew he needed to focus, to think. "You said she's worse. Define worse."

"I'm going to run the usual tests on her blood, but by her quick reaction to being in the workroom, my guess is she's the magical equivalent of a lighthouse. The headaches are a late onset symptom. She has a very powerful, very active spell inside of her. It's seeking release." Jack swallowed another glassful of brandy and got to his feet. He bridged his long fingers on the table and leaned over towards Gideon. "We need to get it out of her. Only that's risky. It needs to safely discharge from the vessel which in this case should have been the Buckle of Isis. Most times, that discharge destroys the vessel, unless it's created to withstand the expulsion of energy. The Buckle, from all my research, was created and owned by one of the first priestesses devoted to Isis, and handed down high priestess to high priestess until one day it vanished. I believe it's built to hold up under discharge."

"And Meg's not built to last under discharge, is she?"

"Nope. Most mortals aren't. Most immortals, too. Why the energy lodged in her, I can't say. Maybe the artifact has a level of sentience and knew its energy was at risk so it sought a safer harbor. What matters is that it will be a bitch to remove."

Gideon splashed brandy into his glass and downed the hot amber liquid, hoping to take the edge off his rapidly building fury. "So I need to get my hands on the artifact."

"And fast. Her body won't be able to contain the energy much longer. She'll stroke out, or go into cardiac arrest."

"The mystics set the timetable as the solstice. I have two weeks."

Jack shook his head, and his eyes darkened ominously. "Four to six days tops."

"Fuck." Gideon sat down hard again and ran a hand through his hair. Forget finding the mage, or saving the world. Four to six days gave him just enough time to save only one mortal: Meg Carter. "Can you buy me more time?"

"I have a charm. If she wears it, the color will tell you if she's running too hot, or if she somehow discharges the spell, and goes 'cool', as we say in the trade."

"She can discharge without you?"

"One of the other risks you run. I don't know what the spell is exactly, though I have my suspicions, so I can't speak to the trigger. If she pops it off prior to getting the artifact, she has a fifty-fifty chance of survival or death."

Gideon rapidly assembled the facts in morbid order. "That's why the mage is after her, he wants to use her in some way."

"That's if you assume the mage knows she doesn't have the buckle. You said the demons ripped up her house. They may have been searching for it." Jack slid back his chair, picked up his glass, kicked his feet up on the table, and narrowed his eyes. "Matt was right, the mage is ceremonial. And he's working Egyptian, which makes him twice as dangerous, three times as mad. Screwing around with magic based on a cult of the dead and immortality is never a sound plan."

This was bad. Really bad. A dull pain spread throughout his chest. "You said you have suspicions about the spell. What do you think it's capable of?"

"Isis has power over healing. You've seen Meg do that firsthand. That's residual power from the artifact, not the real spell. The spell may have elements of that, or, cover one of her other realms of power." Jack stroked the delicate stem of his glass. "The Buckle of Isis refers to Isis's aspect of gate keeper between the dark void and the living realm. The buckle is like the birth canal. In a way, she's a soul keeper. There's one myth where she gives souls to beings made of clay and that results in new life. I think the spell has to do with massive healing, perhaps something to convey immortality, or a version of it, through soul transference."

Gideon's head began to spin. What Jack proposed wasn't all that preposterous. He took a deep, steadying breath, as despair covered him like a shroud. "So I get the artifact and you put the spell back into the magic belt, right? Then I go after the mage."

"I expect if you get the artifact the mage will go after you, which should save you some considerable time." Jack frowned, tossed back his drink, and furrowed his brow. "I can't guarantee Meg will survive spell removal. Technically, with all the juice she's running, she should be dead already. I think she's drawing strength from you. The magic that made you immortal is helping to keep her alive."

Good. At least he was helping her in some small way. "So if I keep her near, her chances of survival improve?"

"Ten fold. In fact, I'm thinking I can use you as a buffer in the removal ritual. That will also help her chances."

So things weren't totally lost. Just partially. "The canopic jar was shipped back to New York a few days ago."

"If I still had some of my old powers, I could locate that thing in two heartbeats. Thanks to your Tribunal, the binding they slapped on me still holds, so I'm useless that way." Jack flashed a wry smile and his eyes cooled with refined anger. "However, I have a contact in New York. I'll have them make a clandestine search of the premises and shipping manifests. With luck, we'll have the artifact in protective custody by morning."

Gideon clung to the shreds of hope. "I need to keep her alive. She can't be a casualty, Jack. No matter what."

Jack studied him with a penetrating gaze. "I've never seen you so worked up over a woman before, Gideon."

"It's not like that."

"Don't talk bullshit. It's me Jack. Fess up."

How could he explain what he himself didn't even understand? He searched for words, searched for sense, and came up empty handed. Once he'd thought it was simple hormones, now he wasn't even sure of that. "She's different, somehow. I can't figure it, Jack. Maybe the artifact—"

"The artifact has nothing to do with your attraction to her, my friend. And it's more than plain chemistry."

Gideon couldn't deny the truth. She was a drug in his blood, and he couldn't get clean, didn't want to get clean. "We click. No big deal."

"Really? And if it comes down to killing her to save the world, you'll have no trouble pulling the trigger, right?"

Gideon's fists clenched. "Don't bait me."

"I'm not. I'm reminding you of who you work for. Not that I think you should do what they want. I think the Wardens are a pack of delusional jackals that have run the range too long in the afternoon sun."

"I don't work for the Wardens. I play by my rules, not theirs." He got to his feet, restless with anger, and pent-up need. "I should check on Meg. She slept through dinner, she might be hungry."

"I had Havers send her a tray. If you need me, I'll be in the study, working on the mage mark and a removal spell." The corner of Jack's mouth twisted up into a wry grin. He gave Gideon a mock salute. "One thing. Be careful. Our kind can't afford to indulge in mortal love. It makes us weak. Look what happened to me."

Gideon glanced sideways at his friend. "You of all people should know I don't have a heart."

"Your heart was only found wanting by the assessors, not missing."

"Same difference."

"Like hell. It's still there, Gid. Just because it's wanting, doesn't mean a good shock to the system can't get it ticking to the right beat again."

"Now who's talking bullshit?" Gideon turned his back on the mage, and Jack's mocking laughter followed him as he stalked out of the ornate dining hall.

He made his way to the main corridor, briefly considered going to the Oasis suite and Meg, and then dismissed it. He needed fresh air, time to think and clear his head, shake off the rage and the helplessness. He took the quickest route to the back gardens and lost himself in the maze of exotic desert and tropical plant life that flourished under Jack's eclectic enchantments.

He wanted to see Meg, hold her close, taste her again, but he couldn't. He had to figure out what he was going to tell her, and right now, he couldn't find a single word that would sound right. *Sorry, Doc, you should have died days ago. Hey, we'll get back the artifact, but getting the spell out of you might make you just as dead. Yeah, sure I told you I'd keep you safe; that was before I knew how impossible that task was...yeah, right.*

Nothing like being good and truly screwed, he thought. The pain in his chest sharpened to a stabbing burn, a fire that wouldn't go out. He sat down on a carved stone bench that rested between two large palms. He promised her he'd keep her safe, he had to keep that promise. He couldn't fail again. He'd spent his own corner of eternity repenting for that one mistake. A second failure, with a woman like Meg, would destroy him.

Gideon went over Jack's words again, and again, trying to find an out. In the end there were only two options: get the magic out of her and into the artifact, or trigger the spell and hope for the best. He didn't care for either, but he didn't have a choice. He did have a choice what to tell her, though. Question was, did he go for truth, or keep up the lies?

Chapter Nine

Meg woke from fitful dreams to find herself alone in the ornate bedroom. The nausea was gone, as was her fatigue. Restless and at odds with what to do, she padded into a marble tiled bathroom that reminded her of a Roman temple and was easily the size of her living room. There was both a sunken bath, and a separate multi-nozzle shower. After a moment of debate, she stripped off her clothes, fired up the shower, and stepped into the marvelous stream of hot water. She stayed inside until her fingers pruned and the restlessness eased to a dull tingling.

She toweled off with a thick Egyptian cotton towel, wrapped it around herself and went to explore further. Back in the bedroom, she found a closet filled with an assortment of gossamer robes and wraps. Jack must entertain women on a regular basis, she thought, selecting a jungle green silk edged with handmade lace. The sensuous fabric slid like a lover's hand over her body, and she shivered, suddenly reminded of Gideon's masterful touch. Her body responded immediately to the memory, her thighs dampening with desire. She had to get a grip, really get a grip. Except it felt so good to let go.

The ringing of a cell phone startled her back to reality. She realized after the third muffled ring, it was hers. Apparently Jack's pocket universe had good reception. She grabbed the cell from her backpack and immediately recognized Stan's private number.

"Hi, Stan." She tried to keep the surprise from her voice. It felt weird to have this intrusion of what was once her real life into this strange and fantastic realm. "What's up?"

"Ethan Keeler had spontaneous, complete remission, Meg!" Stan's enthusiasm rippled across the line. "It's remarkable. Hell, it's a freaking miracle. I've been over the results of his tests a hundred times. I know it's a bad time for you and all, but I thought you might want some good news."

Stunned, she sat down on the plush bed. She'd seen Ethan in the hospital, just before she left on this mad adventure with Gideon. She looked down at her hands as if they belonged to another person. They did. A person who wielded magic, curing what the most advanced science of medicine could not.

"Meg, you still there?"

"Yes." Her voice was a whisper to her ears. She'd cured Ethan. Her touch. Not any of the radiation, certainly not the chemo. "That's wonderful news, Stan. Thank you for calling."

"You don't sound so hot. Things must be tough."

You have no idea. "You know how it is."

"Well, I won't keep you. I just wanted you to hear firsthand from me. Tomorrow it'll be all over the news."

Magic. Not medicine. She couldn't shake that fact. What was science missing, she wondered, and why would the Gods be so cruel as to not share such wonder with mortals afflicted with terrible suffering? "How's everything else?"

"Pharmetrica called an ad hoc meeting in Syracuse tomorrow to discuss the study. Bill's on edge because he can't make it due to conflict. Pharmetrica's team is pissed that I'm subbing in for you. Chang and Lucy are fighting again so the office is a mess. Business as usual. Any chance you'll be back soon?"

"I don't know." And she realized, she didn't. She felt the other life slipping away, like fine cobwebs dissolving in a hard rain. "Listen, Stan, you know your stuff. Don't let the suits get you all stirred up. Give them the imperious doctor line and they'll back down."

Stan laughed lightly. "You're tougher than me, Meg. That's why Bill made you the study liaison. Look, I leave tomorrow for Syracuse. The meeting is two days long. The VP of research and development thinks we're too small to get the job done, so I have to convince him otherwise."

Meg tensed at the news. "What if one of my other patients gets admitted? Who'll cover?"

"Relax. Bill's going to cover for me. He's board certified in oncology and neurology: your kids will be in good hands. His commitment is local, so if someone gets admitted he can be there in twenty minutes. It's all good. Don't worry."

No, it wasn't all good. But that wasn't Stan's problem, or Bill's, or her kids. It was all her own. "Thanks, Stan. Keep me posted if anything else develops with Ethan."

"Sure thing."

She disconnected, tossed the cell phone aside, and looked again at her hands. These hands knew conventional healing, now they were capable of miracles. Would she be able to keep this wondrous power? And if she did, what could she do with it? She thought healing Gideon was a factor of his own enhanced physiology responding to her magic, but her assumption was faulty. Then again, perhaps Ethan's spontaneous remission was due to something else? She had to know for sure.

Meg returned to her backpack, rummaged in her make-up bag, and removed a pocket mirror. She used the end of a heavy candlestick holder from the gilded dressing table to smash the mirror. Then she picked out a shard and carefully drew the edge across her palm. She bit her lip to keep from crying out. Blood sprang up from the gash. It was superficial, but deep enough for the test. She discarded the shard, and then touched the wound, tracing it with her index finger. As her finger moved, the wound closed, pinked up and vanished as if it were never there.

Her asthma had vanished after touching the artifact. It had cured that, and her poor vision. Gideon acted as if her change was horrible, but it wasn't, not if she could keep it. Not if she could use it. Excitement rushed into her veins. She'd need to be careful. She'd need to test her skills, gauge them, learn her limits, then she'd need to be careful about how she applied them. She didn't want to be the center of a media circus.

She grabbed her notebook and pen and moved from the bedroom into the main area of the suite. A covered tray sat on a teak table. Meg's stomach growled, and she ventured over to see what waited. A perfectly prepared cut of lamb rested atop a bed of mint, with roasted new potatoes beside. A smaller plate held a spinach salad, and another, a cut of chocolate cheesecake. The food was divine, especially the cheesecake, and filled her full of energy. After finishing, she added more notes to her book and considered what might and might not be possible if she was a hands-on healer.

Eventually, she put away her book and ventured beyond the walls of the suite, lured outside by the beauty of the still desert night, and the scent of blooming jasmine. The private courtyard was bordered by walls trellised with fragrant, flowering vines. Pristine, white sand surrounded a pool designed to look like an oasis pond ringed with smooth, flat stones. At the end of the kidney-shaped pool was a series of marble columns draped with hot orange and cobalt blue swaths of silk. A low wall of polished stone ringed the columns, creating a private enclosure that allowed one to view the pool, but not be seen.

Inside the circular confines was a large divan covered with rust and gilded raw silk and more jewel-toned pillows. Conical glass candle holders were suspended from gold chain holders linked to the columns, and flames flickered lazily inside. An unlit brazier was set dead center, into the smooth floor, and surrounded by colorful red and gold mosaic tiles. Above was no roof to obscure the majesty of the stars and sky.

The heat of the night, the excitement over Ethan's healing, the beauty and privacy of her surroundings drew out an adventurous side of her. She untied the robe, let it fall in a whisper to the ground, and climbed down the rock ledge steps into the warm, welcoming waters of the pool.

For a while she swam in the moonlight, her eyes closed so her senses could better appreciate the nuances of the night and the water. She finished laps and floated, drifting in the fantasy, pretending she was on vacation at some fancy Sedona resort instead of the magical fortress of a sorcerer, on the run for her life. The breeze picked up and something changed in the surroundings. Current danced like an electric spark through the air.

Meg opened her eyes. Gideon stood in the shadows beside a column, watching her. His body was tensed, his hands shoved into the pockets of his leather pants, his eyes hooded, and impossible to read. She was taking a risk going to him like this. He could reject her again. But she didn't care. She stepped from the pool, naked, water cascading down her body, and answered the call.

"Meg." His voice was husky, needy. "Stay there. We need to talk."

"We can talk later." Meg closed the distance between them, joining him in the shadows. She reached up and touched his face with her palm, tracing the strong jaw, and shivered from the contact. "Tonight's made for other things. Don't you agree?"

She kissed him, and he opened to her immediately, countering her attack. His tongue swept inside her in a savage onslaught, his strong arms locked around her, and he bent her back as he pressed down a searing kiss. Her toes curled and her heart began to race like lightning.

Just when she thought she'd melt from his heat, he broke the kiss. His face was haunted, his eyes liquid night. "This time I won't stop, Meg. Are you sure that's what you want?"

"Never more." She trailed her hands down his chest, enjoying the feel of him. She wanted so badly to take him into herself, to cross the final line and melt together. But there was time tonight. For now she would content herself with returning some of the punishment he'd dealt her way the night before. The devilish notion satisfied her inner siren. She found her way to his waist, undid the button to his pants, and ran her hand inside.

Gideon sucked in a sharp breath. Emboldened by his response, Meg knelt and began her torture. She took her time with the zipper, blowing warm breath on his cock and briefs as they were revealed, inch by maddening inch. Once free, she followed the rigid line, stroked up beyond the fabric with her tongue, and swirled it around the silky head and through the cleft. She tasted the salt of him, and inhaled the musky, exotic masculine scent that was uniquely Gideon. The night was made for them. He was made for her. She for him. She knew this as she knew herself, they were meant to be. Nothing else could be so right.

He buried his hands in her hair and groaned. She sucked

gently and his cock leapt in response.

"Enough," he ground out through clenched teeth. He pulled her up, crushing her with another kiss. Then he swept her up in his arms, carried her into the enclosure of marble columns and laid her down upon the divan.

In moments he shed his clothes, and stood poised above her: naked and magnificent. She reached up for him and he came to her, his kiss ravenous. His cock brushed teasingly against her bare belly. Her juice ran fast with the contact and her blood grew thick. He lowered his head and sucked hard on her nipples, and rational thought receded as erotic pleasure took its head.

She writhed beneath his expert ministrations, turned boneless as he gripped her hips and moved lower still, exploring her folds with the searing tip of his tongue. She parted for him, and a low purr escaped her throat. His mouth was masterful, orchestrating a barrage of sensations spiraling out from her clit, radiating ecstasy to every single nerve in her body. Her orgasm was torrential, sweeping over her like a hurricane. She cried out, clutching his head as her body quivered in the wake of release. Still, she longed for him, still she craved what she'd been so far denied. "I want you inside of me, Gideon."

"We have all night." He lifted his head, moving to her mouth to kiss her in a fluid motion, as he brushed her thighs with his hands.

"Please." Her body hummed with desire, ached for release. "No more waiting."

Gideon kissed her, filling her until she thought she would burst. They were skin to skin, slick, hot, and needy. He gave a short thrust, and a second orgasm shot like lightning through her.

Gideon pushed up on his arms and looked down upon her.

His smile was dangerous, his body a lethal weapon that he used with consummate skill as he began to move with smooth, measured strokes. Somehow he'd turned the tables on her once again. And she didn't have it in her to complain.

"Tell me how you like it, Meg." His husky voice tickled her ears, his breath was hot on her throat. She strained closer, arching her back against him.

"Tell me, Meg," he ordered. He pulled out to the very end of her, then drove in again and thrust up.

Lights exploded in her brain and waves of pleasure churned inside of her. She closed her eyes and danced with him on the edge. She licked her lips, tasting his sweat and sex on them. "Yes. Like that. Faster."

He urged her farther along the path of abandon, his body demanding more and more, until she couldn't hold out. She came hard this time, locking her legs around him and holding him fast. He joined her in the fall, spilling himself into her, body and soul, until she couldn't tell where her pleasure ended and his began. She was wrapped in a seemingly endless orgasm, living in a world beyond that of mortals, and she never wanted it to end.

When her tremors ceased, and she could think to breathe again, Gideon stretched out beside her. The musk of sex thickened the perfumed air. A delicious languor took hold of her as he continued to nuzzle her neck and tease her skin with delicate nips and well-placed licks. She curled against the length of him, surprised he still had the energy to move. The hot desert night stirred itself into a breeze that drifted like smoke across her bare body. His heart beat steadily beside her own, and his breathing matched her easy pace. They fit so well, in so many ways. She pushed aside any other thoughts that might jeopardize what they shared right now. To have this one memory, this perfect moment in time, was worth whatever price she'd pay later on.

She must have dozed for a while, and when she woke, it was to his touch. His hand curved around one breast and he teased her nipple with his thumb and forefinger, rolling it with alternating gentle and forceful pressure until it was puckered and tight. A renewed and dangerous vigor coursed through her. His cock stiffened again, a feat she figured must come hand in hand with being an immortal soldier. Surely no mortal man had this kind of stamina or drive.

He was pure fantasy, yet he was real. Living, breathing, a miracle, and all hers. Her satisfaction shifted into the sublime. She turned on him and pushed him down against the pillows. "Now it's your turn to suffer."

His eyes widened and he gave her a cocky grin. "I wouldn't exactly call this suffering, Meg."

"We'll see." Wicked thoughts filled her mind, triggering carnal impulses she decided to indulge.

She circled her fingers around his nipples in unison. He sucked in a hard breath and shivered.

"You're going to be the death of me."

"You're immortal, you can't die." She licked the six-pack abs, following the treasure line to his waiting cock. When she puckered her lips and pillowed them against the swollen head, he grasped the covers of the divan in a death grip. A drop of his fluid rose to the top. She brought both her hands to his shaft, and used her thumb to move the salty tear around, creating sensual friction.

He made a satisfied, inarticulate sound of male pleasure that had her glowing. Feeling her power, pushed on by his reactions, Meg took the head and shaft into her mouth and sucked deep. He was molten silk inside of her, pulsing with hot life and uncontrolled desire. Her womb contracted, longing to take the pleasure he offered, but there was time for that.

She moved one hand low to cup his tight balls, weighing them in her hand, squeezing with a gentle, rhythmic pressure. In response his cock grew harder still. He laced his hands in her hair, and she began to move, driving him to the edge the way he'd driven her, pushing him beyond any rigid limits or rational, sensible thoughts.

Meg's mouth felt like hot honey pouring over him. Gideon had all he could do to hold back the animal inside while they made love. With her suckling his cock, caressing his balls with her clever hand, stroking his shaft with the other, the beast was sure to slip the chains and run free. Her lush breasts and tight nipples teased his thighs as she moved over him. The scent of her desire filled him. Her hair was silk between his fingers.

He groaned as he waged an inner struggle with uncontrolled need, trying to trap it once more, bind it, put it back in the dark. She had no idea what she was doing. He couldn't handle the strain much longer. He'd want to take her hard, put his mark upon her, make her scream, not just cry out. Tonight, he wanted her to know she belonged to him and no other. He wanted so much he couldn't even describe, things that pulled at him viscerally, primally, things that terrified him and made him crazy with lust-induced insanity. How could a mortal do this to him? Not even the Goddesses took a man this far, pushed this hard, played him so expertly.

He stroked her hair and watched, transfixed by the dangerously hypnotic motions and the sensations she aroused. It lured him into a kind of erotic delirium the likes of which he'd never felt.

The beast inside howled, racing along the razor's edge. Her

tongue darted out once more, pink and moist, and she licked away another drop of his juice. Raw, painful need coursed through his blood. The final illusion of control vanished and Gideon became whole with his uncontrolled desire, directing it at the source of its torment.

Gideon pulled her to him and devoured her mouth with a kiss, and the taste of himself on her lips drugged him further into a tortured state of madness. He needed to possess her, he needed for her to belong completely to him.

Turning her around, he caressed the soft, sweet flesh of her heart-shaped ass, and drove into her from behind. She welcomed him into the hot, velvet heaven, and he shuddered, almost losing control, almost coming without thought. Their union took him so far away from himself, so far from control and rules, he doubted he'd ever find his way back. He wanted her to dissolve in his arms, he wanted to dissolve with her, into the primal oblivion.

Gideon continued his onslaught, driving into her, stroking her clit even as she convulsed with orgasm. She was slick with sweat and soaked with the flow of her juices. Her muscles were weak from pleasure. Her body never felt more full as he pushed the column of male flesh to the very hilt, touching the deepest part of her, working her pleasure centers into overdrive.

This was the Gideon she expected, the demon lover, the demanding one, who pushed her beyond any sensible limits. His one hand was buried in her hair, holding tight as he worked his cock inside of her. His other hand wrapped around her as his fingers tormented her most sensitive spot. She felt completely surrounded, enveloped by him. She was drowning in desire, reveling in untapped sexual abandon.

Her sex swelled as she crested on a tidal wave of pleasure and pain. Her body was ablaze. She couldn't think. She moved on instinct. She wanted his release, and she wanted her own. She moaned low in her throat, a keening sound full of need.

Gideon responded instantly to her call. He moved like a force of nature, unleashing the full of the storm upon her. With three powerful thrusts, she crashed into the torrent of release, and as she went under he cried her name into the dark desert night and drowned with her in the maelstrom.

Gideon collapsed against her, cradling her breasts and breathing softly against the back of her neck. She had never felt more possessed, more fulfilled in her life. She had brought him to ruin, as he brought her, and together, they'd found indescribable bliss. She felt him rumble like thunder above her as he released a growl of satisfaction. He moved and rolled her onto her back, staring down at her with a ferocious gaze.

"Tonight, you're mine, Meg. No matter what comes tomorrow, it doesn't matter. Tonight, you're mine."

She reached for him, unafraid. His jaw was hard against her palm, his skin slick with sweat and blistering hot. "And you're mine."

Chapter Ten

Gideon woke just before dawn, when the world was dark grey and the arrival of day uncertain. He'd made love with Meg for hours, until they were both too exhausted to move or speak. At some point they'd made it back to the suite, finished one last quickie in the shower, then collapsed into sleep on the king-sized bed.

He wished his brief hours of sleep could have been filled with dreams of her. Barring that, he'd have wished for no dreams at all. Instead, he saw the dream of his mortal failure. He buried his wife and children, again and again and again. And each time, his wife's face was Meg's, her gaze accusatory and mocking.

He dressed quietly while she slept and went to stand by the window, wondering what the day would bring. Would they find the jar and the Buckle of Isis? Would Jack save Meg? Would Gideon screw up somehow and damn them all?

He glanced back at the bed where Meg slept, nestled amongst a tide of pillows and the thick scarlet comforter. He felt a stab of guilt burn through his chest. Last night he meant to tell her the complete truth, as Jack had told him. Then he came upon her as she slipped out of the silk robe, and into the dark waters of the pool. All his plans turned to dust. He couldn't look away, he couldn't turn off the desire. It was too strong, too insistent. It claimed him in madness, and he let it get the best of him.

She was a wildcat, a seductress, an innocent, a complex woman that unraveled him and turned him into a savage. She stripped away his facades, his civility, his airs, reaching the bare core of him and rattling his bones until his soul quaked in fear. He blinked hard, ran a hand through his hair, and swore. What the hell had he gotten himself into? Worse, what had he gotten her into?

Just before they fell into sleep, she'd looked at him and he knew. This wasn't just sex. It wasn't just one night. Not for her. She was falling for him, and instead of doing the right thing and stopping her in her tracks, he'd let her fall. She made him feel things he'd not felt in centuries, and he'd indulged his ego at her expense. No wonder he was damned. She had no idea how worthless he was, what a piece of shit. And when she found out, it would be worse than death. He turned back to the tentative dawn, knowing the day to come would bring harsh, cruel reality. He couldn't let Meg drift down the path of "what if". There could be nothing between them. She needed to know the truth. All of it. About her. And, about him.

Meg woke to find Gideon staring out at the rising sun. Weak fingers of yellow light clawed into the room, but none seemed to touch him. He stood tall and alone in the shadows of the retreating night. His body was rigid, and in profile, his jaw set tight. The room had a decided chill. She drew the comforter closer as she sat up in the bed. "Good morning."

He glanced back at her and nodded. "We need to talk."

Her rising spirits took a spill.

"If you're going to lecture me about how things can't work between a mortal and an immortal, save it." She took a deep breath and fixed him with a pointed stare. “We’re good together. You can’t deny that. And you want me just as much as I want you. That’s all that matters.”

He moved away from the window and crossed his muscular arms. “You’re going to die, Meg.”

Her breath left her in a rush, and her chest tightened making it hard to draw in another one. “How? Why?”

“You absorbed more magic than your mortal form can hold. If Jack can’t remove it, you’re dead. Even if he can, you stand a chance of dying.”

“Okay.” She struggled to absorb the facts he so casually and coldly tossed out at her. She knew he was framing things this way on purpose, to drive her away, to keep her at arm’s length. She forced herself to count to ten before responding. “So I have a fighting chance.”

“We need to get the artifact. You need to stay with me, though. Something about my immortality is keeping you alive.”

More good news. “Did you know this last night?”

He gave a curt nod. “I could have told you, but I wanted to fuck you and I figured it would kill the mood.”

“Like I said yesterday, you’re really not a morning person, are you, Gid?” She laughed at his shocked look. “What? Did you think I’m an idiot? I’m on to you. Someone put a hurting on you, so now you want to keep everyone else away. That includes me. Only I’m under your skin, and last night proves you can’t keep me away. What happened? Who hurt you so bad that you’d cut yourself to keep someone else from making you bleed?”

He drew back as if slapped. Something slipped inside of him, turning his eyes to a cold, harsh, inhuman black. Meg pulled the covers tighter like a shield, sensing her words had broken something in him.

"I told you before, it's not who hurt me, Dr. Carter, it's who I hurt." He laughed harshly, a sound that sent a shiver up her spine. "I lied when I told you I lived before William's time. I came after. I was one of the thugs called a knight that subdued the land. I got a local bride in the bargain. She was a whey-faced Saxon with a tight little body. I had two kids on her before she knew what hit her."

His voice dripped with self-loathing. Meg was horrified by the way he spoke. She knew he was trying to hurt her, to scare her, but his words made her heart ache for him. "So you were a man of your times. That's nothing unusual."

"Oh, I was a man of my time all right. I loved to fight. Couldn't turn down a chance to increase my holdings, so when an ally needed a hand in beating down a pillaging neighbor, I packed up my men-at-arms and went. Alys warned me off going. Said she had some premonition of doom." He balled his hands into fists and shoved them into his pockets. "Superstitious, she was. I couldn't stay, but in deference to her, I left one of my finest soldiers to keep an eye on her. That fine man raped and killed her and my two sons, with the help of his cousin and a band of bloodthirsty mercenaries. While my house was laid low, I was fucking a whore, too drunk to even know where I was."

Her dream. Except it wasn't a dream. It was his past. Meg felt her heart break. "You couldn't have known."

"Yeah, well here's the punch line, Doc. I didn't really love Alys. She was a possession, just like my house, or my cattle. But when she was gone it was like a part of me was torn from my body." He stalked the room, pacing like a caged tiger. "I took to the road, spilling blood for those too weak to spill it themselves. I paid vengeance trying to work penance. I turned my back on my God, and when I died several years later near Cairo, the Egyptians came for me when my soul sat unclaimed."

Meg got out of the bed and went to him. She wanted to heal him, to take away the raw pain, to banish the wound that had festered inside of him for countless years. "That's in the past, Gideon. Let me help you."

"You can't." His voice was raw, his face ravaged with pain. He drew back from her like she was cursed. "These Egyptians assess the dead in a death ceremony. They weigh your heart. Mine came up short. I couldn't love, so I was flawed. It worked for them, that's why I got my job with Bast. But my heart, it's still the same. It's wanting, Meg. It can't love. I can't love. And you deserve far better than that. You may not realize it, but I do, and I'll be damned if I'm going to let your life get ruined the way I did to Alys all those years ago."

"That's impossible." But even as she said the words a part of her knew it was true. If he said he couldn't love because part of him was broken, in this crazy rabbit hole world of magic, mad Gods, and mages, then that was very likely true.

"It is possible." He moved towards the door, his shoulders slumped, his face ashen. Shame clouded his eyes. "Get dressed and packed. I'll meet you back at the main house."

Meg's mind raced and her heart burned. He couldn't love. His heart was wanting. He was beyond imperfect, beyond her reach. But she wanted him, and no other. And she believed in him, even if he didn't believe in himself. In that terrible moment, she knew a truth that defied logic and touched her to her very soul. Not only did she want him, but she was falling for him. The how or why didn't matter, the fact couldn't be denied.

He opened the door and started to cross the threshold, stepping into a shaft of dawning light. If she let him go now, he'd be lost to her forever. A moment of calm fell over her and clarity settled in.

She straightened her spine and stood tall in the face of his fear and doubt. "I don't care that your heart is wanting, or that you can't love. I've got heart enough for both of us."

He paused. "I wasn't sent to save you, Doc. I was sent to kill you."

The cold storm in his words blew around her. She'd thought that was the case when she grilled him in the car and he admitted the Gods were after her. His admission chilled her, but didn't deter her. "Maybe so, Gideon. But you didn't kill me. You saved me, and have protected me ever since. A lot has happened since that night. I told you. Heart enough for both of us."

His jaw worked as if he was going to speak, then he shook his head, and left, closing the door in his wake. She'd reached him with her words. She knew she had with absolute certainty. In that moment, she'd bridged his abyss with hope. Now she breathed a prayer she'd live long enough to see the results.

Chapter Eleven

Gideon headed for the main house. Meg's scent was everywhere on him, the feel of her burned into him like a brand. He couldn't escape and worse, he didn't want to. He'd tried his best to push her back, to put things to right, but what passed between them had altered them both irrevocably.

I have heart enough for both of us. Her words touched him to his rotted core, settling in amongst the skeletons and charred bits of memories, growing green in a patch of earth he thought forever burned. He almost believed she could heal him, but he'd gamed for too long, knew himself and his situation too well. There was no use even trying. Best to focus on what he could control, and tuck last night's experiences into a safe, and secret, place.

He felt the familiar ache in his chest, a constant reminder of his deficiency. It didn't matter that he could love her all night, or drown her in wave after wave of erotic pleasure. He couldn't give to her the thing he most wanted to give.

He grabbed his gear and met Jack in the hall on the way to the master living room. "How'd you do with your contact?"

"The jar was never returned to the shipping warehouse. Only an empty box arrived. No way to trace who along the line removed the jar, or if it was ever in the box in the first place. Probably a standard arrangement. The company is a front for dealing in stolen antiquities."

Gideon swore. If the artifact wasn't there, it would be hell to find. And every hour that ticked by brought Meg closer to death. "Tell me there's an upside to this."

"I looked into some of Meg's coworkers last night, specifically Dr. Liebers. I suspect he never sent it back."

Meg waited placidly, perched on the edge of a leather chaise inside the large living room. He grabbed Jack by the shoulder and pulled him back into an alcove before he could be seen.

"What did you do?" With Jack, it could be all manner of things that might come back to bite them both in the ass. No one took risks like Mad Jack. It was an asset and a liability.

"A little detective work. I called Matt and had him check on Liebers. Very interesting financials. He was in debt up to his eyeballs until the appearance, and disappearance of the artifact. He's your lynch pin, not the mage."

Gideon processed the information. "He's the front man for someone." The news was good. It meant he was finally one step ahead of the mage. Providing the mage had no idea of Liebers' involvement. "Has anything hit the black market yet?"

"Not according to my sources."

Even better news. If he got the artifact from Liebers, he could fix Meg, stash her with Jack, and move on to lure the mage and any conspirators in the Council out into the open. The pieces were falling into place. He had to believe Meg would survive, that she was the good part of the fifty-fifty odds. Jack was the son of a God, and even with most of his powers bound, he was still a considerable magical player. Gideon believed he'd get the job done right. "Can you get me back to Troy via a passage?"

"I've got the route mapped and a guide standing by. You'll be there by nightfall. Havers packed you food to go. Hope you don't mind breakfast burritos and chicken salad."

"Thanks, Jack."

"Don't thank me yet. You're still in the thick of it." Jack glanced over his shoulder to make sure Meg hadn't moved, and then stepped closer to Gideon. "I ran preliminary tests on her blood. She's a sun about to go nova. If she blows, get clear, or she'll takc you with her."

He fisted his hands. "Can't do that."

"Figured as much, but I had to give you fair warning."

"Any luck with the mage mark?"

Jack frowned. "Nothing's turned up yet. Whoever this guy is, he's dangerous and skilled. That means he may know how to kill your kind, so watch your back."

Gideon nodded tightly, and they joined Meg.

She smiled at them both, and Gideon felt the bottom drop out of his gut. The urge to take her to him and kiss her was near unbearable. The memories of last night ran through his brain, and his dick stirred hopefully.

"Liebers still has the artifact," he ground out.

Meg's smile faltered. "That means..."

"We go back to Troy, shake him down and see what we find."

"He's in Syracuse. He won't be back for two days."

Fuck. More delays. "Fine. We'll toss his house. Then we'll go get him if we don't find what we need."

"Stan's involved? This is crazy."

"Magic usually is," Jack said smoothly. "Which reminds me. I whipped this up for you in the lab last night. Keep it on at all times. It will help you manage the worst of your symptoms."

He handed her an oval rose quartz pendant suspended on a

close-fitting, thick silver band. Meg put it on and it rested like a metallic snake close against her skin. Gideon's hands and body remembered well the silken feel of that creamy skin, the way it heated and flushed like fresh blooming roses when she came. He shut his eyes for a moment and rubbed the bridge of his nose, trying unsuccessfully to shut out the erotic pictures flashing through his brain.

"Thanks," she said. "Does it come with instructions?"

"Keep it on, don't take it off. If you feel a headache or vertigo coming, focus your attention on the feel of the stone and silver on your body, and it will draw down the energy."

Gideon stepped forward and grabbed her overnight bag. "We're leaving now, Meg. Jack's sending us back through another passage."

She cast him a sidelong look, her eyes mischievous. "Good. That will give us plenty of time to talk."

Venice, Italy

Salazar woke in his bedroom. His favorite blazer hung carelessly off the doorknob to his walk-in closet. He still wore his clothes. Memories flooded into his brain and he jumped from the bed, looking for a fight. He felt none of the aftereffects of the vampiric acid, but he knew that would be short lived. The headache would soon set in, followed by the blinding pain.

A figure emerged from the dark shadows gathered in the farthest corner of the room. "Good afternoon, Ramon. I trust you slept well? It's been almost two days."

Two days? "Seth? What the hell are you playing at now?"

"Is that anyway to address the God who saved your ass?"

The red-headed Egyptian emerged into the light. “Your house is dirty, Salazar. The mystics are compromised. I’m giving you a broom. It’s only fitting an elder Warden does the cleaning.”

Salazar fought for control as the creature he was in the past begged for release, as rage welled up inside like a caged, rabid tiger. He couldn’t fathom the God’s motives. Such an overt strike against the Wardens was against every rule in the quite extensive book. “You don’t know what you’re playing with.”

“Nor do you, or any of your mystics. That’s why I followed you, and why I’m giving you a helping hand to do the right thing. I don’t want to take the fall because I’m the most likely candidate to want the war to re-open. That means you need to figure this out, and fast.” Seth put his hands on his lean hips and stared at Salazar with merciless black eyes. “Ian hasn’t given anything of use, yet, nor has that creature Skathi. However, I let it leak at last night’s Tribunal hearing what you’d caught on your hunt, and since then your head mystic has acted very strangely. If I didn’t know better, Ramon, I’d say Elsa isn’t drinking the Council Kool-Aid anymore.”

Seth’s words swirled round in his brain, knocking against it like loose, grinding rocks. The Egyptian God of Chaos was notorious for twisting truth to the very limit and luring the unwary to dooms of their own making. Could he be right about Elsa, the lead mystic in Venice? More, why would he care? A more sinister thought took shape then. Seth must have had his own mystics check the vision, and they came up with something different. The Egyptian would relish a war unless he was on the losing side.

Salazar tucked the notion away for further exploration, or exploitation, and refocused on the dire matter at hand. “You’re torturing them?”

"No. They're being interrogated, by your man, per your instructions. I have complete deniability."

Ramon's anger chilled to fear. "Ian's an innocent. You can't do this to him. You'll destroy him."

"No one is innocent in this game. Besides, you were planning to kill the Scot in Monte Carlo."

"Death is better than torture."

"Don't be a savage. It's not the old days. This kind of thing is far more sanitized now."

Salazar felt acid settle in the pit of his stomach as he realized how and who had tipped off Seth. There was only one being who could have alerted the God of Chaos. The one he called for a favor back at the Amici. His darker side rallied at this thought. He'd asked for help, here it was, albeit in an odious package. Seth was right, he'd planned to kill Ian. Too sentimental given the dire circumstances. Salazar rubbed his face and used the moment to set aside the last of his outrage and grief over what had transpired, and what was to come. "Who called the Tribunal hearing? You?"

"Horus."

That was unexpected. Perhaps Seth pushed Horus into calling for a hearing. Seth was a master at manipulating the younger God. "What was the result?"

"Gideon Sinclair was deemed rogue and a hunter dispatched to take him out of play."

"Who did the Tribunal send?"

"Lucas Preacher."

Good. Preacher was methodical and deadly, but not inclined to act with undue haste. A tactical decision that indicated Bast and some of the other Tribunal members believed in Gideon. They satisfied their overt mandates and continued playing covert games, just like those they policed. He got to his feet.

Seth cleared his throat, and leaned in close. Ramon smelled the cloying scent of frankincense and trouble that clung to the God, and it made him sick to his stomach.

"I called Bast," Seth said in a sonorous voice. "The Tribunal will most likely bring in their interrogation team, unless you have something by then and can persuade them to allow you to finish extracting information."

That was Seth, a true entity of chaos with a tendency towards evil: play all sides against each other and sit back to watch the show. Ramon knew going into a rogue op meant getting dirty, he'd just forgotten how dirty that could be. The operation was spiraling out of control. Swift action was necessary to maintain control. If the Tribunal sent in their own people it could spell doom for Ian, and trouble for the Council of Wardens.

He sighed, undid his cuff links and rolled up his sleeves as he ran a plan of action in his mind. "How long until she arrives?"

"She's at an unrelated Tribunal Council. You have three hours."

"That should be enough to start." He pulled his cell phone from his pocket and hit speed dial.

After the first ring his most trusted paladin answered. "Where the hell have you been?"

"Working. We have a vermin problem."

"Who?"

"Elsa Ulfsdottir. Bring her to me. Be discreet and quick."

"Consider it done."

Salazar hung up and shoved the cell in his silk pants. He

felt a familiar dread mixed with grim anticipation. “So many centuries have passed between the then and the now, and yet, in the blink of an eye the years vanish and the then becomes the now.”

“I picked you for a reason, Ramon. You’ll get this done, whatever the cost. Very few beings can truly say that about themselves. You can call yourself by whatever name you choose, that will not alter what’s in your blood or your soul. None of us can escape who or what we are.”

The Egyptian was right of course. Salazar looked down at his hands and flexed his fingers, preparing for what he knew would be an ordeal, on him and his subjects. “I certainly hope not. For all our sakes.”

Chapter Twelve

Gideon made a complete search of Stan Liebers' house and found nothing other than questionable financial dealings. There was no magic, not a single thing to link him to the artifact, or hint at its whereabouts. Gideon's frustration level at another failure spiked dangerously. He wanted to trash the place, destroy the pretentious modern furniture and precious art, all bought at the expense of one woman's life. Gideon had found all manner of purchase receipts for these things, obtained after the arrival of the artifact. Liebers was the missing link, Gideon was certain of it, and he was ready to take the guy to the mat to get the answers he needed.

He swallowed his fury, maintained discipline and left the house as he'd found it. He cut through the backyard, keeping to the darkness and shadows, emerging on another street. Meg waited around the corner in the car, parked just beyond the radius of light. The last hours in her company hit him in a hard rush. They'd talked through the journey, and she'd taken it all from him, every scrap of detail of his past, every bit of who he'd been, and who he'd become since then. He wanted to keep it back, but he felt he owed her that much, since he couldn't offer her anything else. Somehow, instead of feeling worse, he'd felt lighter at the end. She never judged him, just listened, questioned, and considered as the story of him poured out.

She didn't ask him about tomorrow or long term, she didn't ask him about what he couldn't give her. In all his centuries he'd never met someone like her, never wanted to have what was forbidden to him.

Gideon gave a quick look around, got in the car and fired it up. "I didn't find anything."

"I didn't think you would. Stan is a typical addict, a master at compartmentalization and secrecy."

"We need to make the call. Are you ready?"

Her lips compressed into a thin line. "Never more." She had her cell in her hand, flipped it open, and dialed. "Hi Stan, it's me Meg. Don't talk, just listen. I want the artifact. I know you have it. No more games. Get back to Troy. Now."

She fell silent for a moment, then her eyes narrowed. "I don't care about Pharmetrica, and don't throw the kids at me. This isn't about them. If you don't meet me I'm coming after you. Gideon's coming with me. Trust me, you won't like what he has in mind for you."

She paused. "You need to get it? How long will that take?"

She chewed her lower lip for a moment. "Fine. The office. Ten-thirty tomorrow night."

She snapped the cell closed and looked at Gideon. Her eyes were wild with anger. "Do you believe he tried to guilt me with the kids to buy more time? He had the nerve to tell me that if he didn't meet with the executives tomorrow, they'd yank the study and the kids would suffer. Bastard."

Gideon put the SUV into drive and headed out. "Why can't we meet tonight?"

"He has the thing stashed somewhere for safe-keeping. It will take him that long to get his hands on it and get back. He heard about the demon attack on me and got spooked. He doesn't want the mage and his cronies chasing him down."

Gideon didn't like that answer. There was too much time between now and then, too much time to set up an ambush. Then again, it did make sense, keeping the thing on ice. Particularly after what happened to Meg. "At least we know the mage doesn't have it yet."

"What if Stan double-crosses us and doesn't bring it?"

"Leave Stan to me, Meg. This is my game, my field of expertise. He'll hand it over."

She turned to look out the window as he drove through the sleepy town. "I don't suppose we can spend the night at my place?"

"I was going to head back up to the Pine Motor Lodge."

"I know. It's silly, right? My cape isn't exactly a safe haven."

"It's too dangerous. We're so close now, I don't want to take any unnecessary risks. Once it's over you can go back."

But even as the words left his mouth, he recognized them for a lie. She couldn't go back to her home or her normal life, no more than he could go back to what passed for his home or normal life. Too much had gone on between them, too much had happened to reclaim the peace offered by the past.

For the first time, Gideon really contemplated living minutes, hours, days, without Meg. He could scarce imagine a moment without her, let alone eternity. He felt an eruption of pain start in his chest and spread into his veins and finally his soul. The profound sense of loss was paralyzing and terrifying. He gripped the steering wheel, holding on for support, and waited for the worst of the physical sensations to pass. In its wake, his blood ran cold and his eyes saw his future: empty, bleak, meaningless. Even the heat of the scorching, erotic bliss they shared last night failed to warm him this time.

This morning he'd told himself he needed to push her away, that it was the right thing to do for her. She broke down every wall he threw up. She owned his soul. She completed him. And she would leave him. She'd have no choice. He'd have no choice. His mouth went dry with fear. He'd become obsessed with her, so completely obsessed that he barely cared about the conspiracy, barely cared that the world hung in the balance. His focus was her, and when she was gone, he would be nothing.

Stan's hands trembled as he waited through rings across a distant line. After an eternity, the line connected and the answering machine beeped.

"She called. We're on for tomorrow night. Ten-thirty. My office. Don't be late. That guy she's running around with is a freaking monster. No telling what he'll try when it goes down."

He hung up and began to pace. He had so much to do. He couldn't believe this was happening. He forced himself to still and took a drink of bland hotel water from the glass pitcher. When that didn't work, he popped a valium and chased it with a shot of gin from the mini-bar.

He lay back on the king-sized bed and stared at the shadows on his ceiling. His heart pounded like a jackhammer. By this time tomorrow, he'd be done with all the bullshit. He'd be free and rich beyond his wildest dreams. All he had to do was hold it together for the next twenty-four hours.

Meg cleaned up in the horrid little motel bathroom and

changed into her single set of pajamas. The light blue cotton was a far cry from the jeweled silk of the night before. Everything seemed so distant from that one moment in time. The talk with Gideon was surprising, cleansing, and frightening. Knowing the mortal man as well as the immortal soldier didn't change her feelings, only confirmed them. His mortality, his failings, made him approachable and real, gave her hope that somehow they could make it work once the worst of this trial had passed.

She dried her face with the harsh towel and stared at herself in the mirror. The fluorescent lighting gave her skin a ghoulish cast. Jack's necklace glowed an eerie dusky pink, full of a life all its own. *This will all pass.* Whatever was inside of her, that crazy desert hermit Jack would pull it out of her. Gideon would catch the bad guy. There would be a happily ever after for them. If she'd learned one thing fighting the battle against cancer, faith mattered. Those patients with a positive attitude and belief in a good outcome had far better responses to treatment, and far better chances of survival. She would survive. She didn't just find the man of her dreams only to lose him to some cosmic battle between ancient Gods and crazed wizards. Love was within her grasp, she'd be damned if she'd let it go.

She stepped out into the chilly air of the small, dated motel room. This wasn't the unit they had that first night, but it was identically decorated and reinforced the feeling of coming full circle.

Gideon sat on the bed, cleaning one of his numerous guns. His exotic scent filled the tiny room. Meg took a deep breath, recalling in vivid detail how that scent mixed so well with the musk of sex. He looked up at her, his sharp features drawn and tight, his dark eyes haunted. Silently she went to him, took the gun from his hands, and pushed him back onto the bed. He offered her no resistance as she stripped him bare and made love to him. She followed an aggressive, erotic, driving need, straddling him and riding him wildly until he cried out her name and came undone beneath her touch. Her own release was next: quick, volcanic, transforming. She'd marked him as hers, as surely as he'd made his mark upon her last night.

She looked down upon him through a mist of passion, but her mind and heart were clear as day. "I love you."

"Meg—"

He made to speak but she laid a finger across his lips. "I know you think you can't. I don't care. I told you, heart enough for both of us. Don't forget."

Chapter Thirteen

Gideon watched the parking lot of the Russell Clinic as darkness settled over the city. A hard rain fell from a sky full of angry clouds. One by one, cars left the lot, until the only one remaining belonged to the security guard on duty. There was only one way in and out of the lot, so it made his job easy. It didn't account for all the non-traditional methods of egress and entry into a place, but it was something.

Meg sat in silence beside him in the SUV, sipping strong black coffee. "Looks like everyone's left today."

"Near as we can tell. That's not saying much."

She flashed a bemused grin. "We've been watching this place since dawn. And I've been on the inside. I didn't see anything out of the ordinary."

"Your boss wasn't in today."

"Bill? I told you, he was giving a lecture at Albany Medical College. Besides, it's his day off."

"He always stops in at the office, unless he's out of town."

"How would you know that?"

"It was in the file. And, I did surveillance for a while before we formally met."

She had another sip of coffee. "One of these days you're going to have to show me my 'file'."

One of these days meant in the future, a future he was certain they didn't have. His hands flexed as the adrenaline circulated in his veins, mixing with lust and something else he couldn't quite name. "Forget your file. The real thing is far more impressive."

She shook her head and laughed lightly. "You immortals are awfully glib in the face of danger. Must be because you can't die."

"I can die. Just not in the traditional sense."

She snorted. "So your God resurrects you, that's not the big sleep."

No, it wasn't, but it hurt like hell and was a major pain in the ass. But it was better than the death they could suffer. Rare, it was, but final. No get out of jail free cards or resurrections. "We can be killed. Certain types of enchanted weapons, or very rare poisons can wipe me out. If I get hit with that, I wind up back where I started, facing the real death that was planned before Bast intervened."

"The lake of fire thing? With Sokar the Snake Goddess?" Meg shivered and her eyes clouded with fear.

He realized his mistake immediately. She needed to believe he was invincible. He wanted to sometimes pretend he was a regular Joe. The two didn't mix. "Don't worry, Doc. They're very rare, hard to obtain, even harder to use."

"The magic I absorbed heals me, too," she said in an offhanded manner.

Gideon swore. Just like Jack said. There were things that would happen to her he couldn't predict, or couldn't see on the surface. Signs the magic was escalating. Gods, he had to end this, and soon. His hands itched for a fight. "When did you figure this out?"

"I cut myself at Jack's and I healed, the way you do when I

touch your wounds."

He gave this some thought. It could work in her favor. If she healed that rapidly, she had similar immortal powers. She'd have a better chance of surviving during any kind of attack. And he was certain they'd face another tonight, he just didn't know when, or from whom. Liebers, the mage, both, or a player to be named later. It was anyone's game at this point, the most dangerous odds of all. "Try to stay out of trouble, anyway. You don't know how reliable the healing powers are, or how long they'll work. The last thing you want is to suffer a fatal wound and not have enough juice left to fix it."

"Good point." She straightened in her seat. "That's Liebers. The silver Volvo."

Gideon's gut tightened. Show time.

He glanced at the clock. It was just past nine. "He's early. We told him ten-thirty."

"Do we follow him in?"

"Give it a few minutes. We want to make sure no one else arrives. We go in too early, we could get caught short by someone riding up our six."

Meg nodded silently, capped her coffee and put it in the drink holder. She folded her hands in her lap and chewed on her full lower lip. Gideon recognized the signs of her keyed-up nerves. He put a reassuring hand on her shoulder.

"Don't worry, Doc. Play it just like we discussed. I go in first. Any signs of trouble, you bail, call Matt. He's got a team nearby."

She nodded tightly. "I'll be fine. So will you."

"Right."

Five more minutes passed in silence, then ten, and no other cars turned into the clinic lot. Gideon started the car, and drove the short distance to the clinic, parking out of camera range as he'd done the first night.

They used the side entrance and bypassed the security station without event. When she went for the private elevator, he stopped her.

"Stairs. The hall that leads to the elevator is a perfect ambush spot."

She stayed close while they made the uneventful climb to the top floor. Once there, he had her wait while he turned to mist and filtered through the top floor. No one was there, including Liebers. His office was empty. He met her back on the stairs and motioned her inside.

"Liebers isn't here," he said softly. "Any idea where he might be?"

"We could try paging him. He doesn't expect us until ten-thirty. He could be anywhere in the building, checking labs, who knows."

Gideon didn't like the idea, but he didn't want to conduct a search of the entire building either. That would leave them vulnerable to ambush. "Fine. Do it from the internal phone system."

They went around the two corners to the reception desk. Meg dialed the beeper number, hit a few more numbers and hung up. "He'll call to the switchboard. If he uses an in-house line, I can tell where he is. If he responds with his cell, we won't know."

Moments passed in tense silence. Meg's brow furrowed and she touched Gideon's arm. "Did you hear that?"

He listened to the silence, but his acute hearing picked up nothing out of the ordinary. "No."

"I think I hear something beeping." She started to walk

down the hall to the small break room. As she did, she scratched her arm. “All this cloak and dagger is giving me hives.”

After a few feet Gideon detected the soft beeping sound Meg had picked up. He stepped in front of her and into the break room. The light from the microwave flashed twelve as if the power had been cut and restarted. Gideon summoned his blade and hit the light. He sniffed the air, detecting the gathering scent of spilled blood.

“Stay alert, Doc. We’re hot.”

He zeroed in on the scent and sound coming from behind the door to the small pantry. When he pulled it open a headless body fell out.

Meg screamed. Gideon took a step back, all his senses on alert. “Go, Meg. We’ve been compromised.”

They ran into the hall, and the elevator doors ground open with a metallic screech. His blood began to hum. A Keeper and a first guard demon rushed into the hall, followed by an entire squad.

“Run.” With his free hand he pulled out the Glock. Thank the Gods he’d packed it with full-strength vampiric acid loads. It wouldn’t stop the Keeper and the first guard, but it would kill the others dead. “Get to the stairs. Call Matt.”

Gideon fired a few rounds softening up the ranks, and backed down the hall, drawing them up the narrow corridor so they wouldn’t surround him. He was aware of Meg, still at his back.

“Go, Meg. I’ll be right behind you.”

Gideon came alive with sword blows and bullets, all the while moving steadily back. Meg hit the speed dial on the phone as she raced around the corner of the office and down the hall towards the stairs. “Help! Demons! Fourth Floor,” she screamed into the line as she ran. “Hurry!”

The door was within her reach. Gideon battled the Keeper, and she watched in horror as he discarded the now empty gun and pulled out the shotgun. He hit the larger thing in the gut, and sent it flying back into the others, buying enough time to back further towards her.

“Come on, Gideon! Run!”

She pushed the door to the stairs open, ran through, and slammed into Bill Russell.

She bounced off him and fell to the floor. “Bill! Get out of here. You’re going to get killed.”

He smiled benignly at her, grabbed her by the elbow and wrenched her roughly to her feet. Too late she saw the syringe in his other hand.

“I’ll be fine, Meg.” It was in her before she could jerk free. “You were going to rule by my side, Meg. Imagine my surprise, learning the artifact had transferred its energy into your body. Luckily, the vessel doesn’t matter, only the power. I hate to lose you, but it’s fitting somehow, you giving your life so others may live.”

The fast-acting sedative turned her limbs to spaghetti, making it impossible to fight. Bill’s crazy words echoed in her head like a chorus of a thousand. She sagged in his arms. “Let me go.” Her tongue was thick, making it hard to speak. “You don’t want to do this, Bill.”

He laughed maniacally. “I’ve been waiting thirteen years for this very moment. There’s nothing in this world or any other I want to do more.”

Meg tried to speak again but the words were a confused torrent in her brain, and her mouth, along with the rest of her body, had ceased to answer to her commands.

Russell dragged her out into the hall. Gideon howled with rage and lunged towards them. The Keeper got up and tackled him, then Meg's vision dimmed and she blacked out.

Venice, Italy

Salazar emerged from his study. His white shirt was stained red with blood and yellow with gore, his hands similarly marked. He stopped briefly in the half bath beneath the stairs to wash off what he could, knowing the real stains, the ones that blackened his old soul, would forever remain.

The face staring back at him in the mirror had dark eyes glittering with menace, reminding him of who he really was. When they first recruited him into the order, he'd been warned of the sacrifices required, of the rigors of the game. He believed in the sanctity of the Covenant, he knew he needed to protect it and he knew his past made him more able to do that than some of the others. Still, he did not like the side effects. An image of Skathi's tortured face appeared before his eyes, and he blinked hard to clear his mind. There was still work to do tonight, but now, he needed a break.

He stalked into his front parlor and went straight for a bottle of grappa. Whiskey was far too fine to waste on such a low occasion. He wanted to stop feeling, to burn away the last of his resistance, not savor this moment of pure poison.

Bast ceased her pacing, but wisely waited until he'd taken his first drink before speaking. "Did you get us answers, Salazar?"

"I called Preacher. We need to keep the mortal woman alive. Seth was correct, if you can imagine that. Elsa was compromised. She, along with another mystic, blocked the most important part of the vision." He hit the Grappa again and shivered as the hot, sour liquid burned through him. "Ian was in a psychic rut because he was the only one powerful enough to sense artifice at work. The war resumes if the mortal dies after touching the artifact, not because of touching it. Only she can prevent the negative convergence of destiny."

The air before him shimmered and Seth appeared. This time he dispensed with the mortal form, and adopted the traditional head of the abomination. "I hope the Wardens plan to address this travesty."

Bast hissed quietly at him, drawing a laugh from the chaotic deity.

Seth continued, undaunted. "Elsa is the lead mystic of the Venice cell. Her compromise means the entire cell and any visions they've interpreted are suspect."

Salazar shrugged and filled his glass again. "It's a good thing the Wardens maintain containment with the cells. We've discovered the truth early on."

"And this mage, what have you learned of him?"

Seth was impossible to read in this form, but Salazar detected nervousness in the God's rigid body posture and false accusatory tone. "The mage has nothing to do with the compromise of the mystics. The artifacts were stolen by thieves, and sold to different individuals. While I believe they were intended for some grand purpose, I have not confirmed it. Elsa, and whomever she works for, exploited the moment to incite chaos and threaten the line."

Seth's form appeared to relax. Salazar made a mental note to follow up on the God's involvement down the road.

Bast stepped in front of the other God and trapped Salazar by the small bar. "Why did it take so long to learn this information? Do we need to call in a Tribunal interrogator?"

Salazar gave her a cold, hard stare that made her twitch. "Elsa is holding out longer than expected." He took a slow drink this time, closed his eyes for a moment and collected himself. Bast was on his side, he reminded himself. They wanted the same thing. "She hasn't given up the name of who turned her. She only confessed to blocking and warping the vision to keep us tied up and foment chaos, and she admitted to releasing Skathi the Enchanter from her prison. We have no idea what other visions she twisted, or what the real outcome of this convergence will be once the mortal is safe."

Unfortunate, for all of them. Nothing could put the Covenant in more jeopardy. Still, he had to remain focused on the matter at hand. There would be time enough for the bigger picture.

Seth appeared satisfied with the information. "And what did you gather from your pet mystic, Ian?"

"Ian is the only one in the clear. He's been sedated." Salazar held back his rage, put up the now empty bottle of Grappa, and stepped around the two Gods. "There's still more to learn. I'll let you know once the job is done."

"Make it quick." Bast's cold, silky voice curled around him like a deadly viper. "I have damage control to run back at the Tribunal. I can only hold them off for so long. And I don't need to remind either of you what will happen if we don't provide a satisfactory conclusion."

"We know to keep the mortal female alive," Seth said, his sonorous voice echoing in the small parlor. "That means we've stopped the convergence. You should be able to do something with that, Bastet."

Her eyes narrowed dangerously, burning bright with a hot, golden fire. "I've near exhausted the limits of my skills between Gideon going rogue, and the likes of you two teaming up with him. This is a very volatile situation. When the Council of Wardens is at risk, the entire Covenant is suspect. Bring me something soon, Ramon, or I can't promise either of you any protection."

Salazar smiled. There was never protection on rogue ops, and certainly not in situations of compromise. Exposure came with the territory. "Give me another hour. I'll get what we need."

"Meg! No!" He made a critical tactical error by turning his back on the Keeper. The creature took him down and Gideon watched helplessly as Meg collapsed in Russell's arms.

He couldn't shift to mist with the Keeper so close. The magic worked at odds. Instead, he shifted to panther and slashed his way out of the hold. The Keeper didn't expect the change and it gave Gideon the few seconds he needed. He bounded after Russell and made it to the elevator hall just as the doors closed. Another squad of Ash demons filtered out of a side room, blocking his access. Rage misted before his eyes, turning his world to red and boiling his blood over the edge. He turned back to human form and let fury take hold. Nothing would stand between him and Meg. Nothing. He would get her back. He wouldn't be too late this time.

Lucas Preacher walked around the demon corpse that had crashed out the fourth floor window, and now lay on the cement in a broken heap. He knew their kind. It wouldn't stay broken like that for long. A quick slice with his axe turned it to dust and he moved on, entering the Russell Clinic through the front door. A tactical team of local shadow cops led by Matt Reichart were about to descend upon the scene, which should really get the party going. He shifted to mist and flowed through the elevator shaft, materializing in the thick of a heated, protracted battle. At the center was Gideon Sinclair, fighting in a state of maddened abandon. There were at least twenty Ash demons trying to bring him down, and each one finding death at his hands.

Lucas smiled. Just like old times. He summoned his axes again, the twin blades that were his oldest and only friends, and joined the mix. He was glad he didn't have to kill Gideon. Killing demons was far more productive. And enjoyable.

He cut a wide swath through the rear flank before they had a chance to realize what was happening. "Where's the woman?" he screamed over the din.

"Are you here to kill me or to help me?" Gideon's deep voice rasped through the air as he wasted another demon.

Preacher slew two more and a path opened clear to the other immortal champion. There was a momentary lull as more forces amassed at the end of the hall. "I'm here to help. The vision was wrong. We need the woman alive."

"Then get out of my way," Gideon growled and shifted into mist.

In the blink of an eye the mist slipped past him and into the elevator shaft. Lucas found himself facing the remaining armada of Ash demons. There were at least twenty left in condition to fight. Just the kind of odds he liked. He spun his blades and went back to the job he loved.

Meg roused from the blackness and found herself laid out on an old hospital gurney. She tried to move her hands as the world came into focus and found them restrained by thick leather cuffs latched to the side rails.

"Good, you're awake. You can share this wondrous moment

with me, Meg. Of all people, I know you'll appreciate it."

She blinked hard and stared at the man she thought she knew. It was Bill Russell, the whole time, he was the mage. And he was barking mad to boot. He'd traded in his chinos and polo shirt for a funky white robe replete with gold embroidered symbols. He was leering over her as he prepped her arm for an IV line.

The recent past came back to her in a sudden rush that burned inside of her skull. She struggled at her bonds, breaking his concentration. "Let me go, Bill. You don't want to do this." Whatever *this* was.

She lifted her head and looked around. They were in a damp basement with painted gold walls and enough candles to set the whole city ablaze. Off to her left stood a small figure swathed head to toe in bandages. "What the—"

"As I told you earlier, I most certainly want this, Meg. My whole life has been spent in preparation for this moment." He picked the needle up from the floor and checked again for a vein. "I see you've noticed Angel. She's waited many years for this moment too. The Buckle of Isis was meant for me you know. I was going to use it to create a new soul for Angel. The soul would bring life to her body again, and the healing powers would allow me to cure her disease."

Meg felt sick. "Bill, Angel's dead."

"Yes. I was too aggressive with the Melaniprin. I brought about her death. But now I can fix it, Meg. I can fix everything."

"You can't bring her back."

He stopped for a moment and looked at her like she was the crazy one. His blue eyes were lit with insanity, fevered and intense.

"Her original spirit is gone, yes, and that is something I can't retrieve. But I've preserved her body, as the ancient rites dictate. The Egyptians were so much more evolved in their understanding of life, and death. So much more advanced in integrative approaches to treating disease."

Her skin pricked as the needle drove home. He connected in tubing, and she realized that it didn't lead to an IV bag. The tubing was open ended. He capped it off and looked behind her to someone standing to her rear. She could make out a number of shadows. More demons she expected. Her blood began to tingle and her head pound. Of all the times to have the headaches! She needed to think, to get out of here.

Jack's words drifted to her. *Focus on the pendant. Direct your energies there, and it will help.*

Despite every instinct to do otherwise, Meg closed her eyes, and forced herself to relax.

"There, that's better," Bill cooed. "You of all people understand sacrifice. Your blood is filled with the soul creating power of Isis. Just as the old rites say, it will help me mix the clay and create the new soul for Angel. And your power will pass to me. I'll be able to heal all the children. No one will ever suffer the loss to cancer again. It's a miracle, Meg. And you're part of the wonder."

Yep. Barking mad. How had she overlooked this before? Had she been that absorbed in her work that she missed the signs of mania? Or was he just that good at hiding his true self? Then she remembered she'd thought similar things about using the healing power, had similar plans. She went cold all over. Meg bit her lip, tasting her own blood, summoning focus, blocking out the impassioned speech of the madman. Someone else spoke. A woman. Lucy. Of course. She was the one who sent the package back. Half the damned office was insane.

Focus. Shift the pain. She tuned in to the cool feel of smooth stone and silver to the exclusion of all else. The world around her felt suddenly very hot. Though her eyes were closed, she saw all around her clearly, as if she looked down on the scene from above herself. Bill fussed over some kind of altar on an old operating table. Lucy was hanging a bag of heparin. That would keep Meg's blood thin as they siphoned it into a bucket of dry clay dust. Two Keepers and a host of demons and zombies fidgeted at the edges of the room. The floor had all kinds of markings, some she recognized as hieroglyphics, others that made no sense. She noticed she had similar markings inscribed on her forehead and hands. And there was something else, far more disturbing, and terrifying. Standing beside the mummified body of Angel Russell there was a ghostly apparition of a hollow-eyed, bald little girl in a hospital gown.

The ghostly image looked upward, as if she realized Meg's consciousness drifted there. It was Angel Russell, as she'd looked just before she died. Her spirit lingered. She was hit with the sudden realization that the unfortunate child's soul was trapped. Whatever crazy magic Bill had summoned by mummifying his daughter after her death bound the soul to the earth. Bill had to know the old spirit remained. If he was sending in a new soul, what would become of the old?

Tears slid down the apparition's pale, sunken cheeks. Her thin lips trembled then began to move, as if she was speaking. The words resounded inside Meg's head in a sorrowful, tortured voice.

"Help me, Dr. Meg. Set me free."

A blinding white light lit the back of her eyes, and she fell back into her body. The spirit's voice had touched her somehow, triggering more of the magical energy. Her entire body shook from tremors, and her blood heated to an unbearable temperature. Knowledge erupted inside of her. Bill had bartered the old soul to gain enough power to hold his daughter's body in stasis until a new one could be found. Until he himself had enough power to manifest a transfer, and unlock the secrets of resurrection. And immortality.

Strength surged through her limbs as the magical power grew. She had to get to that child. Bill had damned the soul that remained. No wonder he needed a new one. Bastard. He'd condemned his daughter to hell.

Meg stopped pulling at the restraints and began to twist her hands upwards, trying to slide them through the cuffs. The leather abraded and cut at her skin, but as fast as it cut, new skin formed. All she needed to do was touch Angel and the spell would do the rest. She had to save that child's soul. And she had to stop Bill. Then she and Gideon could be free.

Gideon switched to panther form once he hit the long corridor in the basement. Meg's scent filled him. Her essence drew him like a beam of light in a storm. The corridor changed to a tunnel that dead-ended in a room. He estimated this to be a few blocks from the clinic proper. His skin crawled as the waves of magic at work beyond the doors seeped through the barriers. A cold anger drove him onward as he gathered momentum. He leaped for the double doors and shifted into human form at the last minute, adding more mass to his speed. He hit them hard, breaking them asunder and crashing to the ground inside.

He rolled to his feet with the sword in one hand and the dagger in the other, and became death as he waded into the midst of hell. He dusted the first three things that tried to stop him from reaching Meg. He recognized zombies, and kicked them into candle stands, setting them ablaze. Ahead, Lucy faced him with a ritual sword held in shaking hands. Two Keepers flanked her. Beyond them, Bill knelt at an altar, crying out all manner of ear burning magical mantras. Before he could reach Meg, she got free of the bonds, sat up and ripped IV tubing from her arms.

Several more Ash demon soldiers took him on, and he lit into them with renewed fury. She was alive. He had a chance.

Lucy made a move towards Meg, but she shoved the gurney at her and knocked her down. Then Meg was on the move, headed towards the small mummy on the raised dais.

Gideon cut his way towards her, and Lucy tried to trip him. He struck her with his boot, and knocked her cold. The Ash kept coming, slowing him down from his target. Flames climbed the walls and ate at the bodies of zombies. He had to reach Meg and get her out of here. He coughed at the smoke and kept fighting, maneuvering the battle so he was closer to Meg. The Keepers were protecting Russell. Gideon could tell they ached to join the fray, but they were bound by Russell's will. Gideon knew the mage wouldn't stop his spell unless there was threat of bodily harm or interruption. He guessed the symbols on Meg's head were entwined with the ritual, so even if Meg was mobile, she was still at risk. He'd need to strike at Russell. If he broke concentration, the Keepers would snap. It was risky, but a good distraction that might give him what he needed to get Meg free.

Gideon switched and moved the fight closer to Russell. As if realizing something was finally going wrong, Russell stopped the crazed chanting. He stood and stepped just beyond one of the Keepers. His eyes locked on Gideon and he frowned. He spoke a single word, and a deadly looking silver dagger appeared in his hand.

Gideon's blood froze as a noxious, caustic odor burned his nostrils. The dagger Russell held was an enchanted darksoul blade, linked to the corrupt mage. Not only was it made of the same kind of metal as his own soul blade, it was perverted with the blackest of magic, and treated with the one very rare poison that could kill him permanently: Asieraz, the Tears of the Gods. It would also put down Meg just as easily, regardless of the protection of the artifact's magic that swirled inside of her.

Gideon slew a few more demons and the path between him and the mad doctor shortened. One of the Keepers detached and jumped in. Gideon was ready and got it in the sweet spot, bringing it down for the killing blow. Russell's eyes narrowed and the madman turned on Meg. And the mummy.

The scene played out before him in macabre detail. Gideon watched Meg as she moved to embrace the disgusting thing in rags. Russell readied the dagger.

Gideon pushed himself to the brink, moving with the speed only Gods possessed. He laid the killing blow into the Keeper, kicked the falling corpse aside, and went for the mage. His vision narrowed to Meg and Russell, and his heart twisted until he thought it would tear itself in two. He summoned the beast inside and shifted into panther form.

The remaining Keeper tried to engage in battle but wasn't fast enough to stop him as he turned. He easily evaded the creature, leaped through its grasp, and slammed into Russell with lethal force.

Russell crumbled beneath the attack. But as he went down, he mumbled horrible sounds and the dagger vanished. The Keeper reached them, and flung Gideon aside in a desperate attempt to protect Russell. Gideon got in only a glancing blow, but rallied easily to his feet. The Keeper snarled at Gideon, and he returned the gesture. Russell lay motionless on the floor, his skull cracked and bleeding. Meg was almost upon the mummy. The pressure on his heart let up for a moment. He needed to end this. End it now. Gideon returned to his human form and faced the last opponent. He couldn't let anything happen to Meg, and he'd spill every last drop of his blood, and anyone else's that got in his way, to keep her safe.

Meg reached for Angel. The spell would release her soul, setting it free to return to the void. Her spirit would move on, escaping damnation. She would no longer be a prisoner of her crazed father and his insane obsession.

She grabbed Angel in an embrace and the spell surge through her, threatening to tear her limbs and body to shreds. Angel's arms wrapped around her and held her steady. The ground began to quake and a blinding light erupted around them.

A moment later, her vision cleared. The mummified corpse was nothing more than a pile of dust and moldy bandages heaped on the floor. She was weak and cold, and at the same time, she had a burning sensation deep in her belly. She shook off the feelings and turned back to look for Gideon.

He fought the last Keeper, moving with unmatched fury, beating the creature back only to be beaten back himself. Fires blazed all around. She started to cross the room to reach Gideon, to try and help. Perhaps the magic could aid him. Flames raged all around and ash and death filled the air. Gideon was cut in a hundred different spots, battered and bruised from the hellacious army he'd fought. She was still unsteady from the magic, and her steps faltered as she moved, but her need to keep him safe propelled her into action.

Bill was in the process of getting up from the floor. Blood poured from slash marks on his cheek. His skin was ashen, his movements shaky. He managed to get to his feet as she neared Gideon. He moved, creating an effective barrier. They locked eyes and she felt his madness deep inside her soul.

"Why, Meg? I could have healed them all. Saved all the

children, not just Angel."

"You're not a God, Bill." She'd have to go through him to reach her immortal.

"I could have become one. You think you can with the Buckle's Power. You think it will protect you, but it won't. Not from this."

A silver dagger appeared in his hand as if conjured from air. He lunged, closing the distance at a rapid clip. Gideon must have sensed it coming. Before Meg could think to move, he broke from the demon and blocked Russell's attack. His body stiffened for a moment as Russell impacted. Then he took Russell back to the ground.

"No!" She ran through the flames to reach him.

The Keeper stepped aside, a dazed look on its twisted features. It rubbed its eyes and glanced around the room.

Gideon got to his knees, pulled the dagger from his chest, and drove it into Bill's heart. The Keeper reoriented, howled wildly, and grabbed Russell's body from Gideon. It flung the dagger aside, punched through Russell's chest wall, and ripped out his heart. The creature swallowed it whole, and then vanished with the corpse in a cloud of black soot.

Gideon fell over onto his back and Meg knelt by his side. Blood pumped from his wound. It showed none of the normal characteristics she'd come to associate with his kind. It was gaping and raw, and he was going into shock. She realized he was dying.

"Hold on, Gideon." She put her hand over the wound but the blood continued to run, flowing around and through her fingers like a warm river. For some reason, her touch no longer healed. Panic raced through her. "You can't die on me. You're immortal."

He shook his head. A small trickle of blood oozed from the

corner of his mouth. "I'm sorry."

Her tears dropped on him, mixing with his life flow. "Why won't this work! Damn the Gods, it's gone. I can't heal you."

"You have, Doc." He raised his arm, touched her cheek lightly with already cooling fingers. His eyes locked with hers and held her fast. "I love you. You were right. Heart enough for both of us."

She held his hand against her face, felt him chill against her, watched as the light dimmed in his eyes and vanished. Her heart seized, her sobs mixed with coughs as the blaze engulfed the room. The smoke thickened until she could barely see. She stayed holding him, the man she loved, hoping the touch would come back, hoping he would come back. Dimly, she thought she heard voices.

Someone touched her shoulder. "Dr. Carter, it's Matt. We need to get you out of here. It's not safe."

"Gideon," she whispered.

"He's gone." Matt coughed heavily from the smoke. "And he'd kick my ass if I left his job half-done."

"I'm not leaving him."

"He died trying to keep you alive. Don't let his sacrifice be in vain."

The words penetrated the fog of her grief. "Please, bring his body."

"We will. Don't worry."

Chapter Fourteen

Gideon woke in the Hall of the Forty-Two Assessors. His chest burned like hellfire. He was on a slab, and Salazar, Bast and Seth loomed over him.

"Where's Meg? Is she okay?"

Bast nodded, her luminous eyes reflecting his haggard face back at him. "She lives. Because of you."

The pain abated some. Thank the Gods. She was alive. His last memory of her she was holding his hand, crying. Trying to heal him. The spell had discharged. She'd survived. Nothing else mattered. "I'm dead again, right?"

"Indeed." This from Salazar.

He looked as bad as Gideon felt. "You look terrible, Ramon. Don't tell me you're dead too."

The Spaniard smiled wanly. "I'm not that lucky."

Gideon shifted, adjusted to the pain of movement, and sat up. "If I'm dead, how come I'm here? And why can I feel pain?"

Ramon and Bast turned to glare at Seth. The Egyptian God of Chaos raised a brow and waved a hand. Instantly, Gideon felt nothing.

He climbed off the marble table. It had been centuries since his first ordeal, but he knew what was coming. "Did you come to watch the games, Seth?"

"I came to thank you. Your unconventional interpretation of orders saved the mortal world, and preserved the balance. For now." His smile never reached his ice-cold eyes. "And I'm here to make sure Bastet and Ramon follow Council guidelines."

Bast's supple golden body rippled with indignation. She turned her back to the other God and addressed Gideon.

"You have gone well above the call of duty. You have fulfilled your oaths and shown loyalty to the Covenant. Had you expired under different circumstances, I would have offered you a peaceful eternity in the afterlife, for your service has been exemplary."

This was news to Gideon. "No lake of fire, or dismemberment during the darkest hour of night by Sokar?"

"You don't sound pleased," Bast purred.

Peaceful eternity meant a conscious eternity. One where he could remember Meg, what they shared. Pain gripped his heart. He stared down at the still open hole. "You said had I expired under different circumstances, that was my offer. What do these circumstances get me?"

"You can still have that choice, Gideon, your eternal peace." Bast glided across the floor, her movements a mix of regal deity and feline grace. She laid a hand upon his chest, covering the hole with the flat of her soft palm. The ache eased and the hole closed. "Or you can take the test of the dead again. If you can pass Sokar's trial this time and your consciousness can hold up to her scrutiny and stay whole, if you can demonstrate your heart is no longer wanting, the Council and Tribunal have agreed to restore you to mortality."

Mortality. The word held everything for him. Hope. Promise. Paradise. Meg. "Last time I passed through the darkest part of the night, I didn't have anything worth remembering. I wanted my consciousness gone. I didn't care."

Bast's silken lips tilted up in a secretive smile. "When I first found you and put you through the trials, you believed yourself unworthy of love. Your heart came up wanting and you proved of use to us. I take it the years have matured you and you no longer believe such things?"

Gideon hadn't thought of it that way. Now, with all his lives behind him, both mortal and immortal, it all fit. He never allowed himself to love or be loved. It took Meg to break his spell. "I believe I can pass this time."

Seth crossed his bare, muscled arms. His handsome face was tight, his lips thin. "If you don't, Sokar gets to shred you and dine on your entrails. There will be no afterlife. No peace."

Without Meg, eternal paradise might as well be the barren plains of hell. It was a gamble, there were other parts of the trials where he could trip up. But life with Meg was worth any price. Worth any risk. He fixed Seth with an unblinking stare. "Just bring it."

"Bring Dr. Carter into the casting room. We need to post a guard."

Meg watched the fluorescent lights on the ceiling of St. Alban's hospital pass by as they wheeled her out of the emergency room bay, and into the casting room. Matt Reichart was at her side the whole way. He insisted she be sheltered from the madness in the ER, and wanted to make sure she was safe. On the other side of her was the tight-lipped, grim immortal in the leather duster. He was stoic, brooding, and reminded her far too much of Gideon and her loss.

"I'll stand guard," he ground out at Matt.

"Like hell. You guys are the ones responsible for this mess.

I want my team on the job. If you don't mind."

"I do mind, son. Your guys ain't trained to handle things the way we are. We don't know the threat is neutralized."

They continued to argue as the nurse's aide locked the stretcher bed into place and brought over a roll away table.

Meg tuned them out. She'd been in the ER all night. Dawn had come and gone, but the last thing she wanted to consider was facing the new day alone. She couldn't think of anything, not Bill's treachery, not the impact to her career or the clinic, not even the kids in the study. All she could think of was Gideon, and her loss. Her sorrow was all consuming.

She held his cell phone in her hand, the only thing other than her memories she had left. Her eyes burned. She had no more tears left to cry. She let her lids close, let the sound of the hospital and the men drone over her. Her thoughts drifted freely into better memories. If she tried hard, really concentrated, she could almost smell him, almost touch him. In her mind's eye, though, she pictured him clearly. He couldn't be gone. Nothing could be more wrong.

"You gentlemen will need to wait outside," said a new voice. "I need to talk with Dr. Carter alone."

"No," her protectors said in unison.

Meg opened her eyes. Dr. Schwartz, the young ER doctor stood in the doorway in rumpled scrubs. He was thin and looked tired, but showed no signs of backing down.

Meg came to his aid. "I'll be fine. Doctor patient privilege."

Matt and the other immortal, Lucas, didn't care for the idea but they did as asked. The aide fluffed her pillows, poured her fresh ice water and left her with the doctor.

"You're doing great for someone who survived a fire. I saw it on the news. That old house was a few blocks from the clinic.

It's amazing the whole neighborhood didn't go up."

She vaguely recalled the spreading flames, the explosions as Matt carried her to safety. She knew they'd used some cover story for her being in the basement of the old brownstone along the river. She didn't care. Not about that. Not about anything.

"Did they bring in the body of a man in a black leather biker jacket?"

The question caught him off guard. He shifted uncomfortably and glanced at his clipboard. Meg knew the only information it contained pertained to her medical condition and insurance status. Nothing about any other victims. It was a standard doctor tactic, used to stall for time, to regain professional poise. "Uh, nothing about that. I can call the morgue after we're done."

"I'd appreciate that." She didn't trust the Gods not to steal Gideon away from her. She would give him a decent, mortal burial. She would pray for him, visit him, bring him flowers. The world swam before her eyes. She shut them and covered them with her hand. The doctor moved closer to her.

"He was important to you, this man who died?"

She nodded, her throat tight. "He was everything."

Dr. Schwartz touched her shoulder lightly. "Was he the baby's father?"

Baby? Gideon was immortal, sterile. They'd made love less than two days ago.

There may be changes we can't see...

The spell. The magic. They should have considered that, she thought, been more careful. Jack had warned them it might do things to her body, things no one could predict. It must be powerful indeed, to overcome Gideon's problems, and to show lab results only a day later. Impossible. And yet, how much had she once thought impossible, only to be proved wrong by a crazy reality with ideas of its own? Baby. Hers. His. Theirs.

The awesome revelation brought her back to herself. She moved her hand from her eyes and tentatively touched her abdomen. New life. A new soul. Isis, Goddess of Fertility and Life. "Yes," she whispered. "He was the father."

"I'm sorry."

She looked up at the doctor, surprised to see genuine concern in his pale blue eyes. He was one of the good guys, the kind that cared. "So am I."

"You're early in the pregnancy. There's nothing to indicate it's at risk. I know it can't make up for your loss."

"No it can't." At least she'd have something other than memories of him now. She'd have a part of him with her, even if she couldn't have him. She thought again about the spell. "Is there anything else I need to know? Anything out of the ordinary?"

"You're in remarkable shape. In fact, you show no signs of smoke inhalation at all. Mainly, I wanted to let you know that your baby is fine, and we'll be releasing you shortly. Do you have someone to see you home?"

No one that mattered. "Agent Reichart can take me."

"The local police wanted to talk to you but I sent them packing. You can stay here and rest as long as you need to."

"Thanks, Doc."

"If you need someone to talk to, a grief counselor, I can call one."

"Not now. It's still too fresh."

He nodded, made a few notes on his clipboard and left.

The man named Lucas entered.

"You really loved him, didn't you?"

His voice was deep like Gideon's but lacked the rasp, and the warmth. "I did."

"Don't worry. In a few days you'll get a visit from one of the mystics. They'll take care of the memories. It will ease the pain."

Meg sat bolt upright. Her grief morphed into cold fury. "You're not going to steal my memories." *Or my child.* But they would try. She wouldn't put it past them. They had their game, but she wasn't playing anymore. Not by their rules, at least.

"You'll feel better, Dr. Carter. It sounds cruel, but it's the best way."

"Get out!" She grabbed the call buzzer and jammed it down with her thumb. "Matt!"

Reichart burst through the door. "What is it? What did he do?"

"I'm tired. I need to rest. Get him out of here. Please."

The burly agent faced off against the immortal. "You heard her, Preacher, hit the bricks."

The dour immortal hesitated a moment, then complied. "You too, Reichart. Lady needs her rest."

The moment they left Meg sprang into action. She opened Gideon's cell and dialed Jack's number. An answering machine picked up.

"Jack, it's Meg. Gideon's dead. I need your help. Call me."

She climbed out of the hospital bed, got her clothes from the bag stored below, and dressed. There was only one door out of the room. She'd need to pass Lucas. He'd try to stop her. That left the window. Luckily St. Alban's was a small, dated hospital. You could still open windows. Hers lead to a small roof. She surmised it was a one story drop to the rear lot where the ambulance bays were. She had her credit cards and ATM card. She could empty her account, rent a car, and be on the road in a few hours. There was no way she would let those fiends take from her the most precious things she had. No way.

She opened the window, sat on the sill, and stuck one leg outside.

The door to her room swung open.

“Going somewhere, Doc?”

A familiar voice rumbled like thunder through the air.

Meg’s heart skipped a beat. She turned and saw the ghost of the man she loved standing large as life in her room.

“I’m hallucinating.” She couldn’t draw in breath. “You’re dead. I watched you die.”

He crossed to her with a swift stride, slipped his arm around her waist and planted a toe-curling kiss on her lips. She drowned in the contact. He was slow and patient, tasting her, savoring her, exploring as if it was his first time. Or, his last. When he drew back, she knew he was alive. Warm, breathing, holding her, with beating heart and flowing blood.

She held his face and fresh tears clouded her vision. He wrapped her in his embrace and rocked her in his arms as she sobbed, this time with a joy that defied explanation.

“It’s okay. I’m here to stay. I’m not leaving. Not ever.”

She cried so hard his shirt was soaked. His own tears slid down in silence, a strange cool fluid that was alien to him. Meg was wonderful in his arms, he never wanted to let her go. He held her until she calmed, then he carried her back to the bed and set her down gently.

“How?” Her voice was raw, her eyes bloodshot.

“The Covenant owed me. Big time. The Tribunal and Council gave me a shot at mortality. I took the test again.” He’d never seen anyone more beautiful. He’d never felt more loved. He took a tissue and wiped away her tears and his own. “You were right, Meg. You had heart enough for both of us. When I passed through the darkest part of the night of trials, I remembered that, I remembered you, I remembered our love. And I held together. My heart was weighed and came up whole. I passed. They made me mortal again."

"You're not a soldier anymore?"

He lifted his sleeve, exposing a forearm devoid of the magical sword. "I'm a regular guy."

He noticed she still wore the pendant, but the pink stone had changed to an opalescent white. She was free of the spell and the residual energy. Relief washed over him. Bast and Salazar assured him she was free, but Gideon didn't trust either of them any more than necessary. "Do you still want me?"

A ghost of a smile drifted across her berry-colored lips. "I love you, you big idiot. Of course I still want you."

"If you love me, prove it. Marry me, Megan Carter."

She pulled him down to her and kissed him so hard it hurt. The pain was good, reminding him he was human, a man with a woman who loved him. "I take that as a yes."

He lowered the rail so he could sit beside her. She settled against him and for a moment they stayed in silence, holding one another.

"Did they find the artifact?"

"Yes, in Russell's house."

"What about the Gods?" she said after a while. "Are they angry you left?"

"No. We saved the dimension's integrity for now, and their collective asses. They've granted me more than mortality, they've granted both of us immunity."

"I don't understand."

"You saved a damned soul of a child. That counts for a lot

with some Gods, particularly Isis, the Goddess who originally imbued the artifact with the power. She spoke on your behalf, and she has a fair amount of clout." He held her closer and stroked her silken curls. "The Tribunal gave us immunity for our combined actions. I have a lot of powerful enemies. Now, you do too. We'll both live to ripe old ages, Meg, but we can only die of natural causes. Anyone seeking overt, or covert harm, becomes a target. We'll have what's called situational mortality, meaning if we die by anything other than natural causes, it's only temporary. We just need to be careful no one in the normal world finds out about our little secret. We're safe, so are any children we may have."

She shifted in his arms and turned her face up to him. "Speaking of kids, how do you feel about them?"

His gut tightened as memories of his sons surfaced. This time he let them come, along with the grief. He didn't try to hide, or force them away. "I like kids. I had two during my first life and wasn't a very good father. I'd like to try again."

"That's good." The mist cleared, replaced by a clear sparkle. "Remember Jack mentioned the artifact might change me in ways he couldn't immediately see? It didn't just change me, it changed a part of you."

He nodded, wondering where this was leading. "How?"

"I'm pregnant, Gideon. With our child."

His throat went dry, and he touched her cheek with reverence. "I was sterile. And it was only two days ago."

"Isis gives life."

"She does." The thought of his life to come filled him to bursting. He was mortal again. He had a woman who loved him, a woman he loved with all his heart. And he was going to be a father. All the centuries of emptiness, the hollow existence, were worth it to reach this point. Lightness entered his heart as his ghosts began to leave him at last, one by one, until his soul felt clean again. “Let’s go home, Meg. I want to make love with you until the end of forever.”

Epilogue

Atlantis—Three months later

The black sands shifted restlessly beneath Seth's magic. The threads of time and space twisted and turned as he worked the spell to tap into his most powerful mystic's visions. The result released image after image, none of which were the ones he wanted to see. Frustrated, he cursed, and the sands settled with a final gasp into an inert heap.

The Egyptian God of Chaos sat back on his heels and stared into the darkness of the cool, Atlantean cave. "You never should have released Gideon from his terms, Salazar."

"It wasn't my doing, Seth. I suggested we keep him until all the artifacts were located. Bast, however, was determined to allow him his trial, and grant him what he desired." The Spaniard's voice resonated like a God's inside the cave.

As always, Salazar seemed unaffected by everything transpiring, and considering what transpired appeared to be the end of all time as anyone knew it, that was quite a feat. Seth had always liked Ramon. They had more in common than either would ever admit. If Seth had to have an accomplice, there was no better partner in crime than this strange man who was far more than a simple immortal. "How many retrieval teams have failed to find them?"

"Five so far. Are the visions still the same?"

"The paths change, but the end result is worse than what was first believed. The dimension collapses." Seth sighed. Chaos. Such a delicate thing. The neutral fulcrum that kept the universe together. And it was his to watch over, use as he desired, and, on occasion, protect. Three months ago, all he wanted was a single soul committed to him. Today, he knew better. And he wished he didn't. A part of him wanted to go back to the old times, the simpler times, when destruction and wars and the normal business of Gods and men didn't appear to have such impact. The rest of him, however, wanted to settle this matter and ensure his smooth existence experienced no more threats. "This is more than restarting a war between myself and my idiot nephew, Horus. If those artifacts remain in circulation much longer, there will be no turning the tide of fate. Gods and men alike will perish. No realm tied to our dimension will survive. I don't know about you, Ramon, but I like my status quo."

"We're doing our best, Seth. The artifacts are enchanted and off the grid. The Council has our best retrieval specialists working on the task. We are still searching for the primary conspirator. We're tapped out at the moment." Salazar coughed discreetly. "The Wardens are cautious after the most recent problems with infiltration. And I don't need to remind you how untrustworthy you're considered?"

Untrustworthy? The understatement of the age. If Seth could figure a way to locate the last few missing jars, secure the artifacts himself, he would have no cares at all. To leave it in the hands of the fools who ran the Council was to assure the worst ends possible would result.

There had to be a way. Ramon was speaking softly, but Seth blotted him out. His mind reached back into fonder memories of more bold times and a dark idea took shape. He leaned forward, reached his palm out over the sands and they stirred. A man's face appeared in the scrying surface. Seth smiled, and recalled something a Norse God once told him: *Chaos meeting Chaos creates order.* His world right now was far from orderly, and only getting worse.

"Now is not a time for caution, Ramon." Seth looked to the conjured man's face again, and smiled. Not a man really. Part God, part lunatic, perhaps. The embodiment of chaos. Yes. This would work. And if it didn't, at least it would promise a spectacular end. "I have a plan, Ramon. It will take every ounce of cunning you and I possess to pull off, but I think it will bring us both what we desire."

"You are forbidden to act on this, Seth, you know the Tribunal rulings, and the laws of the Covenant."

"I know I don't want to cease to exist and I know you want to protect your precious Covenant. If that means we need to break some rules, it wouldn't be a first. For either of us. Are you in?"

His question hung for a moment in the still cave air. Then there was a rustling sound, like someone smoothing garments, and Seth knew he'd won.

"I'm in." Ramon's voice held an edge of restrained excitement. "But I run this game. Those are my terms."

Seth released his hold on the scrying sands. So far so good, the Spaniard was following form. Just like old times. The God of Chaos warmed to the coming challenge. This was far better than the rush of claiming a single soul for his side of a war he knew he'd never fight. This was what the game was all about. Risking everything to gain everything. Who knew what other rewards he might pick up along the way. "Of course, Ramon. I wouldn't have it any other way."

About the Author

To learn more about Ursula Bauer, please visit www.MuseUnplugged.com or send an email to Ursula Bauer at Ursula@MuseUnplugged.com.

What would you risk to make your darkest dream a reality?

Immortal Illusions

© 2008 Ursula Bauer

The Eternity Covenant book 2.

Outcast sorcerer Jack Madden has waited fifty years to take revenge against the Council of Wardens for wrongly convicting him of a crime, binding his powers beyond repair. When the Council turns to him to help retrieve four missing arcane artifacts, Jack decides it's his best shot at vengeance. And Raine Spencer—fearful of her power and clueless about how to use it—is his perfect mystical surrogate and mark.

Raine loyally serves the Council of Wardens as a top Occult Operations Analyst, but she longs to take the sacred oath and become a knight. With the taint of Elven blood in her veins, she has a snowball's chance in hell of making that dream a reality—until she is chosen by "Mad Jack" to act as a mystical surrogate.

Raine is ready to face down her fear of her wild Elven side, and team up with the most unprincipled scoundrel to ever haunt the halls of the Council of Wardens.

But is she ready to pay the price with her heart?

Warning, this title contains the following: explicit sex, graphic language, violence.

Sleeping with the enemy was never so magical.

Don't Let Go

© 2007 Sydney Somers

Book two in the Spellbound Series.

Private investigator Finn Calder would sooner take a Lancaster witch out to dinner than work another cheating spouse case. Considering the long standing feud between their two families, that's saying a lot. But when gorgeous Bree Jacobs works her way into the middle of his case with one memorable lap dance, Finn starts to think things are finally looking up.

The last man Bree Lancaster Jacobs expected to be attracted to was a cocky P.I. with his share of family secrets. Not even an age-old rivalry can stop her heart from pounding whenever Finn gets too close. As they work to solve a murder they both have a vested interest in, Bree knows she's in real danger of losing her heart to a man who could never love her.

Psychic matchmaker Cally gives everyone their happy ending. But can she ever have one herself?

Touch Me

© 2007 Beverly Rae

When Sloan Janson's best friend makes a sudden marriage after being "matched" by Cally, Sloan is convinced his friend is the victim of a con. He storms into Cally's small Texas town, determined to expose her as a fraud. The minute he meets her, he still wants to expose her, but now in a totally different sense!

Years of matching soul mates, however satisfying, hasn't prepared Cally for the electrical effect Sloan has on her. She's tempted, and terrified—she's always known matchmakers can't have love without blowing the fuse on their gift.

Her worst fears come true when her ability to match deserts her. If she cuts Sloan out of her life, she's sure it will return. But is that a choice she can bear to make—or to live with?

Available now in ebook and print from Samhain Publishing.

Printed in the United States
145003LV00003B/109/P

9 781599 987569